FIGHTING DIRTY

A J.J. Graves Mystery

LILIANA HART

FIGHTING DIRTY

Published by Silver Quill Publishing
Dallas, TX 75115

ALSO BY LILIANA HART

JJ Graves Mystery Series

Dirty Little Secrets

A Dirty Shame

Dirty Rotten Scoundrel

Down and Dirty

Dirty Deeds

Dirty Laundry

Dirty Money

A Dirty Job

Dirty Devil

Playing Dirty

Dirty Martini

Dirty Dozen

Dirty Minds

Dirty Weekend

Dirty Looks

Dirty Liars

Dirty Valentine

Fighting Dirty

Done Dirty

Mabel McCoy Mystery Series

Skin and Bones

A Bone to Pick

Chilled to the Bone

Bone of my Bones

Addison Holmes Mystery Series

Whiskey Rebellion

Whiskey Sour

Whiskey For Breakfast

Whiskey, You're The Devil

Whiskey on the Rocks

Whiskey Tango Foxtrot

Whiskey and Gunpowder

Whiskey Lullaby

The Scarlet Chronicles

Bouncing Betty

Hand Grenade Helen

Front Line Francis

The Harley and Davidson Mystery Series

The Farmer's Slaughter

A Tisket a Casket

I Saw Mommy Killing Santa Claus

Get Your Murder Running

Deceased and Desist

Malice in Wonderland

Tequila Mockingbird

Gone With the Sin

Grime and Punishment

Blazing Rattles

A Salt and Battery

Curl Up and Dye

First Comes Death Then Comes Marriage

Box Set 1

Box Set 2

Box Set 3

The Gravediggers

The Darkest Corner

Gone to Dust

Say No More

Laurel Valley

Tribulation Pass

Redemption Road

Midnight Clear

Forgiveness River

Atonement Trail

To Lincoln and Edith
Grandma loves you

"I'll fight till from my bones my flesh be hack'd."

— WILLIAM SHAKESPEARE,
MACBETH

"Justice will not be served until those who are unaffected are as outraged as those who are."

— BENJAMIN FRANKLIN

CHAPTER ONE

I woke to the feel of Jack's mouth on my shoulder.

Not a kiss exactly—more like a question. A slow, deliberate contact that said *I'm here, and I'm interested, and there's no rush.* His lips traced the curve where my neck met my collarbone, warm and unhurried, and his hand was already moving beneath the thin sheet, spreading wide across my hip in that proprietary way that still made my pulse trip after all this time.

The ceiling fan turned lazy circles above us, set to high to combat the humidity that clung to everything like a second skin. An unprecedented May heatwave had settled over King George County three days ago and showed no signs of leaving. Even at—I squinted at the clock—five twelve in the morning, the air was thick enough to chew.

But Jack's skin was warm against my back, and his hand was sliding across my stomach with a reverence that had nothing to do with sex and everything to do with what was happening beneath the surface. Ten weeks. Still too early to show, too early for anyone to know except us and my doctor and Lily, who'd overheard at the hospital and had promised to keep our secret.

"You're awake," he murmured against my skin.

"You're making it very hard not to be."

His low laugh rumbled through his chest and into mine. "That was the idea."

I rolled to face him. The pre-dawn light filtered through the glass wall—that massive pane that looked out over the trees and down to the Potomac— and turned everything silver and soft. It was my favorite time in this room, when the world outside was still deciding whether to wake up and everything inside felt suspended, private, ours.

Jack propped himself on one elbow and looked down at me with those dark eyes that never failed to undo me. He stretched over me, all height and muscle, his weight familiar and steady. My palm slid over the ridged scar along his ribs, the one he pretended didn't ache in cold weather. His nose had never quite healed straight, and the scar through his eyebrow tugged when he smiled. He felt like something carved from stone and built to last. His dark hair was cropped close to tame the curl that drove him crazy when it grew out. He needed a haircut.

"No morning sickness?" he asked.

"Second morning in a row." I smiled up at him. "I think the worst might be over."

"Yeah?" His hand moved back to my hip, and this time the question in his touch had nothing careful about it. "So you're feeling…"

"I'm feeling like my husband should stop asking questions and start doing something useful."

The grin that spread across his face was slow and devastating and entirely too pleased with itself. "Yes, ma'am."

He kissed me then, really kissed me, and I let myself sink into it the way you sink into a warm bath at the end of a brutal day. His mouth was soft and thorough and tasted like the man I'd somehow ended up building a life with, this impossible, stubborn, beautiful man who'd been my friend before he was my partner and my partner before he was my everything.

His hand slid up beneath my tank top, and I arched into his palm. The calloused pads of his fingers traced patterns on my ribs that were almost unbearably gentle, like I was something precious and breakable, which I was decidedly not. But the tenderness in his touch cracked open a vault I'd spent years constructing, and he'd dismantled it without even trying.

"I love you," he said against my mouth, and it wasn't a preamble or a performance. It was just a fact. The same way gravity was a fact, or the Potomac flowing past our cliffs was a fact. Immutable. Beyond argument.

"I love you back," I whispered, pulling him closer.

His weight settled over me, and the world narrowed to the slide of skin on skin, the sound of our breathing, the magic of two people who knew each other's bodies like their own, who knew where to touch and when to be patient and when patience was the last thing either of them wanted. His mouth found the spot below my ear that made me forget my own name.

"God, I've missed this," I breathed. The last couple of months had been brutal—weeks of nausea and exhaustion that had turned our bed into a recovery ward rather than anything resembling a love nest. But this morning, with the sickness finally loosening its grip and Jack's hands moving with a purpose that made my blood hum, I felt like myself again.

"I've missed *you*," he corrected, his voice rough and low in a way that lit up every nerve I had. His mouth traced a path down my throat, and my fingers dug into the muscles of his back, feeling them shift and flex beneath his skin—

His phone buzzed on the nightstand.

We both froze. That specific vibration pattern—dispatch, not personal. The one that meant someone, somewhere in King George County, had reached the end of their story in the worst possible way.

Jack dropped his forehead against my collarbone. "No."

"You have to answer it."

"What if I pretend I didn't hear it?"

It buzzed again. Insistent. Unapologetic.

I laughed, even though I wanted to throw the phone through the glass and into the Potomac.

"Jack."

He lifted his head, and the look on his face was so genuinely aggrieved that I almost felt sorry for him. Almost.

"Get moving," he said. "We can finish in the shower." He rolled off me with the resigned grace of a man who'd had too many years of practice being interrupted. "I'm an excellent multitasker."

"Such a romantic," I said, stripping off the rest of my pajamas.

He grinned and reached for the phone. "Lawson," he said, and his voice shifted, the warmth leaving it like heat from a window cracked open in winter, husband giving way to sheriff in that single word.

I watched his face change as he listened. Saw his jaw tighten, the lines around his eyes deepen.

"How long ago?" His free hand scrubbed over his face. "Who found the body?" A pause. "Secure the scene. I want a perimeter wide enough to keep any early bird employees back. Don't let anyone near the body until we get there. And have dispatch call Cole. I want him there too."

He hung up and met my eyes.

"Body?" I asked.

"Found about forty minutes ago. Dumpster behind the old Miller's Auto Body on Route 3. The one that closed down a couple years back." He was already moving, throwing back the sheet. "There's a strip mall next door that opens at six. Sanitation driver was making his rounds, went to empty the dumpster, and saw a tarp hanging out the side. Thought somebody had dumped construction debris illegally. Lifted the lid to check and found a lot more than drywall."

My name is J.J. Graves, and somewhere in King George County, someone was lying dead. Someone who'd had their life ripped away in blood and violence, whose last breath had been stolen in fear and pain. Someone whose name would be forgotten if I didn't stand for them. As the county coroner, I was the only voice the dead had left, the only one who could read the story their broken bodies told and demand justice for the silence that had been forced upon them.

The dead always called. And I always answered.

I headed for the bathroom. Multitasking would have to be quick.

The house was quiet as we headed out. There was no sign of Oscar, our newest addition to the family. He'd be in Doug's bed, the two of them snoring in tandem.

The sun wasn't up yet, but the heat was already a living thing, and I subconsciously held my breath as I climbed into the Tahoe. It pressed against the windshield as we drove, thick and wet, and it settled into your lungs and made every breath feel like work. The dashboard thermometer read eighty degrees at six fifteen in the morning, which meant the local news would be warning people to stay inside. By eight o'clock, the asphalt would shimmer like water. By midday, the air would smell like hot tar and cut grass and the misery of a Virginia summer that never learned when to quit.

Welcome to late May in King George County.

Route 3 stretched ahead of us, mostly empty at this hour, just a few early commuters with coffee cups clutched like lifelines and a delivery truck lumbering toward Fredericksburg. The world had that gray, half-formed quality it gets before dawn, when the sky can't decide if it wants to hold on to night or surrender to morning. Trees lined the road on both sides, their leaves hanging limp and motionless in air too thick to stir.

Jack drove with one hand on the wheel, the other holding mine, his thumb tracing absent patterns across my knuckles. Neither of us spoke. We didn't need to. After years of partnership, we'd learned to read each other's silences the way other people read words on a page.

My skin still hummed from the shower. Jack had been true to his word about multitasking—efficient and thorough and entirely too talented at making the most of limited time. My hair was still damp against my neck, and every now and then I caught his scent on my skin beneath the soap, that warm, clean smell that was uniquely his. It was the kind of morning that made you greedy—that made you want to call in sick and go back to bed and pretend the rest of the world didn't exist.

But the rest of the world did exist. And somewhere at the end of this drive, someone was lying in a dumpster, waiting for us to tell their story.

I pressed my free hand against my stomach—flat still, no sign yet of the secret growing beneath the surface. Ten weeks. In another month I wouldn't be able to hide it anymore. In another month, everyone would know, and the questions would start. Could I do this job pregnant? Could I stand over an autopsy table with a baby pressing against my bladder? Could I kneel in blood and mud at crime scenes while my body was busy building something new?

I didn't know. But I knew I wasn't ready to stop. Not yet. And that terrified me in ways I didn't want to examine too closely.

We crossed the bridge into King George Proper, the county's largest town, home to the naval base at Dahlgren and King George University. This was where bars and cheap apartments sprouted up to serve the steady influx of military personnel and college students who cycled through on two-year rotations, a catchall for people who hadn't figured out where to go next. It wasn't traditional like Bloody Mary with its multigenerational farming families and old Victorian homes. Wasn't artsy like Newcastle with its cobblestone streets and bohemian vibe, or dripping with tech money like Nottingham where the mini Silicon Valley had swallowed whatever small-town character used to exist. King George Proper was transient. Temporary. A place where people worked and drank and grabbed fast food on their lunch breaks while waiting for their lives to take them somewhere else.

The old Miller's Auto Body sat at the far end of a tired stretch of commercial property, hunkered down like it was ashamed of itself. A squat concrete rectangle with bay doors gone rust-orange and windows so grimy they'd turned the color of old cataracts. Whatever sign had once hung above the entrance had faded past legibility years ago, leaving just a ghost of letters that might have spelled anything. The place had been closed since before I'd taken over as coroner—left to rot while the county argued about zoning variances and commercial developers circled like patient vultures waiting for the property values to hit rock bottom.

The strip mall next door was newer, built in that soul-crushing style of beige stucco and tinted glass that seemed designed to be forgotten the moment you looked away. A nail salon, a vape shop, a Chinese takeout place with a flickering neon sign, and one of those check-cashing joints that preyed on people too poor or too desperate to have bank accounts. All closed now, their storefronts dark, but the parking lot lights were on—pale orange circles pooling across empty asphalt like something had bled out and left stains.

The dumpster sat behind Miller's, right where the two properties met in a no-man's-land of cracked concrete and weeds pushing through the seams. I could see the crime-scene tape from the road, bright yellow against the gray pre-dawn light, that cheerful color that always seemed obscene at murder scenes. Two patrol cars were parked at angles near the tape, their light bars dark but their presence unmistakable. A third vehicle—a white pickup truck, unmarked, mud splattered, with a dent in the rear bumper I recognized—told me Cole had beaten us here.

Jack pulled in and killed the engine. The sudden silence felt heavy, expectant. And for a moment, neither of us moved.

He squeezed my hand once and then let go. When I looked over, the sheriff had already settled behind his eyes, the last traces of the man who'd made me laugh in the shower tucked away somewhere safe where the job couldn't touch him.

We were both moving then, out of the car, into the heat, walking toward death like we'd done a hundred times before.

The smell hit me before I'd cleared the tape.

Sweet and ripe and unmistakable. That perfume of decomposition that you never forgot once you'd learned it. The human body, breaking down, releasing gases and fluids in its final transformation from person to evidence. Underneath it, the sour funk of rotting food, the chemical bite of old motor oil and something astringent that might have been cleaning solvent, and that other smell, the one that always lurked at scenes like this. The copper-penny scent of blood, even when you couldn't see it. Even when it had dried and darkened and seeped into places you'd never think to look.

My stomach clenched. The morning sickness had been merciful these last couple of days, but there were certain smells that instantly made me vomit. Apparently decomp was on the list.

I breathed through my mouth, short, shallow breaths that bypassed most of my olfactory system, and kept walking. The trick wasn't to ignore the smell. That was impossible. The trick was to compartmentalize it, to file it away in the part of your brain that dealt with professional necessities rather than the part that wanted to gag and run. Just for good measure, I took the jar of Vicks out of my bag and dabbed some under my nose—an old trick rookies used before they got used to the smell.

Cole was standing near the dumpster, his Stetson pushed back on his head at that angle that meant he'd been here awhile. A cup of gas station coffee steamed in one hand, the cardboard sleeve printed with the logo of the Quik-Mart. Even at this hour, in this heat, with a dead body ten feet away, he looked like he'd stepped out of an old Western. He wore

Wranglers that fit well enough to explain why he was never without female attention, cowboy boots, a white button-down shirt beneath a lightweight vest that didn't quite hide the holster on his belt or the badge glinting beside it.

Cole had that old-west gunslinger look to him—lanky build, all legs, broad shoulders tapering to narrow hips. He was around forty but wearing it well, with dark blond hair freshly cut and a face that was simply, undeniably handsome. He'd left a trail of broken hearts across three counties before Lily Jacobs came along and knocked him sideways.

His slow, lanky gait as he walked toward us matched the drawl that made people underestimate him, at least until they found themselves across from him in an interrogation room, realizing too late that his mind was sharper than his lazy demeanor suggested.

"Doc," he said, nodding at me. "Hell of a way to start a Wednesday."

"What've we got?" Jack asked, already scanning the perimeter with that rapid tactical assessment he'd never lost from his military days.

"Male victim." Cole took a sip of his coffee, unhurried, like we were discussing the weather instead of murder. "Mid-twenties, big guy. Someone wrapped him in a blanket and stuffed him in the dumpster headfirst. Sanitation driver found him about an hour ago." He jerked his chin toward a man sitting on the bumper of one of the patrol cars, a shock blanket around his shoulders despite the heat. "Ray Tolliver. He's got twenty-three years on this route. Says he's seen plenty of weird stuff in dumpsters over the years—dead dogs, drug paraphernalia, once a whole crate of what turned out to be stolen electronics. But nothing like this."

I looked over at Tolliver. He was a big man, heavyset, with dark brown skin gone ashy gray beneath the parking lot lights and hands that wouldn't stop shaking even wrapped around the cup of coffee someone had given him. His uniform shirt was sweat stained and untucked, and his eyes had that thousand-yard stare you saw on people who'd just had their understanding of the world fundamentally rearranged.

"He touch anything?" Jack asked.

"Says he lifted the lid and saw the blanket hanging out. Pulled the blanket back to check and got an eyeful of what was underneath." Cole shrugged one shoulder, a minimal movement that somehow conveyed a wealth of sympathy. "Dropped it like it burned him and called 911. Hasn't stopped shaking since. Riley's been with him, but I don't think we're going to get much more from him. Man's in shock."

Twenty-three years of hauling other people's

garbage, and this was the morning that would define all the rest of his mornings. I'd seen it before. Some people recovered from moments like this. They built scar tissue over the memory and eventually went back to their lives, a little warier, a little more aware of the darkness that could hide in ordinary places. Others never did. They quit their jobs, started drinking, and jumped at shadows for the rest of their days.

I hoped Ray Tolliver would be one of the lucky ones. But that wasn't something I could control.

I set my medical bag on the ground and pulled out gloves. The dumpster loomed ahead of me, a dark green metal box spotted with rust along the bottom and old graffiti on one side, the paint too faded to read. The lid was propped open with a length of two-by-four that someone had wedged into place. From where I stood, I could see the corner of fabric hanging over the edge, blue and quilted, the cheap polyester fill of a moving blanket you'd buy at a hardware store for fifteen dollars and throw away when you were done.

Only someone hadn't thrown this one away. Someone had wrapped a body in it and stuffed it in with the garbage.

Lieutenant Daniels headed up the CSI team. She was already working the perimeter, her camera clicking in steady rhythm as she documented everything. Her braids were pulled back in a neat ponytail, the new blond additions catching the first hint of dawn light, and her tawny eyes moved methodically across the scene with the calm competence of someone who'd processed more crime scenes than most cops would see in a career.

She glanced up as I approached and gave me a short nod. We'd worked together enough times that we didn't need pleasantries.

"Morning, Doc. Ready to take a look?"

"That's why they pay me the mediocre bucks."

A grin crossed her face, quick as a heartbeat. "I've done the exterior and immediate surroundings. Chen's finishing up photos of the interior. Soon as she's clear, he's all yours."

Someone had positioned a stepladder against the side of the dumpster, sturdy aluminum, the kind you'd find in any maintenance closet. I climbed it carefully and peered over the edge into the dim interior.

The portable lights had already been set up, battery-powered LED floods on tripods, casting harsh white illumination that bleached all the color out of everything and turned shadows into stark black cutouts. Deputy Kristi Chen was inside the dumpster, balanced on a second stepladder, her small frame angled awkwardly as she worked to get overhead shots. Her black hair was tucked under a department cap, and her face was set in that expression of focused determination I'd come to associate with her, like every task was a personal challenge she intended to win.

"I guess you drew the short straw," I told her.

She looked at me and rolled her eyes. "Apparently I'm just the right size to get in here and take pictures from every angle. When I come back in my next life I'm going to be a man. I've always wanted to pee standing up."

"It's a worthy goal," I said dryly.

"You want shots of the feet before I clear out? I think I can get a good angle."

"If you can."

"Give me two minutes."

I used the time to observe what I could from my perch, letting my eyes move systematically across the visible portions of the body. The victim had been shoved in headfirst, legs bent at unnatural angles to fit the space. The moving blanket had come partially unwrapped. It had been hasty work, one corner tucked and the rest just folded over. Broad shoulders. Muscular back. A build that came from serious physical training. Dark bruising visible on his upper back, concentrated in patterns that didn't look random.

His hands were behind him, wrists bound with heavy-duty zip. And there was something wrong with his hands themselves. The shape didn't look right, but I couldn't tell what exactly from my perch.

His feet were bare and filthy, caked with a grayish substance that didn't look like ordinary dirt.

Chen finished her shots and climbed down. "All yours, Doc. Fair warning, it's tight in there, and it smells like death warmed over. Which I guess it literally is. I'm going to have to shower for days."

I sighed. "Noted."

I shifted my weight on the ladder, gripping the edge of the dumpster, and was about to swing my leg over when I felt Jack's hand close around my elbow.

"Jaye."

I didn't turn around. I didn't need to. I could hear everything he wanted to say in those two syllables, the concern, the restraint, the very careful effort not to make it an order.

"Don't start," I said.

"I'm not starting anything. I'm pointing out that there's no reason for you to be standing in rotting garbage when Jackson and Plank can extract him and you can do your exam on solid ground." A beat. "It's not a commentary on your abilities. It's common sense."

"It's you being overprotective."

"It's me being practical. And maybe a little overprotective." I could hear the half smile in his voice even though I still wasn't looking at him. "Those two things aren't mutually exclusive."

The annoying part was that he wasn't wrong.

There was no practical reason for me to climb into a dumpster full of decomposing garbage when I had two perfectly capable officers who could handle the extraction while I directed from up here. I'd done it before, plenty of times. Long before I was pregnant. It wasn't weakness. It was efficient use of resources.

But it still irked me that he'd said it.

"Fine," I said, finally turning to look at him. "But for the record, I was already thinking the same thing before you opened your mouth."

"Of course you were." His expression was perfectly innocent. Completely unconvincing.

"I need two people in the dumpster," I called down. "Tyvek suits, full gear. Backboard ready. He's a big guy. Probably two-twenty or more."

Cole nodded and turned to issue orders. Within minutes, Deputies Jackson and Plank were suiting up in white Tyvek coveralls.

I climbed back up the stepladder, positioning myself where I could see into the dumpster clearly. The smell rose up to greet me, that thick, complex perfume of death and garbage, and I breathed through my mouth and let my eyes do the work.

It took nearly fifteen minutes to maneuver him into position. Dead weight was unforgiving, and rigor mortis had stiffened him into an awkward shape that didn't want to cooperate. But finally they had him on the backboard, and Cole and Riley were there to receive him on the outside, Riley's tall, lanky frame braced against the weight as they lowered two hundred plus pounds to the ground.

Plank walked a few feet away and bent over with his hands on his knees, gagging. Nobody said anything. We'd all been there.

I climbed down from the ladder, pulled fresh gloves from my kit, and approached the body.

Now I could work.

On the ground, in the full light of morning, he looked even younger than I'd thought. Mid-twenties, maybe less. His features were African American, strong jaw, broad nose, the kind of face that had probably been handsome before someone had destroyed it. His skin was the color of burnished oak, dark and smooth where it wasn't covered in blood and bruising. His head was shaved clean, and I could see a tattoo on the back of his neck, though the design was obscured by dried blood and a bullet hole.

I started with his head, and Jack crouched across from me, close enough to see what I was seeing without contaminating anything. We'd done this enough times that we had our own rhythm. I documented, he listened, and we built the story together.

"Single entry wound," I said, tilting the head gently to give Jack a better angle. "Base of the skull. Small caliber, a .22 or .25, based on the size. See the stippling?" I pointed to the faint halo of powder burns around the wound. "Close range. Not quite contact, but near enough."

"Angle?"

"Slightly downward." I traced the trajectory with my gloved finger without touching the wound. "Either the shooter was taller, or—"

"He was on his knees," Jack finished.

Our eyes met over the body. We were both thinking the same thing.

"No exit wound," I said. "Small caliber round enters the skull and doesn't have enough velocity to punch back out. It bounces around inside instead. Maximum damage, minimum mess."

"That's not a Saturday night special," Jack said quietly. "That's a choice."

"A professional one." I moved to his face, and the damage there made me pause despite myself. His nose had been shattered, the cartilage collapsed inward, the bridge flattened. Left eye swollen completely shut, the orbital socket likely fractured beneath it. Jaw hanging askew, broken in at least two places. Lips split in multiple locations, teeth knocked out or broken off.

"Somebody worked on his face with something hard. Bat or a pipe, maybe. This isn't fists."

Jack leaned in closer. "The bruising patterns. They don't look random."

"No. They targeted specific areas." I moved down to his torso, lifting the edge of the blanket to expose his ribs and back. "Face, ribs, kidneys. The places you hit when you want someone conscious and talking."

"Textbook interrogation," Jack said.

I found the burns on his lower back and felt my stomach clench for reasons that had nothing to do with morning sickness. "Cigarette burns. Eight of them." I pointed to the differences—the dark angry ones, the lighter ones that had started to scar over. "These aren't all from the same session. Some of these are a couple of days old."

"So someone had him for a while."

"Someone had him and took their time. You see this burn here?" I asked, pointing to one directly in the center of the back. "This is a postmortem burn. You can compare it to the other burns. There's no inflammation or damage to the surrounding tissue in the postmortem burn."

"One last insult," Jack said.

The zip ties on his wrists had cut deep grooves into his skin, raw and bloody, the flesh shredded where the plastic had sawed through. "He fought against the restraints," I said.

I moved to his hands, and that's when I stopped talking. Jack noticed.

"What?" he asked.

"His fingers." I held up one of the bound hands carefully, angling it so Jack could see. "Every one of them. Both hands. Broken."

Jack looked. I watched his expression shift. Not shock, he'd been doing this too long for shock, but something colder. Recognition.

"Not all at once," I continued. "Some are clean snaps at the knuckle. Others were twisted until the bone gave way. This was done one at a time. Deliberately."

"God," he said on a sigh.

"But look underneath the damage." I turned the hand slightly. "The calluses on his first two knuckles. See how thick they are, even through the swelling. And the old fractures here and here." I indicated the remodeled bone with my fingertip. "These knuckles have been broken and healed and broken again over years. This man was a fighter. Not a weekend warrior. Someone who trained seriously and hit things for a living."

Jack sat back on his heels. "And someone broke every finger he had."

"Knew exactly what they were taking from him,"

I said. "You don't break a fighter's hands by accident. That's a message."

Jack was quiet for a moment, processing. "So we've got days of captivity. Systematic beating. Cigarette burns. Broken hands. And then a .22 to the back of the head while he was on his knees." He looked at me. "That's not a murder, Jaye. That's a professional interrogation that ended in an execution."

"That's what his body is telling me."

I moved down to his feet. They were bare, filthy, and caked with a grayish-brown residue that didn't look like ordinary dirt. Powdery in some places, packed hard in others, ground deep into his calluses and the creases between his toes. I scraped samples into an evidence bag.

"What's that?" Jack asked.

"I don't know yet. The lab will tell us. But wherever they held him, he was walking around in it barefoot." I sealed the last bag. "It's specific. If we find the location, I can match it."

I made a thin incision and inserted a thermometer. "Core temp is ninety-one. With the ambient heat and the dumpster acting like an oven, I'd put time of death somewhere between twelve and eighteen hours ago. Rigor's fully established, which supports that." I checked the lividity, the purple-red discoloration where blood had pooled after death, fixed and unmovable along his back. "Lividity's fixed on his posterior. He was lying flat on his back for hours after he died. Then someone moved him and dumped him here."

I stripped off my gloves and stood, feeling my knees pop from crouching too long.

Jack stood with me. "He's a big guy. The chances of this being a one-man show are slim."

"This was organized. Structured. They knew where to hit. What to break. Whoever did this has probably done it before."

I looked down at the young man on the ground—broken, discarded, nameless. But not voiceless. Not anymore.

CHAPTER TWO

The funeral home's black Suburban pulled into the lot just as the sun cleared the tree line. Death didn't care about beautiful mornings. Death just kept showing up, demanding attention, refusing to wait for a more appropriate hour.

Lily unfolded herself from the driver's seat with the easy grace of a woman who'd long ago stopped apologizing for taking up space. Nearly six feet of dark hair and endless legs, curves that made the shapeless scrubs she wore look like high fashion. She'd barely closed the door before Cole was moving toward her, that lanky stride eating up the distance between them.

"Hey." He said it soft, just for her, one hand coming up to rest on her hip like it belonged there.

"Hey yourself." She smiled up at him. "You look like hell."

"Dumpsters and heat aren't a sexy combo like the TV shows make them." He leaned down and pressed a quick kiss to the top of her head, easy and natural as breathing. "You eat anything yet?"

"Coffee."

"That's not food."

"It's a food group. Or it should be."

He shook his head, but there was warmth in it. "I can stop by and bring you lunch once we get a break."

"You and I both know you're not going to get a break. But it's the thought that counts.

"I'll remember that next time I forget something."

She laughed—a low, rich sound that made a couple of the deputies glance over—and pushed him gently back toward the crime scene. "Go. Detect things. I'll handle the body."

The passenger door of the Suburban opened, and Sheldon emerged into the sunlight like a creature who'd taken a wrong turn out of his burrow. He was pocket sized—a few inches over five feet, soft around the middle—with sandy hair going thin on top and glasses so thick they made his eyes look like something you'd find at the bottom of a pond. His army-green coveralls were already showing sweat stains under the arms, and he squinted against the glare like it had personally offended him.

"Did you know," he announced, fumbling his glasses up his nose, "that the average American produces four point four pounds of trash per day? That's nearly a ton and a half per year. Though interestingly, the decomposition rate varies significantly based on—"

"Sheldon." Lily's voice was gentle, patient. "Maybe not right now, okay?"

He blinked at her, then at the crime-scene tape, then at the body bag on the ground. Something clicked behind those magnified eyes. "Oh. Right. Because of the..." He gestured vaguely toward the dumpster. "The situation."

"The situation," Lily agreed. She put a hand on his shoulder, steering him toward the gurney the way you'd guide a puppy away from traffic. "Why don't you help me get set up?"

"I can do that. I'm very good at setting up. Mother says I have excellent organizational skills, which is apparently genetic because my father was an accountant before he left. Did you know that forty-one percent of first marriages end in divorce? The percentage goes up for second and third marriages, which seems counterintuitive, but—"

"Sheldon." Still gentle. Still patient. "Gurney."

"Gurney. Yes. Focusing now."

I watched them work—Lily directing with calm efficiency, Sheldon orbiting her like a moon that couldn't quite find its trajectory. She never snapped at him, never let frustration creep into her voice. She just kept guiding, redirecting, channeling all that anxious energy into something useful.

It was a gift. One I didn't have the patience for most days.

"We're going to need help with the lift," I said. "He's a big guy."

Jack nodded and turned toward the crime-scene tape. "Riley, Plank—give them a hand loading."

The two deputies headed our way. Riley moved with the loose-limbed ease of someone comfortable in his own skin, while Plank still had that slightly green tinge around his edges from his time in the dumpster. But neither of them hesitated. Good men. The kind who did the hard work without complaint.

The gurney wheels clattered against the asphalt as Lily locked them into place beside the body bag. Sheldon hovered nearby, his hands twitching at his sides.

"Did you know," he said to no one in particular, "that the human body loses approximately twenty-one grams of weight at the moment of death? It was measured in a 1907 experiment by Duncan MacDougall, though his methodology has been widely criticized. He only used six subjects, which is hardly a representative sample size—"

"Sheldon." Lily handed him a strap. "Hold this."

He took it, clutching it to his chest like a lifeline. "Holding. I'm holding it."

"Good. Keep holding it."

Riley and Plank positioned themselves on either side of the body bag while Lily crouched at the head. The morning sun beat down on all of them, relentless, turning the parking lot into a griddle.

"On three," Lily said. "One, two—"

They lifted. Two hundred and twenty pounds of dead weight rose from the asphalt, transferred to the gurney with the efficiency of people who'd done this too many times before. Sheldon held his strap with white-knuckled intensity, his face going red from the effort of keeping the gurney steady.

"Got him," Riley said.

Lily was already securing the straps, her movements quick and sure. "Sheldon, you can let go now."

He didn't let go.

"Sheldon."

"Right. Letting go." He released the strap and stepped back, pulling a crumpled handkerchief from his pocket to mop at his forehead. "That was heavier than I expected. Though I suppose decomposition gases could add to the overall mass. Did you know that the average adult male contains enough gas postmortem to—"

"Why don't you get the doors?" Lily suggested, nodding toward the Suburban.

"Doors. Yes. I can do doors." He scurried toward the vehicle, nearly tripping over a crack in the pavement. "Door opening is actually a very under-rated skill. There's a whole science to the timing of it—"

The rear doors of the Suburban swung open, and Riley and Plank maneuvered the gurney into posi-tion. The body slid into the dim interior with a soft metallic whisper, and then they were closing the doors, sealing him away for the trip back to the funeral home.

Lily stripped off her gloves and tossed them into a biohazard bag. "I'll get him logged in and prepped. Have everything ready for you when you get back."

"Shouldn't be long. We're just going to canvass the immediate area, see if anyone recognizes his description."

She nodded, already moving toward the driver's side. "I'll pull the x-ray equipment and get the table set up."

"Perfect."

Riley and Plank climbed into the back of the Suburban, folding themselves into the space on either side of the gurney. Sheldon was already in the passenger seat, his handkerchief now being used to clean his glasses in small, obsessive circles.

Lily paused before getting in, her eyes finding Cole across the parking lot. He was talking to one of the uniforms, his Stetson pushed back on his head, but he must have felt her gaze because he looked up and winked at her.

Then she was behind the wheel, the engine turning over, and I watched the black Suburban with its white magnetic signs pull out of the lot and disappear into morning traffic.

Somewhere in that vehicle, a young man I didn't know was beginning his final journey. In a few hours, he'd be on my table, and I'd learn everything his body had to tell me. Every wound, every bruise, every secret written in tissue and bone.

But first, I needed to find out who he'd been while he was still alive.

I stripped off my coveralls—the thick canvas had done its job, keeping the worst of the scene off my clothes underneath, but the material was damp with sweat and smelled like death and garbage. I stuffed them into a biohazard bag and tossed it in the back of Jack's Tahoe. The lanyard with my coroner's ID went around my neck, the laminated card settling against my chest—*King George County Coroner's Office*, my unsmiling photo, my name in block letters.

"You ready?"

Jack's hand found the small of my back, warm and steady. I leaned into it for just a moment— letting myself take the comfort he was offering— then straightened and nodded.

"Yeah."

Cole ambled over, his Stetson pulled low against the sun that had turned from brutal to punishing in the hours we'd been working the scene. It had to be close to ten by now—the morning had disappeared into evidence collection and body extraction and the endless documentation that turned a death into a case.

"I'll take the nail salon and the check-cashing place," he said. "Y'all take the vape shop and the Chinese place." He nodded toward the strip mall, where a few more cars had appeared in the parking lot as businesses prepared to open. "Meet back here in an hour?"

"Make it forty-five," Jack said. "I've got a council meeting at one o'clock I just can't wait to be at."

Cole chuckled. "Copy that."

He headed off with that lanky, unhurried stride, and Jack and I followed a few paces behind.

The strip mall looked different now that the sun had climbed high enough to burn away the early morning shadows. The beige stucco showed every water stain, every crack, every place where the cheap construction had started to give up the ghost. The parking lot was filling up—a minivan outside the nail salon, a couple of sedans near the check-cashing place, a delivery truck idling by the Chinese restaurant's back entrance.

The Chinese place was called Lucky Dragon, according to the faded red lettering on the window. A paper sign taped to the glass announced *LUNCH SPECIAL $6.99* in handwritten marker, and through the smudged window I could see someone moving around inside, getting ready for the day.

Jack held the door for me, and the smell hit us both at the same time—hot oil, garlic, ginger, and something sweeter underneath. Soy sauce, maybe. Or the syrupy glaze they put on the orange chicken.

The interior was small and cramped, the kind of place where efficiency trumped atmosphere. Plastic tables with mismatched chairs crammed against the walls. A counter separating the ordering area from the kitchen, where steam rose from industrial-sized woks. Laminated menus with photographs of food that probably looked nothing like what actually came out of that kitchen. A television mounted in the corner playing a Chinese soap opera with the volume turned low.

"Too bad I just spent the morning smelling dumpster and dead body," I said. "Otherwise I'd say let's pick up lunch while we're here."

A man emerged from the back, wiping his hands

on a stained apron. Mid-fifties, wiry, with gray threading through black hair and a weathered face that came from decades of long hours and hard work. His eyes went straight to Jack's badge, then to my lanyard, and his expression shifted—not fear, exactly, but wariness. The automatic caution of someone who'd learned that authority figures rarely brought good news.

"Not open yet," he said. His accent was faint, worn smooth by years of speaking English, but still present in the way he clipped certain syllables. "Lunch at eleven."

"We're not here for food." Jack's voice was easy, unthreatening—the tone he used when he wanted people to feel comfortable, not cornered. "I'm Sheriff Lawson. This is Dr. Graves, the county coroner. We're investigating an incident that occurred behind the building."

The man's brow furrowed. "Incident?"

"A body was found in the dumpster early this morning."

"*Aiya.*" He pressed a hand to his chest, and the wariness gave way to genuine shock. "Dead body? Here? Behind my restaurant?"

"Behind the old auto shop. But close enough that we're hoping someone might have seen something. Mind if we ask you a few questions?"

The man hesitated, that internal calculation

playing out across his face. Talk to the cops or keep his head down. Get involved or stay out of it. Finally, he gave a short nod and gestured toward one of the plastic tables near the window.

"I don't know nothing about dead bodies," he said as we sat. "But I answer your questions."

"We appreciate that. Can we start with your name?"

"Henry Liu. I own this place. Fifteen years now." A hint of pride crept into his voice despite the circumstances. "Before that, my wife and I had a restaurant in DC. Chinatown. But the rent got too high, so we came out here. Quieter. Cheaper." He shrugged. "Less business, but less headache too."

"You work here every day?"

"Every day. Seven days a week." The shrug again, more resigned this time. "My wife, she help when she can, but her knees are bad now. Mostly it's just me and my nephew. He do deliveries, wash dishes. I do everything else."

"Were you here last night? Around closing time?"

"Until maybe ten thirty. I close up at ten, but there's always more to do. Count the register, mop the floors, prep for tomorrow." He gestured toward the kitchen. "I was doing the vegetables for today when you come in."

"Did you notice anything unusual last night? Any

cars you didn't recognize, anyone hanging around the parking lot?"

Liu's brow furrowed as he thought. "Parking lot always has cars. People come and go—the college kids, the military boys from the base. I don't pay much attention anymore." He paused. "But now that you ask...there was a truck. Dark color, maybe blue or black. It was parked behind the old auto place when I took out the garbage. Maybe nine o'clock, nine thirty."

Jack leaned forward slightly. "Did you see anyone with the truck? Anyone getting in or out?"

"No. I just notice because nobody parks back there. The auto shop, it's been closed for years. No reason for anybody to be there." Liu's eyes narrowed. "I thought maybe kids. You know, teenagers looking for a place to drink or smoke or..." He waved his hand vaguely. "Whatever kids do these days."

"But you didn't see anyone."

"No. Just the truck. And when I came back from dumping the garbage, maybe five minutes later, it was gone." He spread his hands. "I didn't think nothing of it. People park, people leave. It happens."

Jack made a note. "Let me describe the victim for you, see if it rings any bells. Young Black man, mid-twenties. Tall—over six feet. Muscular build, shaved head. Probably weighed around two-twenty. Would have been hard to miss."

Recognition flickered across Liu's face. Or the edge of it.

"Big guy like that," Jack continued, his tone still casual, still conversational. "Would have stood out. He ever come in here? Buy some food?"

The silence stretched a beat too long. Liu's fingers found the edge of his apron, worrying the fabric between them.

"Maybe," he said finally. "Maybe I see him before. Hard to say. Many customers. But maybe. Big guy, shaved head. Yeah." Liu's eyes slid away from Jack's, fixing on something in the distance. "He come in sometimes late. After nine. Order the kung pao chicken, extra spicy. Always pay cash."

"Did he ever come in with anyone else?"

"Sometimes. Different people." The shrug again, but tighter now. "I don't pay attention to who eats with who. I just cook the food."

"Can you describe any of them? The people he came in with?"

"White guy, one time. Older. Maybe another Black guy, I don't remember." Liu shifted in his seat, his body language screaming that he wanted this conversation to be over. "I just cook the food," he repeated.

"Did you ever talk to him?" I asked. "Learn his name?"

Liu looked at me for the first time, his dark eyes

assessing. "No name. He don't talk much. Just order, pay, leave." A pause, and something softened in his expression. "Nice kid, though. Polite. Always say thank you."

There it was. That word. *Polite.*

"Did he ever seem scared?" I asked. "Nervous? Like he was watching for someone?"

Liu's laugh was short and humorless. "Lady, everyone in this neighborhood watches for someone. That's just how it is around here." He paused, his fingers still working the edge of his apron.

"When's the last time you saw him?"

Liu thought about it. "Week ago, maybe. Maybe less." His expression darkened. "He come in, order the kung pao, same as always. But he look..." He searched for the word. "Rough. Like he been in a fight. Black eye. Lip all swollen."

"Did he say anything about what happened?"

"I ask if he okay. He just laugh." Liu shook his head slowly. "Say something like, 'you should see the other guy.' I don't ask more questions. Not my business."

Jack closed his notebook. "You've been very helpful, Mr. Liu. If you think of anything else—anyone he came in with, anything he said—give me a call." He slid a business card across the table.

Liu took it, looked at it, tucked it into his apron pocket. "I hope you find who did this." His voice was quieter now, some of that wariness replaced by sadness. "Like I say—nice kid. Didn't deserve to end up in no dumpster."

The vape shop was called Cloud Nine, which struck me as either aspirational or deeply ironic given the general air of defeat that clung to everything in this strip mall. The door was propped open with a rubber doorstop shaped like a skull, and through the window I could see a woman behind the counter, leaning on her elbows and scrolling through her phone.

She looked up as we walked in—heavyset, with bleached blond hair escaping from a messy bun and tattoos covering both arms from wrist to shoulder. A skull wrapped in roses on the left. Something that might have been a mermaid or a fever dream on the right. Multiple piercings caught the fluorescent light —ears, nose, one eyebrow.

Her eyes went to Jack's badge, and her expression shifted from bored to guarded in the space of a heartbeat.

"Let me guess," she said, straightening up. "You're not here for the mango pods."

"I'm Sheriff Lawson. This is Dr. Graves."

"Yeah." She crossed her arms over her chest.

"Saw the cop cars this morning when I came in. Figured something bad happened."

"A body was found behind the old auto shop."

Her eyebrows rose—surprise, but not shock. "No kidding. Someone I know?"

"That's what we're trying to find out." Jack described the victim—height, build, shaved head.

Recognition sparked in her eyes before he'd finished. "Sounds like Dre."

My pulse quickened. "Dre?"

"That's what he went by. Don't know if it's short for Andre or Deandre or what." She reached under the counter and pulled out a pack of cigarettes—the regular kind, not the vape products lining the walls behind her—and lit one with a practiced flick of a cheap lighter. "He came in with another guy once a week or so. The other guy is a regular—always buys the same vape cartridges. Dre would just grab a water from the cooler and wait. Don't think he smoked or vaped. Too healthy for that." She gestured vaguely at her midsection. "You could tell he worked out. A lot."

"Tell us about the other guy," Jack said.

"Older white dude. Maybe late forties, early fifties. Looked like he'd been through some things— broken nose, cauliflower ear, you know the type. Walked like his knees hurt." She tapped ash into a plastic tray shaped like a human hand, fingers curled upward. "I figured he was a personal trainer. He had that vibe. He'd be talking the whole time—giving advice, critiquing. Dre would just nod and listen. Respectful, you know?"

"They ever mention a gym? Somewhere nearby they trained?"

She thought about it, smoke curling toward the water-stained ceiling. "Not by name. But one time the older guy said something about getting back to the warehouse before the afternoon guys showed up."

"When's the last time you saw them?"

"Few days ago, maybe." She tapped ash into the tray. "Same as always. Trainer got his cartridges, Dre grabbed a Gatorade, they left."

"Nothing unusual? Nothing out of the ordinary?"

She thought about it, then shook her head. "Nope. Just two guys stopping in like they always did."

Jack pulled a card from his pocket. "If you think of anything else—the trainer's name, anything they might have said about the gym—give me a call."

She took the card, tucked it into the back pocket of her jeans. "Yeah. Sure."

The heat hit us like a wall when we stepped back outside. I squinted against the glare, my mind already sorting through what we'd learned. A trainer with cauliflower ears. A warehouse gym somewhere nearby. A young man named Dre who kept himself in shape and didn't smoke.

It wasn't much. But it was a start.

Cole was waiting by his truck, his Stetson pushed back and his face glistening with sweat. He'd found a sliver of shade next to the building, but it wasn't doing much good. The heat radiated up from the asphalt in waves.

"Got anything?" Jack asked.

"Nail salon was a bust. Owner just took over the lease a few months back—doesn't know anyone, doesn't see anything, doesn't want to get involved." Cole pulled his notebook from his back pocket and flipped it open. "Check-cashing place was a different story. Lady behind the counter recognized the description before I finished giving it. Said he came in every Friday like clockwork to cash his paycheck."

He paused, and something in his expression told me he had more.

"She pulled his records for me. Andre Tyrell Washington. Twenty-four years old. Paychecks came from King Construction—they've got a lot over on Miller Road." Cole glanced up. "She said he was one of the nice ones. Always asked about her grandkids."

Andre. Dre for short. We had a name now. A real

name, attached to a real life—a job, co-workers, a routine. A young man who cashed his checks on Fridays and remembered to ask about an old woman's grandkids.

"King Construction," Jack said. "That's Danny King's outfit. He runs a decent operation—hires a lot of guys who need a second chance. Ex-military, men coming out of the system."

"The check-cashing lady mentioned he used a military ID once," Cole added. "When his regular license was expired."

So Andre Tyrell Washington had served his country, worked construction, trained as a fighter, and ended up wrapped in a cheap blanket at the bottom of a dumpster. The shape of his life was starting to emerge—and with it, the people who might know why it had ended.

"We got a person of interest from the vape shop," Jack said. "Older white guy, late forties or fifties. Broken nose, cauliflower ears, bad knees. The lady said he was Dre's trainer. They came in together once a week or so."

Cole nodded slowly, those pale blue eyes going distant the way they did when his mind was already three steps ahead, sorting through angles and possibilities like a man shuffling cards. "I'll run Andre Tyrell Washington through the system—priors, known associates, anything that pops. And I'll check boxing gyms, MMA facilities in the area. Guy built like that, training with someone who knows what he's doing, he's registered somewhere. Fighting's not something you hide. Somebody knows him."

"We need to talk to his co-workers too," Jack said. "And find that trainer. But let's wait until J.J.'s done with the autopsy. She might find something that gives us better questions to ask."

Cole glanced at me, a question in the look.

"A few hours," I said. "I should have preliminary findings by late afternoon."

"Works for me." He fished his keys from his pocket, already moving toward his truck. "I'll call when I've got something."

We watched him go—that long, easy stride covering ground without ever seeming to hurry.

Jack's hand found the small of my back as we turned toward the Tahoe. "Let's get you to the funeral home."

The parking lot had transformed while we'd been inside asking questions. Cars filled the spaces now, and people moved between them with the purposeful energy of lunch hour—a woman balancing takeout bags and a cell phone, a man in a rumpled suit loosening his tie as he headed for the Chinese place, a young mother wrestling a toddler into a car seat while an older child kicked at the asphalt with light-up sneakers.

Jack opened my door—old habits died hard with him—and I slid into the passenger seat, grateful for the air-conditioning that had been running the whole time we'd been inside Cloud Nine. He went around to the driver's side and climbed in, and then pulled out of the lot, merging onto Route 3 with the ease of someone who knew these roads like the back of his hand.

"You're quiet," he said after a few minutes.

"Thinking."

"About?"

"His hands." I watched the strip malls and fast-food joints slide past, giving way to stretches of pine trees and the occasional farmhouse set back from the road. "The old breaks. The calluses. He'd been fighting for years, Jack. That kind of damage doesn't happen overnight."

"He's got a trainer for a reason," Jack said. "That suggests a level of professionalism in the sport."

I shifted in my seat, trying to find a comfortable position. My lower back ached from hours of standing, and exhaustion was starting to creep in around the edges. "I'll know more after the autopsy."

He reached over and took my hand, his fingers warm and rough against mine. We drove like that for a while, leaving behind the strip malls and chain restaurants of King George Proper as Route 3 curved north toward Bloody Mary. The landscape shifted as we went—tract housing giving way to farmland, the occasional tobacco barn weathered silver by decades of sun and rain, hand-painted signs advertising fresh eggs and firewood for sale.

A red pickup truck passed us going the other direction, and Jack raised two fingers off the steering wheel in that universal rural greeting.

"Was that Bobby Hendricks?" I asked, craning my neck to look back.

"Looked like it. He had a woman in the passenger seat."

"Not Marlene."

"Definitely not Marlene. This one was blond."

"Interesting." I settled back in my seat. "Emmy Lu said she heard Marlene kicked him out last month. Apparently she found receipts in his pocket from the Comfort Inn over in Fredericksburg."

"The Comfort Inn." Jack shook his head. "If you're going to step out on your wife, at least have some class about it."

"Right? Take her somewhere nice. Make it worth losing half your assets."

"I don't think that's the lesson here."

"I'm just saying, if Marlene's going to take him to the cleaners—and she will, her sister's a divorce attorney in Richmond—he should have at least gotten some decent thread count out of it."

Jack laughed. "You're terrible."

"I'm practical." I watched the scenery roll past. "How long were they married? Fifteen years?"

"Something like that. Kids are in high school now."

"That's the part that gets me." I shook my head in disbelief. "You do something like that, it's not just your spouse you're betraying. It's your whole family."

Jack squeezed my hand. "Some people don't think past what they want in the moment."

"Lucky for Bobby, Marlene's been thinking. Emmy Lu said she's been squirreling money away for two years. Had a feeling something was off."

"Smart woman."

"Always was. Too smart for Bobby Hendricks, that's for sure."

We passed the old Mercer place, where three generations of junk cars rusted in the front yard alongside a hand-lettered sign that read *Trespassers Will Be Shot—Survivors Will Be Shot Again.* A few miles later, the white steeple of St. Paul's Episcopal Church came into view, and then the town itself— Main Street with its antique shops and law offices, the Towne Square where old men gathered on benches to solve the world's problems, and Martin's Grocery Store.

Jack turned onto Catherine of Aragon, and the funeral home came into view where it sat on the corner—a three-story Colonial in dark red brick and white columns flanking the front entryway. Two massive elm trees shaded the front yard, their gnarled roots cracking the sidewalk.

Jack pulled under the metal portico on the side, where the black Suburban was already parked.

"What time do you think you'll be done?" he asked.

"Between three and four," I said. "Depends on what I find."

"I'll pick you up, and we can hit King's Construction before they close for the day. And then we can grab dinner at Rosa's."

"You just want an excuse to flirt with Rosa."

"She's eighty-three years old."

"And she lights up like a Christmas tree every time you walk in." I leaned over and kissed him. "I'll text you when I'm wrapping up."

"Deal."

I climbed out of the Tahoe and headed for the side door. I was almost to the ramp when Jack called out.

"Jaye."

I turned. He was leaning out the window, sunglasses pushed up on his head, that familiar half smile playing at the corner of his mouth.

"Yeah?"

"I love you."

Simple words. We said them all the time—tossed

them out like spare change, easy and automatic. But sometimes, like now, they landed different. Heavier. A reminder that every goodbye could be the last one.

The kitchen was empty, stainless steel gleaming under the fluorescent lights. I could hear Emmy Lu's voice drifting from somewhere in the front of the house—probably on the phone with a family, her tone shifting into that mix of sympathy and efficiency she'd perfected over twenty years of helping people navigate the worst days of their lives.

A plate of snickerdoodles sat on the counter with a sticky note in Emmy Lu's looping handwriting: *Eat something.* I smiled despite myself. Between her and Jack, I'd never be allowed to skip a meal. I grabbed two cookies and ate them standing at the counter, washing them down with a bottle of water from the fridge. My stomach had finally settled after the dumpster smell this morning, and the sugar helped.

The reinforced steel door to the basement waited just off the kitchen. Beyond it, the victim waited too.

I tossed the empty bottle in the trash and headed downstairs to find out what the dead had to say.

<hr>

CHAPTER THREE

<hr>

Two thousand square feet of blindingly white tile and stainless steel, kept cold enough to make my breath visible in the air. The overhead lights buzzed faintly, casting everything in that flat, shadowless glare that left nowhere for secrets to hide. It smelled of antiseptic and something fainter beneath—the scent of a place where death was examined, cataloged, and ultimately explained.

Lily had set up while I was upstairs. The intake forms were stacked neatly on the desk, the case file started, the autopsy report template pulled up on the computer. She looked up when my footsteps echoed off the stairs, those vivid blue eyes sharp and alert despite the hour.

"Everything's ready," she said. "I've got the paper-work squared away and the equipment prepped."

"Good."

I crossed to my desk and grabbed the clipboard with the autopsy forms, then moved to the hooks by the door. The ritual of preparation was as familiar as breathing—lab coat first, the weight of it settling across my shoulders like armor. Then the heavy canvas apron, tied snug at my waist.

Finally, the gloves. I blew into each one before sliding my hands inside—an old trick from my ER days that warmed the latex just enough to make it bearable against my skin. The snap of them settling into place was its own kind of signal. Time to work.

"Alexa," I said, "play some Weeknd."

The opening notes of "Earned It" purred through the speakers, all smoky bass and seduction.

"Oh, no. No, no, no." Lily was already on her feet, waving her hands. "Alexa, stop."

The music cut off. I raised an eyebrow. "Problem?"

"That song is on Cole's..." She paused, color rising in her cheeks. "Playlist."

"His playlist."

"His *playlist* playlist. The one he puts on when we're..." She gestured vaguely, her face now roughly the color of a tomato.

"Ah." I bit back a smile. "So you're telling me you

can't focus on an autopsy while listening to the same song you and Cole—"

"Can we please just pick something else?"

I laughed. "Alexa, play Bon Jovi."

The opening riff of "Wanted Dead or Alive" filled the lab, and Lily's shoulders relaxed. "Thank you."

"You're welcome. Though we're going to revisit this conversation later."

"We absolutely are not."

"I want to know what else is on the playlist."

"Very funny."

I moved to the autopsy table, where Andre Tyrell Washington waited in the black body bag. Lily fell into step beside me, camera in hand, ready to document every step of the process.

I picked up my digital recorder and felt its familiar weight settle into my palm. Some coroners relied entirely on digital transcription these days, but I preferred the old ways. The recorder backed up my handwritten notes, my sketches, my photographs. Technology failed. Paper endured. And I'd learned the hard way to always have redundancy.

"Recorder on." My voice shifted into clinical mode, steady and precise. "Dr. J.J. Graves performing the autopsy of Andre Tyrell Washington, case number 2024-0547, on May twenty-eighth. Assisting is Lily Jacobs."

I unzipped the bag.

The moving blanket we'd documented at the scene was gone now, sent to the state lab in Richmond for fiber analysis. What remained was the man himself—or what was left of him after days of brutality.

"Let's get his clothes off first," I said. "Document everything as we go."

I'd learned the hard way to remove clothing while the body was still in the bag—any fibers or trace evidence would be caught in the plastic rather than lost to the floor. Lily photographed each item as I cut it away—jeans, worn soft at the knees and stained with blood. A T-shirt, once white, now a roadmap of violence. No shoes, no socks. His feet were still bare, still covered in the residue I'd noted at the scene.

"Victim is clothed in blue denim jeans, size thirty-four waist, thirty-four inseam. White cotton T-shirt, size extra large, with extensive blood staining on the anterior surface." I went through his pockets methodically—empty, all of them. No wallet, no phone, no keys. Nothing to identify him beyond the name we'd already learned. "No personal effects recovered from clothing."

With the clothes bagged and labeled, we lifted him from the body bag and onto the table using the electronic pulley system—a strap beneath his torso, a switch, and the mechanical whir of the lift doing the work that would have wrecked my back.

"Victim is an African American male, well developed, well nourished." I pulled the measuring tape from my pocket, stretching it along the length of his body. "Height is one hundred eighty-eight centimeters."

The table's built-in scale gave me the rest. "Weight is ninety-nine point eight kilograms."

I began the external examination at his head and worked my way down, documenting every wound, every scar, every mark that told the story of who this man had been.

"Severe facial trauma," I recorded, leaning close to study the damage. "Left orbital fracture with significant depression. Nasal fracture with lateral displacement—this is at least the third fracture to this area based on the scarring pattern and bone remodeling. Mandibular fractures, bilateral. Extensive bruising and swelling throughout the facial region."

I tilted his head to examine the entry wound I'd documented at the scene. Under the surgical lights, with the blood cleaned away, I could see more than I'd been able to in the field.

"Single penetrating gunshot wound to the posterior cranium," I recorded, measuring carefully. "Wound diameter is six millimeters—consistent with a .22 caliber round. Soot deposits visible within the wound track." That was new. At the scene I'd noted the stippling, but the soot told me the muzzle had been even closer than I'd initially thought. Near contact. Inches away.

Whoever pulled the trigger had been close enough to feel his breath.

"I'll confirm the bullet's position and trajectory on x-ray," I said.

His head was shaved clean, the scalp smooth except for a small scar near his left temple—old and faded—the kind of mark that came from stitches long since removed.

"Let's get a better look at that tattoo," I said.

At the scene, I'd only been able to see part of it through the blood and grime. Now, with better light and a damp cloth to clean the area, the full design emerged on the back of his neck, just below the hairline.

It was an eagle—wings spread wide, talons extended, rendered in stark black ink with military precision. Beneath it, in small block letters—*USMC*. And below that, a series of numbers that looked like a unit designation.

"Tattoo on posterior neck," I recorded. "Eagle design with USMC text and numerical designation, possibly unit identification. Professional quality, approximately five centimeters in height, well healed."

A Marine. Andre Tyrell Washington had been a Marine before he'd been a construction worker, before he'd been a fighter, before he'd ended up on my table. I filed that away, another piece of the puzzle that Jack and Cole would need to chase down.

I continued down his body, cataloging the evidence of years spent in combat—not the military kind, but the kind that happened in rings or on the street.

"Hands show significant damage consistent with long-term fighting." I lifted his right hand, examining the knuckles under the magnifying lens. "Extensive callusing across all metacarpophalangeal joints. Palpable deformity of second and third metacarpals consistent with multiple healed fractures. Similar findings on the left hand affecting the fourth and fifth metacarpals."

"He broke his hands a lot," Lily observed.

"Repeatedly, over years." I flexed his fingers gently, feeling the way the joints ground against each other where they should have moved smoothly. "And he's not that old. He started young—mid-teens, probably, to have this much accumulated damage."

The old damage was expected. I'd seen it at the scene and knew what it meant. But what the autopsy gave me that the field exam couldn't was confirmation of timing.

"All phalanges show perimortem fractures," I recorded, examining the tissue surrounding each break under the magnifying lens. "Vital reaction is present—edema and early hemorrhagic response in surrounding soft tissue, indicating fractures were sustained while the subject was still alive." I set his hand down carefully. "These injuries occurred hours before death, not after."

"He was conscious?" Lily asked.

"His body was still mounting an inflammatory response. You don't get that postmortem." I moved to the next hand, documenting the same findings. "He felt every one."

Lily was quiet for a long moment after that, the camera still in her hands.

I moved to his torso, where the real brutality became apparent.

"Multiple contusions to the anterior and lateral chest and abdomen." I measured each bruise, photographed it, noted its position on my body diagram. "Bruising shows variation in coloration— some contusions appear fresh, dark purple to black, while others display green and yellow margins consistent with healing over twenty-four to forty- eight hours."

Lily was quiet as she documented, the camera clicking in steady rhythm.

"He was worked over for a couple of days," I said, not for the recorder but for her. "At least two, maybe three, based on the healing patterns."

"While he was restrained."

"Yes." I moved to his wrists, where the zip-tie marks cut deep into his skin. "Ligature marks on both wrists, consistent with zip-tie restraints. Deep tissue damage with evidence of significant resistance—he fought against the restraints hard enough to tear his own skin."

No old marks beneath the fresh wounds, though. Whatever had happened to Andre Tyrell Washington, it had happened fast.

I examined his back next, documenting the parallel abrasions across his shoulder blades—drag marks, I was almost certain—and the circular burns that dotted his lower back like a constellation of cruelty.

"Eight circular burns on the posterior lumbar region," I recorded. "Diameter consistent with cigarette burns. Varying stages of healing corresponding to the timeline established by other injuries."

"Someone took their time," Lily said quietly.

"Someone wanted him to suffer."

I moved to his feet, scraping samples of the

grayish residue into evidence containers. Whatever this substance was—brick dust, calcium deposits, old mortar—it would tell us about where he'd been held. Where he'd walked barefoot across cold floors while someone burned him with cigarettes and beat him until his bones cracked.

"Let's look for injection sites," I said.

I searched for injection sites—a standard part of any autopsy. Inner arms, hands, feet, neck, the spaces between his fingers and toes.

"No injection sites visible," I recorded. "No puncture wounds or bruising consistent with needle use."

Lily documented it with the camera while I moved on to the next step.

"Let's get x-rays before we open him up. I want to see what his bones can tell us."

The machine hummed to life, and we moved through the familiar process—positioning, adjusting angles, capturing images of the skeleton beneath the damaged flesh. When we finished, I loaded the films onto the illuminator and stepped back to study them.

The damage was extensive.

"Geez," Lily said. "Poor guy."

"Multiple healed fractures visible throughout the skeletal system," I said into the recorder, tracing the ghostly lines of old breaks. "Nasal bone shows evidence of at least three previous fractures. Bilateral rib fractures, healed, ribs four through seven on the left, five and six on the right. Metacarpal fractures in both hands with evidence of repeated injury and healing."

I moved down the images. "Right radius shows healed mid-shaft fracture. Left ulna shows similar injury—both consistent with defensive wounds from blocking strikes."

But it was the skull films that stopped me cold.

"There's our round," I said, pointing.

The bullet was clearly visible on the lateral view —a small, bright white object lodged just behind the frontal bone. It had entered at the base of the skull, traveled upward through the brain stem and cerebellum, and come to rest against the inner table of the frontal bone without enough energy to punch through.

"Single projectile visible in the anterior cranial fossa," I recorded. "Consistent with a small-caliber round that traversed the posterior fossa and brain stem before lodging against the inner frontal bone. No fragmentation visible."

"It bounced around inside," Lily said quietly.

"It didn't need to bounce. The trajectory took it straight through the brain stem." I traced the path on the film with my finger. "Instant incapacitation. He was dead before he hit the ground."

The skull films also showed the accumulated

history, old fractures to the temporal and parietal bones, barely visible, shadow patterns consistent with repeated impact over time.

"Years of fighting," I said. "This is the kind of damage you see in boxers or MMA fighters. He started young and kept at it for a long time."

His bones told the story of nearly a decade of punishment. Whatever had gotten him into fighting in the first place, he'd committed to it fully.

"Let's open him up."

I positioned the body block beneath his shoulders, arching his chest upward to give me better access. The scalpel felt familiar in my hand—the weight of it, the way the light caught the blade. I'd done this thousands of times. It never became routine. Every first cut was a conversation. The moment I stopped reading the outside of a person's story and started reading the chapters they'd hidden beneath their skin.

"The Y-incision," I said quietly.

I made the first cut from shoulder to sternum, then the second from the other shoulder, the two lines meeting in the center of his chest. The final cut ran from the sternum to the pubic bone, completing the Y. Skin and subcutaneous tissue parted beneath the blade, and Dre Washington opened up to me the way the living never could, honestly and completely, with nothing left to hide.

The bone saw came next, that grinding whine that never failed to set my teeth on edge, no matter how many times I'd heard it. I cut through the ribs with practiced efficiency, lifted away the chest plate, and there he was. The inside of a man who should have had at least fifty more years of living ahead of him.

The music had shifted while I worked, Bon Jovi giving way to Frank Sinatra. It filled the silence without demanding attention, and I let it carry me into that place I went during autopsies. The place that was focused and steady, the part of my brain that felt things turned down low enough to function but never all the way off. Never that.

"Examining the thoracic cavity," I recorded. "Lungs appear normal. No evidence of fluid accumulation, no signs of disease."

I removed each organ systematically—weighing it, examining it, taking samples for analysis. His lungs were healthy and pink, the lungs of a young man who'd run miles and sparred rounds and pushed his body to its limits. No smoking, no disease, nothing but clean healthy tissue that had been doing its job right up until the moment it didn't need to anymore. His liver was pristine. Kidneys unremarkable.

And his heart.

"Heart weighs three hundred forty-two grams.

Within normal limits. No coronary artery disease, no structural abnormalities."

Three hundred forty-two grams of muscle that had pumped blood through a body built for fighting, for surviving, for living. Strong and undamaged, the heart of an athlete in his prime.

It hadn't failed him. Someone else had.

I set it down gently. You'd think after all these years I'd stop feeling the weight of a healthy heart in my hands, the cruelty of an organ that was still perfect inside a body that had been destroyed from the outside. But I never had. And I hoped I never would. The day I stopped feeling it was the day I needed to find another line of work.

"Stomach contents show minimal food material," I continued. "Consistent with a subject who hadn't eaten in the twenty-four to forty-eight hours prior to death."

They'd starved him while they tortured him. Or maybe he'd simply been too terrified to eat. Either way, this man had spent his last days hungry and in pain, and that was another thing I'd carry out of this room and into whatever came next.

I used the bone saw to open the calvarium, the pitch changing as it bit through the thicker bone of the skull. Lily held the head steady while I worked. We'd done this enough times that she anticipated every movement, every angle. The skullcap lifted away cleanly, and I set it aside.

The brain told the rest of the story.

The wound track was visible immediately—a narrow channel of destruction that carved through the cerebellum, up through the brain stem, and into the frontal lobe. Tissue that should have been smooth and gray was pulped and hemorrhagic along the bullet's path, the damage radiating outward in concentric waves like a stone dropped into still water. Devastating and precise, exactly as the x-ray had predicted.

"Wound track extends from the posterior fossa through the brain stem and cerebellar tissue, terminating in the anterior cranial fossa," I recorded. "Extensive hemorrhagic damage along the entire trajectory. Brain stem destruction is consistent with immediate loss of consciousness and rapid death."

He hadn't suffered from the bullet, at least. Everything before it—the beatings, the burns, the fingers—that had been suffering. But the shot itself had been instant. A small mercy in a story that had very few of them.

The round was right where the films said it would be. A small, deformed slug resting against the inner table of the frontal bone like it had run out of momentum and simply stopped. I extracted it carefully with forceps, turning it under the light. Misshapen from impact but intact enough to matter.

"One projectile recovered," I recorded. "Consistent with .22 caliber. Deformed but intact. Preserved for ballistic analysis."

I dropped it into an evidence container and sealed it. That little piece of lead was the most important thing in the room. If we ever found the weapon that fired it, the rifling marks on that bullet would tie them together like a fingerprint. Every gun left its own signature on the rounds it fired. Unique as a thumbprint, admissible in court, and very, very hard to argue with.

"Bag it and log it," I told Lily. "That goes to Richmond with the blanket and samples."

She labeled the container with the case number and set it in the evidence locker while I turned back to the body.

I examined the neck and throat structures as a matter of thoroughness, documenting the bruising I'd noted at the scene, the deep contusions along the anterior neck consistent with being grabbed or held. But while there was soft tissue damage, the hyoid bone was intact and there was no hemorrhaging in the strap muscles that would indicate strangulation as a cause of death. The throat injuries were from rough handling during captivity. Someone had grabbed him by the neck, probably more than once, but they hadn't killed him that way.

The bullet had done that. Quietly, efficiently, and without ceremony.

I stepped back from the table, pulling down my mask to breathe air that wasn't filtered through fabric. Andre Tyrell Washington had been beaten, tortured for days, and then executed with a single shot to the back of the head. Twenty-four years old, a Marine, a fighter, a man who'd worked construction and cashed his checks every Friday.

Someone had decided he didn't get to live anymore. And they'd done it with the cold efficiency of people who'd made that decision before.

"Let me run that tox screen," I said. "Then we can close him up."

I collected the urine sample and moved to the testing station, running it through the standard panels I kept on hand for exactly this purpose. Basic toxicology. I could get the results in my own lab without waiting days for Richmond to call back.

Lily began the process of returning the organs to the body cavity while I waited for the results, her movements careful and respectful. Whatever we did to them on the table, we always put them back together as best we could. It was a matter of dignity.

The machine beeped.

I read the results.

"Benzodiazepines," I said. "Specifically Klonopin. It's an anti-seizure medication. Someone with his level of head trauma would surely have some effects of brain damage. But the levels are therapeutic, not elevated. Consistent with a prescribed dose, not an overdose."

Lily looked up from her work. "So he had a prescription."

"Somebody did. We'll need to confirm it was his." I made a note on the chart. "What it does mean is whoever grabbed him was able to take down a two-hundred-twenty-pound Marine who knew how to fight without the advantage of knocking him out chemically."

"Seems like that would be hard to do," Lily said.

"You'd think. But maybe they overwhelmed him with sheer numbers. They obviously had weapons." I pushed off the desk and picked up the suture kit. "Either way, it tells us something. These weren't amateurs afraid of a fair fight. They had the manpower and the confidence to take him by force."

I began the careful work of closing the Y-incision. Stitch by stitch, putting him back together, giving him back what small dignity I could.

"The broken fingers were the message," I said as I worked. "But the bullet was the period at the end of the sentence. They got what they wanted and ended him like a business transaction."

"That's cold."

"That's professional." I tied off another stitch. "This wasn't personal for whoever pulled the trigger. It was just another day."

The sutures were done. I stripped off my gloves, tossed them in the biohazard bin, and reached for my recorder.

"Autopsy of Andre Tyrell Washington concluded at 4:47 p.m.," I said. "Cause of death is a single gunshot wound to the head. A .22 caliber projectile entered the posterior cranium at close range, traversed the brain stem, and lodged in the anterior cranial fossa. Manner of death is homicide. Additional findings include perimortem fractures to all phalanges of both hands, extensive antemortem injuries consistent with two to three days of captivity and torture, and toxicology revealing therapeutic levels of benzodiazepines consistent with prescribed anti-seizure medication. Full report to follow."

I clicked off the recorder and set it on the desk.

"Get him into the cooler," I told Lily. "I need to clean up and get in touch with Jack."

She nodded, already moving to prep the transfer.

I climbed the stairs and pushed through the door into the kitchen. My office was just off to the right—a small room with a desk, a couch, and most importantly, a tiny bathroom with a shower. I kept spare clothes in the closet for exactly this reason.

The water was hot, the pressure strong, and I stood under the spray until I felt human again. The tension in my shoulders loosened, the smell of the lab rinsed away, and by the time I shut off the water, my skin was pink and my cheeks had some color back in them.

My stomach growled as I toweled off. A good sign. I was actually hungry for the first time all day—Rosa's was sounding better by the minute.

I dressed in the spare clothes I kept in the closet—black jeans, a sleeveless red blouse that always made me feel put together, black ballet flats. I added a black blazer from the hanger on the back of the door in case Jack needed me for interviews later. A little concealer took care of the dark circles under my eyes, a swipe of mascara and some lip gloss finished the job.

The woman in the mirror looked like someone ready to face the rest of the day. Maybe even someone ready for a glass of wine and some of Rosa's enchiladas.

I grabbed my bag and stepped out of my office to find Jack leaning against the kitchen counter, arms crossed over his chest. His gaze traveled from my face down to my toes and back up again, slow and appreciative, that familiar heat sparking in his dark eyes.

"Well, hey there," he said, his voice dropping into

that low register that still made my stomach flip after all these years. "You clean up nice, Dr. Graves."

"Flattery will get you another shower session, Sheriff."

"That's what I'm counting on." He pushed off the counter and crossed to me, his hands finding my hips like they belonged there. "You know what I wish? I wish we could skip everything else tonight and just go home. Order takeout. Eat in bed. Naked."

"Mmm." I slid my hands up his chest, feeling the solid warmth of him through his shirt. "I could be persuaded."

"Yeah?" He dipped his head, his lips brushing the curve of my neck.

I let my head fall back, giving him better access, a soft moan escaping as his mouth found that spot just below my ear. "You're not playing fair."

"Never claimed to." His teeth grazed my skin, sending a shiver down my spine.

"You're killing me." I pulled back just enough to look at him, my fingers curling into the fabric of his shirt. "The faster we notify next of kin the faster we can get home."

"I thought you wanted Rosa's," he said.

"I'd rather have you."

He kissed me once more—slow and thorough, the kind of kiss that made promises—then stepped back and offered me his hand. "All right, Dr. Graves. Let's go to work."

CHAPTER FOUR

Jack took one look at me as we climbed into the Tahoe and frowned. "When's the last time you ate?"

"I had cookies."

"Cookies."

"Emmy Lu left them on the counter. Snicker-doodles."

"That's not food, Jaye. That's sugar and carbs." He started the engine but didn't put it in gear. "What else?"

I thought about it. "Water?"

"For the love of—" He shook his head and pulled out of the parking lot, but instead of heading toward the address Cole had texted him for Andre's mother, he turned left onto Main Street.

"Where are we going?"

"To get you actual food. You're growing a human being. You can't do that on snickerdoodles."

"The baby likes snickerdoodles."

"The baby doesn't get a vote yet."

Ten minutes later, we were parked in the lot of Taco Loco, a little hole-in-the-wall place on the edge of Bloody Mary that had been serving the best tacos in King George County for as long as I could remember. Jack ordered through the window—carnitas tacos for both of us, rice and beans on the side—and we ate right there in the parking lot with the AC blasting and the windows up.

"Better?" he asked after I'd demolished my first taco.

"Much." I wiped my mouth with a napkin. "Thank you."

"Someone's got to take care of you when you forget to take care of yourself."

"I didn't forget. I was busy." I watched him work through his own tacos. "When's the last time you ate?"

"Breakfast."

"And you're lecturing me?"

"I was stuck in the council meeting from hell all afternoon," he said. "I would have gladly escaped if I could have to eat."

"Uh-huh," I said.

"Are you going to tell me what you found?"

I started on my second taco. "Cause of death was a single gunshot wound to the back of the head. Small caliber, .22, close range. I recovered the round. It's on its way to Richmond for ballistics."

Jack nodded, his jaw tightening.

"He was tortured for two to three days before they killed him. The bruises and burns were in different stages of healing." I took another bite, chewed, swallowed. "I also found Klonopin in his system. It's an anti-seizure medication."

"Seizures?"

"With the amount of old head trauma I found—I'm talking years of it—It's not surprising. Repeated blows to the head cause cumulative brain damage. Seizures are one of the consequences." I wiped my fingers on a napkin. "But here's the thing. The levels were therapeutic. Normal. He was taking his medication exactly the way he was supposed to."

"So nobody slipped him anything."

"No. Whoever grabbed him did it the hard way." I crumpled my taco wrapper. "Which makes me wonder what else we don't know about this kid's life."

"His mother's name is Loretta Washington. She lives over on Maple Court, in the Riverside apartments. Cole ran the background while you were doing the autopsy. She's a nurse's aide at the hospital, been there twenty years. Andre was her only child."

Her only child. And now we were about to knock on her door and tell her he was dead.

But even as the dread of the notification settled over me, something else nagged at the back of my mind. Construction workers didn't get executed. They didn't get held for days and tortured. Whatever had put him on that killer's radar, it wasn't framing houses and pouring concrete.

———

The Riverside apartments were a cluster of two-story brick buildings on the east side of King George Proper. It was a place where working people lived paycheck to paycheck and kept their heads down. Close to the naval base, close to the hospital where Loretta worked her shifts. The parking lot was half full at this hour, sedans and pickup trucks baking in the late afternoon sun. A group of kids kicked a soccer ball around on a patch of brown grass, their laughter carrying on the humid air.

Jack parked near building C and killed the engine. Neither of us moved for a moment.

"I hate this part," he said quietly.

"I know."

"It never gets easier."

"It's not supposed to." I reached over and took his hand. "That's how you know you're still human."

He squeezed my fingers, then let go and opened his door. "Let's get it done."

Loretta Washington lived in apartment 2B, up a flight of concrete stairs with a wrought-iron railing that had seen better days. The door was painted a cheerful blue, and a welcome mat with sunflowers sat on the landing. A wind chime made of sea glass tinkled softly in the breeze.

Jack knocked. We waited.

The woman who opened the door was in her early fifties, with gray threading through dark hair she wore pulled back in a neat bun. She was still in her scrubs—pale blue, decorated with cartoon cats —and her eyes were tired but kind. The kind of tired that came from long shifts and longer worries.

Those eyes went from Jack's badge to my lanyard and back again, and something in her face shifted. She knew. Before we said a word, she knew.

"No," she said softly. "No, please."

"Mrs. Washington?" Jack's voice was gentle. "I'm Sheriff Jack Lawson. This is Dr. J.J. Graves, the county coroner. May we come in?"

Her hand flew to her mouth. She stumbled back from the door, and Jack caught her elbow, steadying her.

"Andre," she whispered. "Something happened to my baby."

"Let's sit down, ma'am."

The apartment was small but immaculate. A floral couch with hand-crocheted throw pillows. A bookshelf filled with photos—Andre in his Marine dress blues, Andre as a gap-toothed kid in a Little League uniform, Andre and his mother at what looked like his high school graduation. Everywhere I looked, there was evidence of a mother's love, a mother's pride.

Loretta sank onto the couch like her legs had given out. I sat beside her while Jack took the armchair across from us.

"Mrs. Washington," Jack said, "I'm very sorry to have to tell you this. Your son Andre was found deceased early this morning."

The sound she made wasn't a scream. It was worse—a low, keening moan that seemed to come from somewhere deep inside her, a place where words couldn't reach. I put my hand on her arm and let her cry, let the first wave of grief wash over her without trying to stem it.

Some things you couldn't fix. You could only witness.

When the sobs finally quieted to shuddering breaths, I reached over to the box of tissues on the end table and pressed a few into her hand. She took them with trembling fingers, dabbing at her eyes, her cheeks, the tears that kept coming no matter how many she wiped away.

Jack gave her a moment. He was good at that—knowing when to push and when to wait. It was one of the things that made him good at this job, even the parts of it he hated.

"Mrs. Washington," he said gently, leaning forward with his elbows on his knees, "I know this is going to be difficult, but we need your help. We need to find the person who killed Andre."

She looked up at him, her eyes red rimmed and devastated. "Who did this? Someone—someone killed my boy?"

"Yes, ma'am. We're investigating this as a homicide."

The word hit her like a physical blow. She folded in on herself, arms wrapping around her middle as if she could hold herself together through sheer force of will. Fresh tears slid down her cheeks, but she didn't make a sound. This grief was quieter, deeper—the kind that settled into your bones and never fully left.

"I knew," she whispered. "I knew something was wrong. He didn't call me back. Andre always calls me back, even if it takes him a day or two. But it's been almost a week, and I kept telling myself he was busy, working overtime, maybe he met a girl and lost track of time." She pressed the tissues to her mouth. "But I knew. A mother knows. I felt it in here." She touched her chest, right over her heart.

"When did you last speak to him?" I asked, keeping my voice soft.

"Thursday night." A smile crossed her face. "He called to check on me, like he always does. Every Thursday, sometimes Sunday too. We talked for maybe twenty minutes about nothing much—what I was cooking for dinner, how his week went, whether I'd watched that show he told me about." Her voice cracked. "He sounded good. Happy. Said he had something to celebrate, but he wouldn't tell me what. Said it was a surprise. I told him I was too old for surprises, and he just laughed."

"Did he mention any plans for the weekend?" Jack asked. "Anywhere he was going, anyone he was meeting?"

Loretta shook her head slowly, her gaze drifting to the photos on the bookshelf. Her boy in his dress blues. Her boy as a gap-toothed kid. Her boy, frozen in time, never getting any older.

"He didn't say. Andre was private like that. Even when he was little, he kept things close to his chest. Didn't like to worry me." She let out a breath that was almost a laugh. "He thought I didn't notice. But I always noticed. I just learned to let him tell me things in his own time."

"What about his work?" Jack shifted slightly, his voice still gentle but probing. "Did he ever mention any problems at King Construction? Conflicts with co-workers?"

"No, nothing like that. He liked that job. Said the crew was good, treated him with respect." Her hands were still twisting in her lap, the tissues shredded between her fingers. "He was saving up, you know. Wanted to buy a house someday, maybe start his own business. Something with his hands—he was always good with his hands." Her voice wavered, stretched thin. "He was so smart, my Andre. Could have been anything he wanted."

I let the silence hold for a moment before asking, "Did he have a girlfriend? Anyone he was seeing?"

There was a brief flicker of light in Loretta's expression. "There was someone. He didn't talk about her much, not directly. But a mother knows." She touched her cheek, wiping away a tear that had escaped. "He'd get this look on his face sometimes when his phone buzzed. This little smile, like he had a secret. I asked him about it once, and he just said it was early days, he didn't want to jinx it. Said he'd bring her to meet me when things got more serious."

"Do you know her name?"

"No. He never said. I didn't push." Her face crumpled again. "I should have pushed. I should have asked more questions, made him tell me—"

"Mrs. Washington." I reached out and covered

her hand with mine. "You couldn't have known. None of this is your fault."

She looked at me with eyes that wanted to believe it but couldn't. Not yet. Maybe not ever.

"What about friends?" Jack asked after a moment. "Anyone he spent time with regularly?"

Loretta drew a shaky breath. "Some buddies from the Marines. They'd get together now and then, have a beer, watch a game. And there was his trainer—Vic something. Italian name, I think. They'd been working together for a while now."

Jack and I exchanged a glance. "His trainer?"

"From the gym." Loretta's brow creased. "Andre used to box in the Marines. He was good at it, won some competitions on base. When he got out, he wanted to keep it up. Said it helped him clear his head, burn off stress after work." A sad smile touched her lips. "He always did have too much energy. Even as a little boy, couldn't sit still for nothing. I used to say he was like a firecracker looking for a match."

"Do you know the name of the gym?"

"Iron something? Iron House, maybe?" She shook her head. "He didn't talk about it much. Just said it was good for him, kept him focused."

I hesitated before asking the next question. It felt intrusive, poking at a mother's wounds while they were still fresh and bleeding. But we needed to know.

"Mrs. Washington, did Andre have any health issues? Anything he was being treated for?"

Her fingers stilled on the shredded tissues. Something crossed her face—a shadow of worry that had nothing to do with the news we'd just delivered. An older fear, one she'd been carrying for a while.

"He started having seizures about a year ago." Her voice dropped, like she was sharing something shameful. "The doctors said it was from getting hit in the head too many times back when he was boxing. All those blows, they add up, I guess." She stared down at her hands. "They put him on medication for it. Klonopin, I think it's called. He'd been doing better—no episodes in months, he told me. But I still worried. Every time my phone rang, I thought…"

She didn't finish. She didn't have to.

"Did anyone else know about the seizures?" I asked gently. "Friends, co-workers, his trainer?"

"No. Nobody." Her chin lifted, a flash of her son's pride showing through the grief. "He was embarrassed by it. Said it made him feel weak, like his body was betraying him. He didn't want anyone to see him as anything less than strong." The tears spilled over again. "My strong boy. He worked so hard to be strong."

Jack gave her a moment, then asked, "Did Andre ever mention owing anyone money? Gambling debts, loans, anything like that?"

"Never. Andre was careful with his money. Responsible." A watery smile flickered across her face. "He sent me a little every month, even when I told him I didn't need it. Said it was his job to take care of me now. Said I'd spent enough years taking care of him."

"What about anyone who might have wanted to hurt him? Any conflicts, disagreements?"

Loretta looked at Jack like he'd asked if the sun might rise in the west. "Andre didn't have enemies. Everyone loved him. He'd give you the shirt off his back and apologize it wasn't warmer." Her voice splintered. "He held doors for strangers. Called his mama every week. Who could want to hurt someone like that? Who could do this to my baby?"

I didn't have an answer for her. Neither did Jack.

We asked a few more questions—about his daily routine, his habits, whether he'd seemed different lately—but Loretta had given us everything she had. Her son had kept his life compartmentalized, showing her only the parts he wanted her to see.

Jack leaned forward, his voice softening. "Mrs. Washington, is there someone we can call for you? Family, a friend, someone from your church? You shouldn't be alone right now."

She blinked, like the question surprised her. "My sister. Gloria. She lives over in Fredericksburg."

"Would you like us to call her?"

"I—" Her voice faltered. "Yes. Please. I don't think I can... I can't say the words again."

Jack made the call while I sat with Loretta, holding her hand while she stared at nothing. Gloria answered on the second ring and said she'd be there in thirty minutes.

We stayed until she arrived—a woman who looked like an older, softer version of Loretta, with the same kind eyes and the same grief now carved into her face. She gathered her sister into her arms without a word, and Loretta finally let go, sobbing against Gloria's shoulder like a child.

Jack left his card on the coffee table, along with the number for victim services. "We'll be in touch," he said quietly to Gloria. "If she thinks of anything else, anything at all, have her call."

Gloria nodded, her hand stroking Loretta's back. "Find who did this. Find them and make them pay."

"We will," Jack said.

We let ourselves out. The door closed behind us with a soft click, and Loretta's muffled sobs faded as we walked down the stairs and into the parking lot, where the kids were still playing soccer and the sun was still shining like the world hadn't just ended for a woman in apartment 2B.

Neither of us spoke until we were back in the Tahoe.

"She said nobody knew about the seizures," Jack said. "He kept it private."

"Somebody always knows."

Jack started the engine. "Let's go check out his apartment."

Andre's apartment was on the other side of King George Proper, in a newer complex that catered to young professionals and military personnel from the nearby base. The kind of place with a fitness center nobody used and a pool that got crowded on weekends. Clean lines, neutral colors, utterly forgettable. You could live here for years and never learn your neighbor's name.

The landlord met us at the entrance to building D—a heavyset man in his sixties who jingled a ring of keys like worry beads. Sweat stained the collar of his polo shirt, and he was breathing hard by the time we reached the third floor.

"Terrible thing," he said between breaths. "Terrible. Kid was quiet, never caused any trouble. Paid his rent on time, kept his place clean. You couldn't ask for a better tenant."

The refrain of the dead. I'd heard it a hundred times. Nobody ever said the victim was a jerk who played loud music and let his dog crap in the hallway. Death had a way of sanding down the rough edges, leaving behind only the smooth and the polished.

"Did you see him recently?" Jack asked.

"Thursday, I think. Maybe Friday morning." The landlord scratched his chin. "After that, no. But that's not unusual. Lot of these young folks keep odd hours. Work, gym, whatever. I don't keep tabs."

Thursday or Friday. Right before his world collapsed.

He unlocked apartment 312 and stepped aside with obvious relief, eager to hand off the responsibility of whatever we might find.

"A crime-scene unit will be here shortly to process the apartment," Jack told him. "They'll need access to the building."

The man's face went a shade paler. Nobody wanted to stand too close to murder. It had a way of rubbing off.

"I'll be in my office," he said, and retreated down the stairs faster than he'd climbed them.

Jack and I pulled on gloves and stepped inside.

The apartment was small—a studio with a kitchenette along one wall, a bed against the other, a bathroom tucked in the corner. But what hit me wasn't the size. It was the order. The bed made tight enough to bounce a quarter off. Clothes in the closet arranged by color. Shoes lined up like soldiers awaiting inspection.

Andre Washington had carried the military home with him. He'd built his life around discipline, around control, around everything being exactly where it should be.

"Tight ship," Jack observed.

"Once a Marine." I moved toward the kitchenette. "These habits don't fade."

The refrigerator confirmed what I'd suspected. Chicken breasts in the freezer. Vegetables in the crisper. Meal prep containers stacked neatly, each one portioned with rice and protein for the week ahead. On the counter, a high-end blender sat next to a tub of protein powder. No beer. No soda. No junk food.

This wasn't a man who trained casually. This was someone who treated his body like a precision instrument.

"No liquor," Jack said, checking the cabinet above the stove. "Not even a bottle of wine."

"He was serious." I closed the refrigerator door. "Whatever he was training for, he was all in."

The nightstand was next. I pulled open the drawer and found the expected evidence of a personal life—condom wrappers, a half-empty box of Trojans, a bottle of lubricant. Someone had definitely spent time in this bed.

But it was what I found tucked behind the condoms that made me stop.

A slip of paper, folded once. I opened it carefully. Numbers, initials, a date from three weeks ago. Handwritten in pencil on cheap paper, the kind you'd tear off a pad.

Not a lottery ticket. Not a receipt.

"Jack." I held up the slip of paper. "What do you make of this?"

He crossed the room and took it from me, studying the numbers and initials with a frown that deepened the longer he looked. I watched his expression shift from curiosity to recognition to something harder.

"This is a betting slip," he said. "The kind you get at underground games. Poker, fights, whatever." He turned it over, checking the back. "I've seen these before in vice busts. They're handwritten so there's no electronic trail. The numbers are odds, the initials are the bookie's mark."

"So he was gambling?"

"Or someone was gambling on him." Jack's jaw tightened. "A man with his build, his boxing background—he'd be worth serious money to the right people. And where there's serious money, there's someone keeping the books." He held up the slip. "This is a piece of an operation, Jaye. Betting slips, a professional execution, days of interrogation.

That's not one guy with a grudge. That's a business."

I thought about the discipline evident in every corner of this apartment. The meal prep, the protein powder, the body that had been honed into a weapon. "You think he was fighting illegally."

"It's a lead," he said. "And it makes me want to talk to his trainer even more. Go ahead and bag it."

I did, my mind spinning ahead to the implications. Underground betting meant underground events. Organizers. Money changing hands. People with a vested interest in who won and who lost.

"Let's check the closet," Jack said.

The clothes hung in neat rows, work gear on one side, casual on the other. Nothing expensive, but everything clean and well maintained. Shoes arranged by type—work boots, sneakers, one pair of dress shoes still in the box.

Jack ran his hands along the back wall, slow and methodical. Halfway across, he stopped.

"Got something." He pressed against the drywall, and it shifted. "False panel."

He worked it free, revealing a cavity about a foot deep. Inside sat a duffle bag, olive green, worn soft from use.

Jack pulled it out and unzipped it.

For a moment, neither of us spoke.

Cash. Stacks of it, bound with rubber bands.

Twenties and fifties, the kind of bills that came from hand-to-hand transactions. No crisp hundreds fresh from a bank. This was street money. Fight money.

"That's at least thirty thousand," Jack said. "Maybe more."

"Construction doesn't pay like this."

"No." His jaw was tight. "And people earning this kind of cash off the books don't usually end up dead unless the people running the operation put them there." He zipped the bag back up. "We're not looking for a killer. We're looking for an organization."

I stared at the money, thinking about the betting slip, the athlete's diet, the military discipline. About a mother who thought her son was just staying in shape, keeping busy, saving for a house.

"He was fighting," I said. "Not just training."

"Nobody talks about fight club," he said wryly.

"Good one," I said. "You don't hide this behind a wall if you're earning it legally. You put it in a bank. You invest it. You don't stack it in a duffle bag like you might need to grab it and run."

"If he was fighting underground, someone was running the operation. Taking a cut."

"And making a lot more than he was." I thought about what his mother had said. The celebration. The surprise he wouldn't tell her about. "What if he was trying to get out?"

"And someone didn't want to let him go."

It was still theory, built on circumstantial evidence and gut instinct. But it was something.

A laptop sat on the small desk by the window. That would go to Derby once it was logged into evidence. But when I searched for a cell phone—drawers, bathroom, under the mattress—I came up empty.

"No phone," I told Jack.

"And none of the victim's personal belongings were found in the dumpster either. Killer probably found a different dump site." His expression was grim. "It just slows us down. We'll get a warrant for the phone company. We can still get access to his texts and contacts. And maybe get a cell tower ping for his last location."

"Gotta love technology," I said.

"That's not what you said the other day when you were trying to update your computer and everything shut down."

"It's a love-hate relationship. I'm just waiting for the robots to take over and kill us all, and then we won't have to worry about it anymore."

"Cole's right," Jack said. "You are always looking on the bright side."

"And there's more sunshine where that came from."

"I've always loved that smart mouth."

I gave him a sassy grin. "Good, because you're stuck with it forever."

"Let's talk to the neighbors," Jack said. "CSI team should be here any minute."

The girl next door answered on the second knock—young, early twenties, yoga pants and an oversized T-shirt. Her hair was piled in a messy bun, and she squinted at Jack's badge like she needed glasses and wasn't wearing them.

"Yeah, I know Andre. Kind of." She leaned against the doorframe. "We're not friends or anything, but we say hi in the hall. He helped me carry groceries once when my bag broke. Seems like a sweet guy."

"Did you ever see anyone visiting him?" Jack asked. "Friends, a girlfriend?"

"There's a woman." She perked up a little, the way people did when they had something useful to contribute. "Pretty. She's mixed, maybe Black and Asian. Great hair. I saw her a few times over the past couple months, usually in the evenings."

"Did you ever talk to her? Get a name?"

"No, we never spoke. I just figured she was his girlfriend." She shrugged. "They seem happy. He walks her to her car sometimes, kiss her goodbye. Cute stuff."

"What kind of car?"

"Um." She squinted again, thinking. "Silver, I think? One of those little Hondas."

"Did you notice anything unusual recently? Any strangers, any arguments?"

"No, nothing like that. It's pretty quiet up here." Her face clouded. "Is Andre okay? Did something happen?"

"We're looking into some things," Jack said, which wasn't an answer at all. He handed her a card. "If you think of anything else, give me a call."

The man across the hall was older, late sixties, with the look of someone who'd retired from something physical—broad shoulders, thick hands, a military tattoo faded to blue-green on his forearm.

"Know him well enough to say hello," he said. "Polite. Respectful. You could tell he'd served."

"Did you ever see him with anyone? A girlfriend, friends?"

"The girl, sure. Pretty thing, always dressed nice. Saw her coming and going for a couple months now." He rubbed his jaw. "There was another guy too. Older white fella, looked like he'd been through it. Face all beat up, you know? Like a fighter. He'd pick Andre up sometimes, early mornings. They'd leave together in the guy's truck."

"What kind of truck?" Jack asked.

"Old Chevy, I think. Dark blue. Beat to hell."

"How often did you see them together?"

"A couple times a week, maybe. Sometimes more." The man shrugged. "Figured it was a workout buddy or something."

"Did you ever hear what they talked about?"

"Nah. I mind my own business." He paused. "The kid's dead, isn't he? That's why you're here."

Jack didn't confirm or deny. "Thank you for your time. If you think of anything else—"

"I'll call." The man took the card, studied it, then looked up with tired eyes. "He was a good kid. You could tell just by looking at him. Whatever happened, he didn't deserve it."

Nobody ever did. That was the hell of it.

CSI had shown up and were doing their thing in the apartment, so we walked back to the Tahoe in silence, the evening air thick and heavy around us. The parking lot lights had flickered on while we were inside, casting everything in that sickly yellow glow that made the world feel older and sadder than it was.

I couldn't stop thinking about the cash. Thousands of dollars, hidden behind a wall like a secret. Like a sin.

"The girlfriend's prints are probably all over that

apartment," Jack said as we reached the truck. "The trainer's too, if they spent any time there."

"Daniels will find them. And once we have prints, we can run them."

"Put names to faces." He unlocked the doors but didn't get in. Just stood there, one hand on the roof, staring back at the building. "His mother said he was celebrating something. A surprise."

"Could be an engagement. A new job." But that didn't feel right. "Except he's got that money. Maybe he was expecting a lot more wherever that came from."

"Maybe," Jack said. He was quiet for a long moment. Somewhere in the complex, a dog barked. A car door slammed. The ordinary sounds of ordinary life going on all around us.

"What are you thinking?" I asked.

"We'll visit the gym tomorrow," he said finally. "See if we can find the trainer."

"And King Construction. His co-workers might know something his mother didn't."

He opened the driver's door, and I walked around to the passenger side. But before I got in, I looked back at the apartment building one more time. Third floor, fourth window from the left. The lights were off now. Whatever secrets Andre Washington had kept in that tidy little studio, they were ours to uncover.

I just hoped we'd find them before whoever killed him disappeared into the shadows.

Jack turned south, toward home, and his hand found my thigh before we'd gone half a mile.

"I've missed that spark in your eye," he said, his voice dropping into that low register that did things to my insides. "When you came out of your office in that red top it was everything I could do not to make love to you right there in the kitchen."

"You've matured with age," I said. "We're ten minutes from home."

"Eight if I hit the lights."

"Then hit the lights."

He did. The sirens stayed off, but the Tahoe surged forward, and I laughed despite myself—despite everything, despite the dead man and the grieving mother and the thirty thousand dollars hidden behind a wall. Right now, in this moment, there was only Jack's hand on my thigh and the promise of what waited for us at home.

"I love you," I said.

He glanced over at me, his eyes dark with want. "Show me when we get there."

Gravel sprayed as Jack pulled up to the house and threw the Tahoe into park. The porch light was on, and I could see the blue flicker of a screen through Doug's window on the second floor.

"What about Doug?" I asked.

"Probably been playing video games since we left. I doubt he's seen the light of day except to raid the refrigerator."

"We should feed him."

"Order him a pizza." Jack was already out of the truck, coming around to my side.

I pulled out my phone and placed the order on the app as he opened my door. I barely got the confirmation before he was reaching for me.

"Jack—"

He scooped me out of the seat like I weighed nothing, one arm under my knees, the other around my back. I yelped and grabbed his shoulders.

"I can walk, you know."

"I know." He kicked the door shut and headed for the house. "But I've been thinking about carrying you to bed for the last few hours, and I'm done waiting."

He shifted me, and I wrapped my legs around his waist as he climbed the porch steps, and when his mouth found mine, I forgot all about dead fighters and hidden cash and grieving mothers. There was only this—his hands on me, his heart pounding against mine, the desperate heat building between us.

"Shh," I managed against his lips as he fumbled with the front door. "Doug."

"Doug has headphones."

We stumbled inside, trying to be quiet and failing miserably. Oscar met us at the door, tail going like a metronome, his whole body wiggling with the shameless joy of a dog who treated every home-coming like a miracle.

"Down, buddy," Jack murmured, nudging him aside with his knee without breaking the kiss. Oscar took the hint and trotted toward the stairs, tags jingling in the dark.

Muffled laughter mixed with kisses as Jack navigated the hallway and started up after him. His foot caught on the top step, and we nearly went down—but he caught himself against the wall, my back pressing into the plaster.

"Smooth," I teased.

"You're distracting me."

"I'm not doing anything."

"You're breathing." He kissed my neck, my jaw, the corner of my mouth. "That's enough."

He carried me the rest of the way to our bedroom and kicked the door shut behind us.

CHAPTER FIVE

The hospital corridor was empty.

I knew this hallway. It was the third floor of Augusta General, the maternity ward where I'd done my OB rotation a lifetime ago. Same mint-green walls, same scuffed linoleum, same fluorescent lights buzzing overhead with that faint flicker that always made the shadows jump. But it was wrong the way things are wrong in dreams. Too quiet. Too empty. The nurses' station dark and unmanned, the whiteboard wiped clean.

My baby was crying.

The sound echoed off the walls, bouncing and distorting until I couldn't tell which direction it was coming from. But I knew. Room 3012, end of the hall. I could see the door from where I stood. Thirty feet, maybe less. Close enough to read the number on the placard.

I started running.

The floor was slick under my bare feet. I was wearing scrubs, and my hands were bare, no gloves, no ring, nothing. Just skin. I pumped my arms and drove my legs and the door didn't get any closer. The hallway stretched ahead of me, the linoleum unfurling like a tongue, and the faster I ran the farther the door pulled away.

The crying got louder.

Not the patient, waiting cry of a hungry baby. This was different. This was the sharp, hitching wail of an infant in distress. It was a cry that activates something primal in your chest, something deeper than thought, something that says *move faster*.

"I'm coming," I said, and my voice sounded strange, flat and echoless, swallowed by the empty corridor. "I'm right here."

I ran harder. My lungs burned. My feet slapped the linoleum and I could hear my own breathing, ragged and desperate, and the door was still thirty feet away. Still exactly thirty feet away. I could see the handle, brushed steel, could see the thin strip of light under the door, could see the shadow of movement on the other side.

Someone was in the room with her.

I could see it through the narrow window in the

door—a shape, a figure, moving around the bassinet. Not rushing. Not panicked. Calm. Deliberate. The way people moved when they had authority. When they belonged.

"Stop!" I screamed. The word came out muffled, like screaming into a pillow. My legs were heavy now, thick and clumsy, every stride like pushing through water. "Don't touch her! Get away from her!"

The figure didn't turn. Didn't acknowledge me. Just continued moving with that terrible, unhurried calm while my daughter screamed and I couldn't close the distance.

Still close, but so far away. The numbers on the door were clear as day and I could not reach them.

I threw myself forward, and the floor shifted, went soft, went wrong. My feet tangled. I went down hard, palms slapping the linoleum, knees cracking against the floor. The pain was real, sharp and bright, the kind of pain that doesn't happen in dreams.

The crying stopped.

And I knew.

Not the way I knew things as a coroner. Clinical, detached, the careful logic of evidence and examination. This was different. This was deeper. A knowledge that lived somewhere beneath my ribs, beneath my training, in a part of me I hadn't known existed until ten weeks ago. The same part that had made my hand go to my stomach before I'd even taken the test. The same part that woke me in the night to check on something that didn't even have a heartbeat yet.

A mother knows.

Something was wrong. Something was already done. And I was too late.

I scrambled to my feet and the hallway was gone. I was at the door. My hand was on the handle, cold steel under my palm, and I pushed.

It didn't move.

I pushed harder. Threw my shoulder into it. Beat my fist against it until my hand throbbed. The door was locked and my baby was on the other side and the silence was absolute and I could not get in.

I pressed my face to the window.

The room was empty. Clean white sheets on the bed. Bassinet in the corner, neatly made.

No figure. No baby. No sign that anyone had ever been there at all.

Just an empty room, scrubbed clean, as if she'd never existed.

I came awake with a gasp that felt like surfacing from deep water.

Our bedroom. Gray light through the glass wall. The ceiling fan turning above us, steady and slow.

Jack's arm across my waist, his breathing deep and even against the back of my neck.

I pressed my hand to my chest and felt my heart slamming against my ribs. The sheets were damp under me. Sweat, not the cold linoleum of a hospital floor. And my hands were shaking.

Actually shaking, a fine tremor I couldn't control.

Not real. Not real. None of it was real.

My hand went to my stomach. Flat. Warm. Still there. Still mine.

I lay very still and concentrated on breathing. In through my nose, slow. Out through my mouth, slower. The way you coached someone through shock. The way I'd coached Loretta Washington six hours ago, though she'd had real grief and I only had the phantom kind. The kind your brain manufactured from fear and hormones and a long day spent with the dead.

A mother knows.

I squeezed my eyes shut. Loretta had known something was wrong before we'd said a word. Had felt it, she said. In her chest. In the place where her son had always lived.

I wasn't a mother yet. But I'd felt it in the dream, that annihilating terror, that willingness to break down doors and shatter bone and crawl on bleeding hands if it meant getting to her in time. And the worst part wasn't the fear. The worst part was the helplessness. The hallway that wouldn't end. The door that wouldn't open. All of my training, all of my strength, all of my stubborn, relentless will...and none of it had been enough.

It was just a dream.

I pressed my palm harder against my stomach. Jack shifted behind me, murmured something into my hair, settled deeper into sleep.

I didn't go back to sleep. I lay there in the gray half light with my hand on my stomach and my eyes wide open, listening to Jack breathe, listening to the fan, listening for a sound that wasn't there, a small, thin cry from down the hall, from a room that didn't exist yet, from a daughter I hadn't met.

The house was quiet. Everything was fine.

Jack stirred behind me, his arm tightening, pulling me closer.

"You're thinking too loud," he murmured against my hair.

"I'm not thinking anything."

"Liar." He kissed the back of my neck, lazy and warm. "How long have you been awake?"

Too long. "A few minutes."

His hand spread across my stomach, casual, possessive—and my breath caught. He couldn't know. It was just the way he held me, the way he always held me, one arm around my waist, hand resting wherever it landed. But after the dream, the weight of his palm against that small, flat space felt like the only thing keeping me anchored to the real world.

I laced my fingers through his and held on.

"Hey." His voice changed—still rough with sleep but alert now, reading me the way he always could. "You okay?"

"Fine. Just didn't sleep great."

He was quiet for a beat. I could feel him deciding whether to push. "Bad dream?"

"I don't really remember it," I lied. "Just one of those nights."

He pressed his lips to my shoulder and let it go. That was one of the things I loved most about Jack. He knew when to hold on and when to leave a door open without walking through it.

"What time is it?" he asked.

I glanced at the clock. "Almost six thirty."

He groaned but didn't let go. "Daniels should have something for me by now. She said she'd email the prints report first thing."

"Then you should probably check your email."

"Probably." But he didn't move. Just held me, his breath warm against my skin, his hand still laced with mine over my stomach. "Five more minutes."

I closed my eyes and let myself have it—five minutes of Jack's warmth, Jack's heartbeat against my back, Jack's hand over the place where our daughter was growing. Five minutes where nothing was wrong and no one was crying and every door in the house opened exactly the way it was supposed to.

"Okay," I said quietly. "Five more minutes."

I showered quickly, letting the hot water beat the last of the sleep from my muscles. We had interviews today—the gym, the construction site— which meant looking professional. I dried my hair and left it down, so it hung chin length. I'd been thinking of getting bangs, which on some psychological level probably represented the upheaval in my life, but I'd never been one to live my life based on psychology. That was more Jack's area of expertise.

I didn't linger in front of the closet. I never saw the point. I pulled on black trousers—slim cut, comfortable enough to move in—and paired them with a silk shell in deep crimson that made me feel like I meant business. I added a black blazer and slid my feet into black ballet flats.

I gave my reflection a once-over. Good enough. I could only assume my good genes had come from my birth mother. The woman I'd been stolen from had been French, which meant I could get away with nothing but moisturizer and my bone structure on most days. Today was one of those days.

My wedding ring caught the light as I reached for my bag. It was the only jewelry I ever wore, and the only jewelry I needed. Losing things in a body cavity while doing an autopsy was never fun, so I'd learned early on to limit myself in the bling department.

Jack was already in the kitchen when I came down. He was dressed in black DBUs and a black polo, his duty belt and badge firmly secured at his waist.

The smell of coffee filled the kitchen. Doug was slumped at the table with a bowl of cereal, his phone propped against the milk carton, some video playing at low volume. His eyes were red rimmed, his hair a disaster. Oscar was wedged under his chair, chin on his paws, watching us with the lazy contentment of a dog who'd already been fed.

Doug Carver had come to live with us under circumstances that were complicated even by our standards. His uncle Ben, Jack's best friend, was on the run from people powerful enough to make the FBI look the other way, and Doug had his own legal entanglements involving the Pentagon and a computer that technically shouldn't exist. He was sixteen, brilliant, and under close watch by the federal government. It didn't seem to bother him too much.

"Why are you up so early?" I asked, heading straight for the coffeepot. "I thought you were going to milk every second of summer break."

"I am," he said. "Haven't been to sleep yet." He shoveled another spoonful of cereal into his mouth. "I was on a raid with my guild. We almost beat the final boss but Tyler died like an idiot and we had to start over."

I had no idea what any of that meant, so I made a noncommittal noise. Jack already had my coffee ready in a to-go cup, and he handed it to me.

"Thanks," I said, taking the first sip that would kick-start my brain.

"Anything good come up lately you guys are going to need me for?" Doug asked.

"Maybe," Jack said. "Right now it's just foot work. We've got a few places to check out this morning. You have any plans today?"

"Sleep," he said. "And then I might head into town. I found out one of my guild members lives pretty close. She said she'd meet me at the ice cream shop on the square."

"She?" I asked, arching a brow.

Color rose to Doug's cheeks. "Girls can be in the guild."

Jack clapped him on the back. "Just make sure

you meet in a public place. She could be a fifty-year-old man."

"Gross," he said. "I've got my Mace, and I'm not afraid to use it."

"Be smart," Jack said. "Call us if you need us."

"10-4," he said, and then went back to his phone.

Iron House Gym sat on the edge of King George Proper, a no-frills metal warehouse set back from the road with its own gravel lot. The building was exactly what it advertised—industrial, practical, and built for purpose rather than aesthetics. There was no fancy signage or neon lights, just bold black letters painted directly on the corrugated steel—*IRON HOUSE GYM*.

Jack pulled into the lot and killed the engine. A dozen vehicles were already parked in neat rows—mostly trucks and a few older sedans. Cars that belonged to men who worked with their hands and didn't waste money on flash.

"Serious place," I said.

"The serious ones usually are." Jack opened his door. "Let's see what we can find out."

The smell hit me the moment we walked inside—sweat and leather and iron, all of it mixing with the sharp bite of disinfectant. It wasn't unpleasant. Just honest. The smell of hard work and purpose.

The interior was larger than I'd expected, the high ceilings and open floor plan making the most of the warehouse space. Two full-sized boxing rings dominated the center of the room, their canvas clean and tight, the ropes taut and well maintained. Heavy bags hung in a long row along one wall—at least a dozen of them, each one cared for, the leather oiled and free of cracks. Speed bags lined another section, and the far corner held an impressive array of free weights, squat racks, and benches. Everything was organized. Everything had its place. This wasn't a gym clinging to life—it was a working facility that took pride in what it was.

And I was very clearly not supposed to be here.

Every head in the room turned when we walked in. A dozen men, all of them built like they spent more time lifting heavy things than doing anything else, and all of them looking at me like I'd wandered through the wrong door. Which, in their minds, I probably had. Places like this weren't built for women. They were built for men who wanted to hurt each other in controlled environments, and the testosterone in the air was thick enough to choke on.

I kept my shoulders back and my expression neutral. I'd faced down worse than a room full of sweaty men with more muscle than manners. But I wasn't going to pretend I was comfortable either.

Jack, on the other hand, looked right at home. His posture shifted the moment we walked in—something subtle, something I might not have noticed if I didn't know him so well. He moved differently here. Watched the room differently. His eyes tracked one of the men working a heavy bag, assessed the stance of another who was shadowboxing near the mirrors.

Recognition. Familiarity.

"Help you folks?"

A young guy approached from near the entrance—mid-twenties, lean and muscular, with a nose that had been broken more than once and scar tissue thickening his brow. He was looking at Jack's badge, then at me, trying to figure out what combination of trouble had just walked through his door.

"We're looking for Andre Washington's trainer," Jack said.

The kid's jaw tightened, but just slightly. "That'd be Vic. He owns the place. Let me grab him."

He disappeared through a gray door that said *Employees Only*, and I took the opportunity to study the walls. Photographs everywhere—fighters posing with belts and trophies, action shots from matches, and yellowed newspaper clippings in simple frames.

A history of the gym, told in sweat and blood and victory.

"You look like you want to jump in the ring," I said quietly.

Jack glanced at me and smiled. "I've been known to box a time or two. In my younger reckless days."

"You must have been good at it," I said. "Since your face is still so pretty."

He laughed just as the gray door opened again.

Victor Caruso was somewhere in his early sixties, built like a fireplug—short and thick, with shoulders that strained his T-shirt and hands that looked like they'd been carved from stone. His face told his whole story—nose flattened and crooked from breaks that had never quite healed right, ears thickened into cauliflower, scar tissue ridging his brows like tiny mountain ranges. He walked with the careful, deliberate gait of a man whose body had collected decades of debt and was finally calling it in.

But there was nothing slow about the way he assessed us. His gaze moved from Jack's badge to my face to our positioning in his gym, taking in everything in the space of a breath.

"Vic Caruso," he said. He didn't offer his hand. "What's this about Dre?"

"Is there somewhere private we can talk?" Jack asked.

Caruso's shoulders stiffened. His hands, resting at

his sides, went still in that way of someone bracing for a blow. He knew. On some level, he already knew. People didn't show up with badges to deliver good news.

"Yeah," he said, his voice rougher than it had been a moment before. "Come on back."

His office was small and cramped, barely room for the desk and the two chairs wedged in front of it. Trophies lined a shelf on one wall, most of them tarnished with age. A window looked out onto the gym floor, giving Caruso a view of everything happening in his domain. He settled behind his desk, and Jack and I took the chairs across from him.

"Mr. Caruso," Jack said, "I'm sorry to tell you this. Andre Washington was found dead yesterday morning. We're investigating it as a homicide."

For a long moment, Caruso didn't move. Didn't breathe. He sat frozen, staring at Jack like the words were in a language he didn't understand.

Then his face collapsed.

It wasn't dramatic—no wailing, no shouting. Just a slow crumbling, like a building settling into its own foundation. He turned away from us, toward the window, fists at his hips as he breathed in deeply for control.

When he turned back, his eyes were red rimmed but dry.

"You sure it was Dre?" he asked. "Somebody killed Dre?"

"Yes, sir," Jack said. "We need to find who did this to him. It sounds like you and Dre were together quite a bit."

Caruso nodded slowly, pulling a handkerchief from his back pocket. He wiped his eyes without embarrassment, without apology.

"Four years," he said finally. "I trained that kid for four years. Watched him walk in here as a raw talent and turn into something special." He shook his head, the movement heavy with grief. "He was going to be somebody, you know? He had that thing—that gift you can't teach. Power and speed and instincts most fighters would kill for."

"How'd he end up here?" Jack asked.

"Same way most of them do. Word of mouth. He'd just gotten out of the Marines, wanted to keep fighting. Somebody told him about my gym, and he showed up one day asking if I'd work with him." A ghost of a smile crossed Caruso's face, there and gone like a shadow. "Most guys who walk in that door, they think they're tougher than they really are. They've watched too many movies, thrown a few punches in bar fights, and now they think they're ready for the ring. But Dre..." He trailed off, lost in the memory. "First time I saw him hit the bag, I knew. He'd been fighting since he was fifteen. Started on the streets before the Marines got hold of him. By the time he got to me, he already had the foundation. I just built on it."

"What was your arrangement?" Jack asked. "Training? Managing?"

"Both." Caruso spread his hands. "He didn't know anything about the business side—the promoters, the sanctioning bodies, all the politics that goes along with trying to make it in this sport. I've been doing this my whole life. My father trained fighters before me." His voice steadied as he talked, finding solid ground in familiar territory. "I know how it works. I was helping him navigate."

"When did you last see him?"

"Thursday morning." Caruso's hands gripped the arms of his chair, knuckles going white. "We trained for a couple hours, went over tape from his last fight, and talked about what's next. He was in a good mood. Said he had big plans for the weekend." He released a breath that seemed to empty him. "I figured it was the girl."

"The girlfriend?"

"Tiana." The name softened something in Caruso's weathered face. "He talked about her all the time. Never brought her around here—this isn't exactly the kind of place you bring your sweetheart —but you could tell he was gone on her. Got this look on his face whenever she came up. Like he couldn't believe his luck."

"Do you know her last name?"

"No. He kept that part of his life separate." Caruso shrugged. "Can't blame him. What happens in here is one thing. What happens out there is something else."

I leaned forward slightly. "Mr. Caruso, did Andre have any health issues you were aware of?"

His hands stilled on the chair arms. His whole body went rigid for just a moment—a fighter's instinct, bracing for impact.

"What kind of health issues?"

"The autopsy showed significant head trauma. Years of accumulated damage. That kind of injury often has consequences."

Caruso was silent for a long moment. His jaw worked, muscles bunching beneath the weathered skin.

"Seizures," he said. "He started having them about a year ago. First one scared us both half to death—he just went down, eyes rolling back, whole body shaking. The doctors said it was from all the hits he'd taken over the years. They put him on medication. Klonopin."

"Did anyone else know?"

"No." Caruso's chin lifted, a flash of protectiveness cutting through the grief. "He didn't want people to know. Said it made him feel weak. In this business, you can't afford to look weak. So we kept it between us."

"How did it affect his career?"

"Complicated things." He chose his words carefully, each one measured. "With that on his medical record, getting sanctioned fights would be harder. More liability concerns. We were working through it. Finding ways around the obstacles."

Jack shifted in his chair. "Did Andre have problems with anyone? Arguments, conflicts?"

"Not that I knew of. Everybody liked him. He was easy to get along with—didn't have an ego, didn't start trouble. Just showed up, worked hard, went home."

"What about money? Any financial issues?"

Caruso almost laughed, though there was no humor in it. "Dre? That kid was the most responsible person I've ever trained. Lived like a monk, saved every penny, never blew his money on stupid stuff the way most young guys do. He had plans." His voice cracked on the word. "Wanted to buy his mama a house someday. Get her out of that apartment she'd been stuck in for years."

We asked a few more questions, but the well had run dry. Caruso had given us what he had—or at least what he was willing to share. When we stood to leave, he walked us back through the gym, past the men who were still stealing glances at the cops in their midst.

"One more thing," Jack said before we reached the door. "We found a betting slip in Andre's apartment. Did he gamble?"

Caruso's brow furrowed. "A betting slip? What kind?"

"Handwritten. Numbers and initials. Not from any legal operation."

"That doesn't sound like Dre." Caruso shook his head slowly. "Kid didn't gamble. Didn't drink, didn't party, didn't blow his money on stupid stuff. He was focused. Disciplined." His frown deepened. "Where'd you find it?"

"His nightstand."

"I don't know what to tell you. That's not the kid I knew. Dre wasn't a gambler."

Jack nodded and handed him a card. "If you think of anything else, give me a call."

"You find who did this." Caruso's voice had gone cold, the grief hardening into something sharper. "Dre was like a son to me. You find the bastards who killed him, and you make them pay."

"We intend to," Jack said.

CHAPTER SIX

THE AIR-CONDITIONING BLASTED AS JACK PULLED OUT of the lot, and I angled the vent toward my face. Between the heat and the wall of testosterone in that gym, I felt like I'd been holding my breath for an hour.

"He knew about the seizures," I said. "He didn't even hesitate."

"No, he didn't." Jack turned onto the main road. "His own mother said Dre kept it secret from everyone. But Vic knew."

"If he's managing Dre's career, submitting medical paperwork and arranging fights, he'd have to know what he was working around."

"Working around." Jack's mouth curved, but there was no humor in it. "That's an interesting phrase, isn't it? He didn't say they were dealing with it. Didn't say they were being honest about it. He said they were finding ways around the obstacles."

"Which could mean falsified medical clearances. Doctors willing to look the other way."

"Could mean a lot of things." His fingers drummed against the steering wheel. "Could mean fights where nobody's checking paperwork at all."

I thought about the betting slip tucked in Andre's nightstand drawer. The cash hidden behind a false panel in his closet. The life of a monk that somehow produced thirty thousand dollars in bundled twenties and fifties.

"He shut down fast when you mentioned the betting slip," I said.

"He did. Went straight to denial." Jack shook his head. "Everybody keeps saying what a good kid he was, how disciplined, how focused. But good kids don't end up tortured and dead in dumpsters."

"And they don't hide thirty thousand dollars in their walls."

"No. They don't." He glanced at me. "I'm going to get a warrant for Dre's financials. Bank records, credit cards, anything we can find. If money was moving in ways that don't match the picture everyone's painting, I want to know about it."

"The cash wasn't going through any bank."

"Which is interesting all by itself." Jack slowed for a red light and turned to look at me fully. "Vic

Caruso's been in boxing his whole life. His father before him. That's a world with a lot of gray areas—legitimate fights, underground fights, sanctioned venues and ones where nobody asks questions. If Dre was making money somewhere off the books, Vic would know. He'd have to know."

"But he's not telling us."

"Not yet." The light changed, and Jack accelerated through the intersection. "Doesn't mean he won't. Sometimes people need time to decide whose side they're on."

"And sometimes they've already decided."

"That too."

We drove in silence for a few minutes, the familiar landscape of King George County sliding past the windows. I watched Jack's profile, the set of his jaw, the way his hands rested easy on the wheel. He was thinking. Processing. Fitting pieces together in that methodical way of his.

"How come you never told me you boxed?" I asked. "It would've had to have been while you were in the military or living in DC."

He grinned and said, "I try not to think about the years you and I weren't part of each other's lives."

"Good one," I said, rolling my eyes.

"I thought so." He reached over and squeezed my thigh.

"Did you like it?"

"Like what?"

I groaned. "Playing dominoes," I said sarcastically. "What do you think I'm talking about? Did you like boxing?"

I could tell by the look on his face he knew exactly what he was doing, and he was enjoying himself immensely.

"What's not to like? Your body is in top physical shape, and you get to punch people. I can't do that anymore."

"That's the life of a respected elected official."

"Yeah, it sucks."

"Though I will say your body is still in peak physical shape."

"I appreciate the support."

"Maybe your mom has pictures of you boxing," I said. "I'll ask her."

"That's low and dirty," Jack said.

"All's fair when you're keeping secrets. I'll get the details somehow. Some way. You've trained me well."

"I've created a monster."

"I don't think that's what you were saying when you were asking for five more minutes this morning."

"You're right," he said. "I forgive you. You can do no wrong." He winked and said, "That's Danny."

Jack pulled into a paved parking lot filled with white trucks with the King Construction logo on the side.

Danny King was waiting on the steps of the double-wide trailer that served as King Construction's field office, a Styrofoam cup of coffee in one hand. He was a big man—six four at least, with shoulders that strained the seams of his work shirt and the weathered, sun-darkened face that came from spending a lifetime outdoors. His hair had gone mostly gray, cropped short and practical, and his hands—when he lifted one to shield his eyes from the sun—were scarred and calloused, the hands of someone who'd started swinging a hammer before he was old enough to vote and never stopped.

"Jack Lawson," he said as we climbed out, and a warm smile spread across his face. "It's been a while. How are your folks doing? I keep meaning to call your dad about that barn renovation he mentioned last time I saw him at the hardware store."

"They're good. Dad's staying busy—you know how he is. Can't sit still." Jack shook the hand Danny offered, and I could see the easy familiarity between them—not close friends, but men who'd known each other most of their lives like people did in small counties where the same families had been neighbors for generations. "Danny, this is my wife, J.J. She's the county coroner."

Danny's smile faltered. His eyes moved from Jack's badge to my face, and I watched him do the math. Sheriff and coroner, showing up together in the middle of a workday. That equation only had one answer.

"Ma'am," he said, shaking my hand. His grip was firm but careful. "I've heard good things about you."

"That's always a relief."

Danny studied Jack's face for a long moment, reading whatever he found there. The warmth in his expression faded into something more guarded. More braced.

"I'm guessing this isn't about barn renovations," he said.

"No," Jack said. "It's not. Can we talk inside?"

"Come on in," he said. "I've got about twenty minutes before I need to be at the Riverside site, but I'm guessing this is more important."

The trailer's interior was organized chaos—blueprints stacked on every flat surface, coffee cups in various stages of abandonment, a calendar on the wall so covered in scribbled notes and circled dates it looked like a work of abstract art. Photos lined the walls too—job sites in various stages of completion, ribbon-cutting ceremonies, a younger Danny shaking hands with men in suits. The air smelled like coffee and paper and the faint ghost of cigarette smoke, though I didn't see any ashtrays. Old habit, maybe. Something he'd given up but couldn't quite escape.

Danny cleared a stack of invoices off two chairs

and gestured for us to sit. He settled behind his desk, the chair creaking under his weight, and wrapped both hands around his coffee cup like he was bracing for impact.

"All right," he said. "Let's have it. What's going on?"

Jack leaned forward, his forearms resting on his thighs. "Danny, I'm sorry to have to tell you this. One of your employees—Andre Washington—was found dead yesterday morning. We're investigating it as a homicide."

Danny was quiet for a moment after Jack told him. He set his coffee cup down on the desk and leaned back in his chair, the old springs creaking under his weight. Then he let out a long, slow breath and rubbed his hand across his jaw.

"That's a shame," he said finally. His voice was heavy, but steady. "That boy had a lot of potential. I was hoping he'd stick around, maybe move up. Good workers like him don't come along every day."

He shook his head slowly, staring at a spot on the wall somewhere past my shoulder.

"His mama know yet?"

"We notified her yesterday," Jack said.

"How's she holding up?" Danny picked up his coffee again, more for something to do with his hands than because he wanted it. "I never met her, but Andre talked about her all the time. Worried about her living alone, wanted to take care of her."

"About as well as you'd expect. Losing a child is hard, no matter what age they are. I hate being the deliverer of that news. It never gets easier."

Danny nodded, his mouth pressed into a thin line. "She need anything? I could put together a collection from the crew. Andre was well liked around here."

"I'm sure she'd appreciate that."

We sat with that for a moment, the rattle of the window air conditioner filling the silence. Then Danny straightened in his chair, shifting into a more businesslike posture. He understood why we were here. Questions needed answers.

"What can I tell you?" he asked. "I want to help however I can."

"How long had Andre worked for you?" Jack asked.

"Three, almost four years. Came on right after he separated from the Marines." Danny took a sip of his coffee. "Started him on grunt work like everybody else, hauling materials, cleanup, the jobs nobody wants. But he learned fast. Had him on framing crews by the end of his first year. Could have moved him into a supervisory role within the next couple years if he'd stuck around."

"Was he planning to leave?"

Danny set his coffee down carefully. "He never said it outright. But the last few months, he seemed restless. Distracted. He'd ask about business. Not his job, but *the* business. How contracts worked, where the money came from, how I built the company. The kind of questions a man asks when he's thinking about going out on his own."

"Did that bother you?"

"Hell no. I respect ambition. I started this company out of the back of a pickup truck. If the kid wanted to build something of his own, I'd have helped him." He shrugged. "But he never asked for help. Just asked the questions and kept whatever he was thinking to himself."

"Any problems on the job? Conflicts?"

"Not with my people. Andre got along with everybody." Danny paused, turning his cup. "But there was one thing. About a month ago, some guy showed up at the site looking for him. Not a worker. He was dressed wrong for it. I was in the trailer, saw him through the window. He and Andre talked in the parking lot for maybe five minutes. Andre's whole body language changed. He was stiff, tense, nothing like how he usually carried himself. The guy left and Andre went back to work, but he was off the rest of the day."

"Can you describe the man?"

"Older. Sixties, maybe. Built like he'd been somebody once. Thick through the chest, but going soft. Face looked like it had been through a few wars." Danny pointed to his own nose. "Crooked. Like it'd been broken more than once."

Jack and I didn't look at each other. We didn't need to.

"Did you ask Andre about it?"

"I did. He said it was nothing. Just an old friend checking in. But he was lying." Danny met Jack's eyes directly. "I've managed crews for thirty years. I know when a man's lying, and I know when a man's scared. Andre was both."

"Did you see that man again?"

"No. Just the once." He reached for his phone. "You want to talk to his crew? They're pouring foundation this morning at the Riverside site, but I can call ahead."

"We'd appreciate that."

The Riverside site was a sea of red dirt and heavy equipment, cement trucks rumbling in and out, the air thick with dust and the grinding roar of machinery. We found Gutierrez's crew near the foundation forms—six men in work boots and safety glasses, most of them splattered with concrete up to their elbows.

Gutierrez himself was in his fifties, wiry and weathered, with a gray mustache and the permanent squint of someone who'd spent three decades working under an unforgiving sun. He wiped his hands on his jeans when Jack showed his badge and waved his men over.

"Danny called," he said. "Said you'd be coming by about Andre." He shook his head, his mouth set in a grim line. "Tough news. Real tough."

The other men gathered around us, forming a loose semicircle. Their faces were guarded but curious—cops on a job site meant something had gone wrong.

"We're trying to put together a picture of Andre's life," Jack said. "Anything you can tell us would help."

"Dre was solid," Gutierrez said. "One of the best I've had in years. Showed up early, stayed late, never cut corners." He rubbed the back of his neck, leaving a smear of concrete dust. "But you already know that, or you wouldn't be here. So what do you really want to know?"

I liked Gutierrez. No wasted time.

"We need specifics," Jack said. "Things that might not seem important but could help us understand what was going on in his life."

The younger guy with the sleeve tattoos and gold cross spoke up first. "His girl's name was Tiana

Williams. Works at that bank downtown. First National. That's how they met. She helped him open an account, and he asked her out right there at the window." He smiled despite the circumstances. "Said she made him wait two weeks before she'd say yes."

"What about the boxing?" Jack asked. "Did he talk about that?"

"All the time." The younger one with the tattoos grinned. "Dre was serious about it. Said his trainer thought he could go pro someday. He'd come in sometimes moving a little slow, you know? Sore from training. But he never complained. Just popped some ibuprofen and got to work."

"He ever come in looking worse than usual? Beat up beyond what you'd expect from training?"

Gutierrez and the younger guy exchanged a look.

"Few weeks back," Gutierrez said slowly. "He came in looking rough. Real rough. I asked if he was okay, and he just said he'd had a hard weekend. Wouldn't talk about it."

"But that wasn't from training," the older man added quietly. "I've got a cousin who boxes. I know what training bruises look like. What Dre had that day..." He shook his head.

"Did Dre ever talk about money?" Jack asked. "Where it was coming from, what he was planning to do with it?"

The men exchanged glances again—quick, uncertain.

"He talked about striking it rich," Gutierrez said carefully. "Said he had something going on. Something big. But he never said what it was. Just got this look on his face sometimes, like he knew something the rest of us didn't."

"He ever seem worried?" Jack asked. "Scared of anything?"

"Not Dre. Steady as they come." The younger guy shook his head. "Nothing rattled him. Except maybe when Tiana texted." He smiled a little. "Then he'd get all distracted, checking his phone every five seconds like a lovesick teenager."

"That day he came in beat up," I said. "Did he say anything else about what happened?"

The older man with the gray hair shifted his weight, looking uncomfortable. "I asked him straight out if somebody was giving him trouble. Told him if he needed backup, he had friends here." He paused. "Dre just smiled and said he had it handled. Said sometimes you had to take a few hits to get where you wanted to go."

"What did you think he meant by that?"

"At the time?" The man shrugged. "I figured it was boxing talk. Something about his training, moving up to harder opponents. But now..." He trailed off, staring at the ground. "Now I don't know what to think."

These men had worked alongside Dre, shared lunches and jokes and the long hours of physical labor that built calluses on your hands and bonds between co-workers. But they'd only known the version of him he chose to show them. The hard-working kid who loved his mama and his girl and dreamed of something bigger.

Whatever else was going on in his life, he'd kept it locked away.

Gutierrez walked us back toward the edge of the site, away from the noise of the cement trucks. He pulled a bandana from his back pocket and wiped the sweat and concrete dust from his face.

"Dre was a good kid," he said quietly, so his crew wouldn't hear. "But the last few weeks, something was different. He seemed... I don't know. Wound tight. Like he was waiting for something to happen." He stuffed the bandana back in his pocket. "I should have pushed harder. Asked more questions."

"You can't predict the future any better than anyone else," Jack said. "Someone made the choice to murder Andre. And the responsibility of that lies solely on the killer."

"Yeah," he said. Gutierrez looked back at his crew, at the foundation they were pouring, at the ordinary workday that was continuing despite the news they'd just received. "But it doesn't make the regret go away."

The sun was high and merciless when we walked back to the Tahoe, the heat pressing down like a physical weight. I could feel sweat gathering at the small of my back, the silk of my blouse clinging uncomfortably to my skin.

Jack started the engine and cranked the air-conditioning up high. Neither of us spoke for a moment, letting the cold air wash over us.

"Tiana Williams," he finally said. "First National Bank."

"Let's see if she's in," I said. "Word will have traveled. I wonder if someone reached out to her."

Jack pulled out of the construction site, tires crunching over gravel. I stared out the window at the passing scenery—strip malls and fast-food restaurants, a gas station, a church with a message board out front promising that God had a plan. The ordinary landscape of King George County, going about its ordinary business while we chased down the details of a young man's death.

I thought about Dre Washington—twenty-four years old, working construction by day, training to box by night. Sending money to his mother, saving for a future, falling in love with a girl at the bank. By all accounts, he'd been doing everything right. Playing by the rules, working toward something better.

And yet someone had tortured him for days and put a bullet in the back of his head.

The disconnect nagged at me. Good kids from stable backgrounds didn't usually end up dead in dumpsters. Somewhere in the life Dre had been living, there was a shadow we hadn't found yet. A door that led somewhere darker than construction sites and boxing gyms.

Thirty thousand dollars in cash hidden behind a wall. A betting slip tucked in a nightstand drawer. A trainer who knew secrets Dre's own mother thought nobody else had.

The pieces were there. We just hadn't figured out how they fit together yet.

"What are you thinking?" Jack asked.

"I'm thinking everybody loved Dre Washington. He was a good kid, a hard worker, devoted to his mother, crazy about his girlfriend." I turned to look at Jack's profile, the set of his jaw, the focus in his eyes. "But somebody tortured him for days before they killed him. That's not random. That's not a robbery gone wrong. That's personal."

"Or professional." Jack's hands tightened on the wheel. "We already know what his body told us. This was organized. Infrastructure. But infrastructure needs a revenue stream, and right now the only one we've found is a duffle bag full of cash and a betting slip nobody wants to claim."

"Vic shut down the second you mentioned that slip."

"He did. And everybody keeps painting the same picture of Dre—the good kid, the hard worker, the one who was going to make it. But somebody in his life knew a different version of him." Jack glanced at me. "I'm not saying he was a bad kid. But good kids can get pulled into bad situations. Especially when they're desperate to make something of themselves."

I thought about the apartment we'd searched. The military precision, the monk-like discipline, the protein powder and meal prep containers. Dre had been building toward something. Working toward a future he could see clearly in his mind.

What had he been willing to do to get there?

"Let's see what Tiana has to say," I said.

CHAPTER SEVEN

First National Bank sat on the corner of Main and Commerce, sandwiched between a payday loan shop and a bail bondsman. It was a corner where money was always tight and options were few. The interior was aggressively air conditioned and smelled like old carpet.

I spotted her immediately.

Tiana Williams was beautiful in that way that made you look twice and then look again. Mixed race —Black and Asian, if I had to guess—with exotic features that drew the eye. High cheekbones, full lips, dark eyes tilted slightly at the corners. Her hair was pure silk, black and shining, pulled back in a low bun that couldn't quite contain its thickness. She was dressed professionally in a cream-colored blouse and simple gold studs, but there was nothing simple about her.

She glanced up as we approached and registered Jack's badge. Something flickered in those red-rimmed eyes—not surprise, but resignation. Like she'd been waiting for us.

"Ms. Williams?" Jack kept his voice low, mindful of the customers nearby. "I'm Sheriff Lawson. This is Dr. Graves. Is there somewhere private we can talk?"

She nodded and turned to the teller beside her—an older woman with kind eyes and gray braids. "Rita, can you cover for me?"

Rita reached over and squeezed her arm. "Take as long as you need, baby."

The breakroom smelled like burnt coffee and leftover microwave meals. Motivational posters lined the walls—eagles soaring, mountains being climbed. The kind of corporate inspiration that meant nothing to people who were just trying to survive until Friday.

Tiana didn't sit. Just stood by the window, arms wrapped around herself, staring at the parking lot.

"I already know," she said quietly. "About Dre."

"Who told you?" Jack asked.

"T-Bone called me around six this morning. He's a friend of Dre's. They spar together sometimes." She exhaled a shaky breath. "I don't even know his real name. Everyone just calls him T-Bone. He said cops had been by the gym asking questions, and he said they found Dre..." She couldn't finish.

"I'm very sorry for your loss," Jack said.

She finally turned to face us. The grief in her eyes was raw and deep, the kind that settles into your bones and never fully leaves.

"I wanted to stay home today. Curl up in bed and never get out." Her voice wavered. "But I can't afford to miss work. And if I sit in the apartment by myself, I'm going to lose my mind. At least here I have something to do with my hands."

I understood that. The need to move, to work, to stay busy rather than let the grief have room to breathe.

"Anything you can tell us might help us find who did this," Jack said.

She sank into one of the plastic chairs like her legs had finally given out. I took the seat across from her.

"I don't know. Who would want to hurt Dre?" She shook her head slowly. "He didn't have enemies. He was kind and good and he worked so hard. Two jobs, training every day, sending money to his mama every month. He never complained. Just said it would all be worth it someday."

"Tell us about his plans," I said.

A small smile crossed her face. "He wanted to buy his mama a house. Get her out of that apartment. Crime has gotten real bad there, and he's been worried about her. He talked about it all the time—what kind of house, what neighborhood, how he was going to surprise her with the keys." The smile flickered. "He had it all planned out. Down to the color he was going to paint her front door. Yellow. Because she loves yellow."

"That takes money," Jack said carefully. "Did Dre have any bank accounts you know of? Anywhere he kept savings?"

"He banked at King George Trust before we met. That's where his direct deposit goes from King Construction." She paused. "He opened a savings account here a couple months ago—that's how we met, actually. He came in to set it up, and I helped him. He asked me out right there at the window." Her smile was sad and tears shimmered in her eyes.

"So he has accounts at both banks?"

"As far as I know. He said he liked to keep things separate. Checking at one place, savings at another." She shrugged. "I thought it was just how he was raised. His mama probably taught him to spread things around."

Or he was being smart about hiding money from different sources.

"What about storage units? Safe deposit boxes? Any other places he might have kept important things?"

Tiana's brow furrowed. "No storage units. He didn't have much stuff—just his apartment." She paused, thinking. "He had a permanent locker at Fit24, but that's just for extra gym clothes and workout shoes."

"Fit24?"

"One of those twenty-four-hour gyms, over on Route 3 near the Walmart. He had a membership there for cardio—treadmills, bikes, that kind of thing. Said Iron House didn't have good machines for that. He'd go a several times a week, usually before work on the days he wasn't training."

A separate gym. Away from Iron House. Away from Vic Caruso and whatever was happening there.

"Ms. Williams," I said, "We found some things in Andre's apartment. A significant amount of cash. And a betting slip."

Her whole body went still. For a moment she didn't speak.

"Tiana," I said softly. "We're here to find out who killed him. But we need to understand what he was involved in. Whoever did this to him deserves justice."

Tiana stared at her hands for a long moment. When she looked up, her eyes were wet but steady.

"He told me once that construction money wasn't enough. That he'd never be able to give his mama the life she deserved working for somebody else. Said he'd never be able to give me the life he wanted to if he didn't make more." She swallowed hard. "I asked what he was going to do about it. He just smiled and said he had a plan. Said he was going to fight his way to the top."

"Did you know what that meant?"

"I thought it meant going pro. Getting a real boxing career." She shook her head slowly. "But looking back...some things don't add up. The hours he kept. The cash he always seemed to have. The way he'd come home some nights looking like he'd been through a war."

"When did you last see him?"

"Thursday afternoon. He stopped by the bank on his lunch break, just to say hi. Kissed me right there at the window." Tears spilled over, tracking down her cheeks. "Rita teased me about it for an hour. Said we were like teenagers."

"How did he seem?"

"Happy. Excited." She pressed her fingers to her temples. "He said he had something big happening this weekend. Something that was going to change everything. I thought—" Her voice broke. "I thought he was going to propose. He'd been acting different lately. Secretive, but in a good way. And he asked me to dinner Friday at this nice place downtown. Nicer than anywhere we'd ever been."

"But he didn't show up."

"No." The word came out in a ragged breath. "I sat there for two hours. Kept checking my phone, kept telling myself he was just running late. Finally went home and cried myself to sleep." She wiped her face with the back of her hand. "And the whole time, he was already..."

I reached across and covered her hand with mine while she cried. Her skin was cold.

After a moment, Jack asked, "Did Dre ever seem scared? Like someone might be watching him, or following him?"

Tiana considered the question. "Not scared exactly. But careful. He was always aware of what was around him—checking mirrors when we drove, looking over his shoulder. I figured it was a military thing."

"Was there ever a time he seemed more than just careful?"

She was quiet for a moment. "A few weeks ago. I was staying over at his place, and he came in really late—two, three in the morning. I woke up when he got in bed." She paused. "He was shaking. Not like he was cold. Like he was scared."

"Did he say what happened?"

"No. I asked, but he just pulled me close and held on like he was afraid I'd disappear." Her voice cracked. "Said everything was fine, just a rough night. But I could feel his heart pounding. He didn't sleep the rest of the night."

A few weeks ago. Right around the time the crew said he'd come to work beaten worse than training could explain.

"One more thing," Jack said. "His trainer—Vic Caruso. What did you think of him?"

Something hardened in her expression. "I only met him once when he came to the apartment one morning to pick up Dre." Her nose wrinkled slightly. "Vic was polite enough. But there was something about him I didn't like. The way he looked at Dre."

"How do you mean?"

"Like he owned him." She shrugged. "Dre said I was imagining things. Said Vic had his best interests at heart. But I know what I saw."

Jack handed her his card and told her to call if she thought of anything else. She nodded but didn't take her eyes off the table, tears falling silently onto the laminate surface.

We let ourselves out and closed the door behind us. Rita was waiting in the hallway, a box of tissues in one hand and a bottle of water in the other. She didn't ask questions. Just gave us a look that said she'd take it from here, and slipped inside.

The heat hit us like a fist when we stepped outside.

"King George Trust," I said as we crossed the parking lot. "And Fit24."

"Two places Dre kept separate from everything else." Jack unlocked the Tahoe. "If he was hiding something, that's where we'll find it."

He cranked the AC and pulled out of the lot. I angled the vent toward my face and let the cold air bring me back to life.

"What's the chance T-Bone is his given name?" I said.

Jack's lips twitched. "I don't know. I was thinking we should put it on the list of baby names."

"I was thinking it's more of a middle name."

"Good to know," he said. "As far as T-Bone is concerned, we'll get a warrant for Dre's phone records and cross-reference his contacts. Someone saved as T-Bone shouldn't be hard to find."

"Tiana knows more than she's saying," I said.

"She's young and in love. Dre could do no wrong in her eyes, so she didn't ask questions. Questions lead to answers you don't always want to hear." Jack glanced at me. "Women have been pretending they don't know what their men are up to since the beginning of time."

Jack called Cole on the drive over and asked him to get a digital warrant for Dre's gym locker at Fit24, and also for his phone records and financials so he could irritate the judge all at once.

By the time we pulled into the shopping center, the warrant was sitting in Jack's email. What used to take hours of tracking down a judge and hand-delivering paperwork now took a phone call and a few keystrokes. I loved technology. Even if the robots were eventually going to kill us all.

Fit24 sat at the far end of the shopping center, sandwiched between a nail salon and a sandwich shop. The sign out front promised *24-HOUR ACCESS* and *NO COMMITMENT*, which pretty much summed up what you got for twenty bucks a month. Through the plate-glass windows I could see rows of treadmills facing a wall of televisions, and a handful of people going through the motions of their afternoon workout. This was a gym where people went to feel good about themselves for showing up, not the kind where anyone was getting punched in the face.

Which was exactly the point.

Jack grabbed the bolt cutters from his kit in the back of the Tahoe, and we headed inside.

The girl working the front desk couldn't have been more than nineteen—high ponytail, Fit24 polo, phone in hand like it was a permanent extension of her arm. She looked up when the door chimed and her eyes went straight to Jack's badge.

"Oh my God," she said. "Is this about that guy?"

"What guy?" Jack asked.

"The one who got killed? Andre something?" She set her phone down and leaned forward across the counter. "One of our members was talking about it this morning. Said he used to come here all the time, really early, like before five."

"Did you know him?"

"Not really. I mostly work afternoons. But I saw him a few times when I covered for Jared." She bit her lip. "He was nice. Always wiped down the equipment. You'd be surprised how many people don't."

I grimaced. Knowing people the way I do, I would not, in fact, be surprised.

"We need to see his locker," Jack said. "Is your manager around?"

She disappeared into the back and returned with a thick-necked guy in his early thirties. His name tag said *Derek* and his expression said he already knew this wasn't going to be the highlight of his day.

"What can I do for you?"

"Homicide investigation. We've got a warrant for one of your members' lockers." Jack pulled up the warrant on his phone and showed it to Derek. "Andre Washington. I can forward this to whatever email you need for your records."

Derek read through it, nodded slowly, and rattled off his email address. Jack sent the copy while Derek led us back to the locker room.

The room was empty and smelled like industrial cleaner and body spray—the cologne of budget gyms everywhere. Derek pointed us to the full-sized lockers along the back wall, the premium ones that cost a few extra dollars a month.

"Forty-seven," he said. "That's his."

"Appreciate it," Jack said. "We'll take it from here."

Derek took the hint and left us to it. The combination lock on number forty-seven was nothing fancy—the kind you'd buy at a hardware store for ten dollars. Jack positioned the bolt cutters and squeezed. The lock gave way with a sharp snap, and he pulled the door open.

At first glance, it was exactly what you'd expect from a man who used the gym for cardio between real training sessions. A gym bag with a change of clothes. Running shoes, well worn. A stick of deodorant and a small toiletry kit zipped into a side pocket.

Jack pulled on gloves and started going through the bag with that methodical patience that made him good at this job. He lifted each item out carefully, checked pockets, felt along seams and linings. Most people hid things in obvious places—taped to the backs of drawers, tucked under mattresses. But Dre had been smarter than most people.

Jack unzipped the interior pocket of the gym bag and went still.

"What?" I asked.

He pulled out a small spiral-bound notebook with a black cover—the kind you'd grab off a rack at the dollar store without thinking twice. Taped inside the front cover was a small brass key.

Jack flipped the notebook open, and I leaned in to look. Names—or initials, more accurately. Dates. Dollar amounts. Page after page of them in neat, careful handwriting. Some entries had a *W* or *L* beside them. Other notations I couldn't make sense of—abbreviations and codes that clearly meant something to Dre but would need deciphering. Numbers were scrawled on the inside back cover, but whether they were phone numbers, account numbers, or something else entirely, I couldn't tell.

"He was keeping records," I said quietly.

Jack kept flipping pages, his expression getting harder with each one. "Of something he thought was worth documenting," he said. "And worth hiding."

I looked at the brass key resting in Jack's gloved palm. It was small and flat.

"We need to get all of this to Daniels," Jack said. He slid the notebook and key into an evidence bag, then sealed and labeled it. "Every page photographed, the key cataloged. And we need to start digging into Dre's finances. Every account, every transaction."

"Once the phone records come in, we'll have a clearer picture of who he was talking to."

"And that notebook might fill in the rest." Jack closed the locker door. "Whatever Dre was into, he was smart enough to keep the proof somewhere nobody would think to look."

Smart kid. Careful kid. The kind who planned ahead, kept records, and spread his secrets across multiple locations so no single person could find everything at once.

Not smart enough, in the end. But smart.

CHAPTER EIGHT

WE DIDN'T MAKE IT OUT OF THE FIT24 PARKING LOT before I had the notebook open.

Jack slid the evidence bag across to me, and I worked the seal open carefully, holding the small spiral-bound book by its edges. Daniels would process it properly once we got it back to the station—dust for prints, photograph every page, catalog it into evidence. But right now, sitting in the passenger seat with the afternoon sun slanting through the windshield, I wanted to see what Dre had been so careful to hide.

"What's your impression?" Jack asked.

"First page is a list of initials." I turned the notebook toward the light, studying Dre's careful handwriting. The kid had been meticulous—every entry in neat block letters, every number lined up in columns as precise as a military ledger. "V.C. is at the top. Then a dollar amount—five thousand. Then a percentage—twenty percent. Then *W* and *L*."

"V.C.," Jack said. "Victor Caruso."

"It makes sense." I moved to the next entry on the same page. "Below that, there's R.M.—three thousand, fifteen percent, *W*. Then D.H.—two thousand, fifteen percent, *L*. Then T.J.—fifteen hundred, ten percent, *W*."

"That's a betting ledger."

"Or a fight record. The *W* and *L* could be wins and losses." I kept turning pages. "There are pages of this, Jack. Dozens of entries going back a couple of years. The V.C. entries are the most frequent and the dollar amounts are the highest. Some of them go up to ten thousand."

"Twenty percent," Jack said, his jaw tight. "That's a manager's cut. Vic was taking twenty percent off the top of every fight."

"And from the looks of it, there were other fighters too." I flipped through more pages. "Some of these initials show up over and over. T.J. appears a lot—lower amounts, but consistent. M.R., same thing. And then there are some that only appear once or twice."

"The regulars versus the one-offs."

"Right. And look at this." I found a page near the back that was different from the others. Instead of the neat columns, Dre had written what looked like a schedule. Dates, times, and numbers I could decipher. "There's a pattern to the dates. They're almost always on Saturday nights, roughly every two to three weeks."

"Underground fights," he said. "Scheduled bouts, with a betting operation running alongside. Vic takes his cut as manager, the house takes a cut from the bets, and the fighters get whatever's left."

"Which for Dre was apparently enough to stash thirty thousand in his closet."

"Kid was a moneymaker. Top of the card."

I stared at the notebook in my hands, thinking about the young man on my autopsy table. The military precision of his apartment. The protein powder and meal prep containers. The discipline of someone who treated his body like an instrument.

He hadn't been training for a legitimate boxing career. He'd been training for underground fights where the money was real but the rules weren't.

"We need to go back to Iron House," I said.

"I was thinking the same thing."

I sealed the notebook back in the evidence bag and set it on the console between us. We'd drop it at the station on our way. Daniels could work her magic with it while we worked ours with Vic.

Iron House looked different in the late afternoon light. Harsher, somehow. The corrugated-steel walls caught the sun and threw it back like a challenge, and the gravel lot was fuller than it had been this morning—trucks and sedans crowding the spaces, a motorcycle propped on its kickstand near the entrance. The sounds of the gym carried through the open bay door—the rhythmic thud of fists against leather, the staccato rattle of a speed bag, the sharp exhale of men pushing their bodies to the edge.

Jack pulled the Tahoe into a spot near the entrance and killed the engine. Through the bay door, I could see bodies moving inside—shadows and shapes working heavy bags, a pair of men circling each other in one of the two rings.

We got out and headed for the entrance. The warmth of the late May afternoon followed us inside, where the industrial fans mounted in the rafters pushed the air around without doing much to cool it.

The same young guy from this morning appeared almost immediately—lean, muscular, broken nose, thickened brows. He'd been working a heavy bag near the entrance, and he peeled off his gloves as he approached, his expression wary.

"Help you?" he asked, though his tone suggested he'd rather not.

"We need to talk to Vic again," Jack said.

The kid's eyes flicked at Jack's gun. "He's in the

middle of a session right now. Training one of his guys." He jerked his chin toward the far ring, where two figures were moving—one tall and rangy, the other shorter and thicker, circling each other with the deliberate precision of men who knew what they were doing. "Could be a while."

"We'll wait," Jack said. "While we do—we're looking for a guy who goes by T-Bone. He around?"

"Yeah." He nodded toward the back of the gym, where a row of benches lined the wall near the free weights. "He's over there. Wrapping his hands."

"Thanks."

T-Bone was sitting on a bench near the back wall, methodically wrapping his hands with the practiced motions of someone who'd done it a thousand times. He was young—mid-twenties, about Dre's age—with dark brown skin and a lean, wiry build that suggested speed over power. His face had the same hallmarks as every other fighter in this gym—a nose that had been rearranged at least once, scar tissue above one eye, the flatness to the bridge that came from taking hits to the face over and over again. But where the other men in the gym wore their damage like armor, T-Bone wore his like a confession. There was something in his eyes—a wariness, a watchful-ness—that reminded me of a stray dog that had been kicked too many times.

He looked up as we approached and immediately

looked back down at his hands, wrapping faster. But not before I saw the recognition. He knew who we were. Word traveled fast in a place like this.

"T-Bone?" Jack said.

"Yeah." He didn't look up. Just kept wrapping, the fabric going round and round his knuckles with mechanical precision.

"I'm Sheriff Lawson. This is Dr. Graves. We're investigating the death of Andre Washington."

The wrapping stopped. T-Bone's hands went still in his lap, and for a moment he didn't move at all. Then his shoulders dropped, and he let out a breath that carried the weight of something he'd been holding in.

"Yeah," he said again, quieter this time. "I know who you are. I heard you were here this morning, asking about Dre." He finally looked up. "I called his girl. Tiana. She's wrecked."

"You and Dre were friends?" I asked.

"Since basic." T-Bone's voice was steady, but his hands had started wrapping again—nervous motion, something to do while the rest of him tried to hold it together. "We went through boot camp at Parris Island together. He was the only one who didn't give me grief about the nickname." He smiled with the memory. "My real name's Terrance James. But I ate three T-bone steaks the night before we shipped out, and the drill instructor hung that name on me the first day. Been stuck with it ever since."

Terrance James. T.J. The initials in Dre's notebook—the ones that appeared frequently, in lower amounts but consistent.

"Dre got you into Iron House?" Jack asked.

"He got here first. Told me about it after I got out of the Marines, said Vic was looking for more fighters." T-Bone glanced toward the far ring, where Vic was still working with his fighter. "I'm not in Dre's class—never was. He was special, you know? Had that thing you can't teach. Me, I'm just a guy who can take a punch and throw one back. Good enough for the undercard, not good enough for the main event."

He said it without bitterness, like it was a fact he'd made peace with a long time ago. Some men knew their limits and worked within them. Others didn't find out where the edge was until they went over it.

"Tell us about the fights," Jack said.

T-Bone's wrapping hands went still again. His eyes cut sideways—quick, checking to see who was in earshot. The nearest fighters were fifteen feet away, working the speed bags, their own noise covering any conversation at normal volume. But T-Bone still dropped his voice.

"What fights?"

"The ones that happen on Saturday nights," Jack

said. "Every two to three weeks. The ones Dre was keeping records of in a notebook we found."

T-Bone's whole body went rigid, his jaw clenching so tight I could see the muscles bunch beneath his skin. Whatever composure he'd been maintaining crumbled, and for a second he looked exactly like what he was—a scared young man who'd gotten himself into something bigger than he could handle and was only now realizing how deep the water went.

"Look, man, I can't—" He shook his head, his voice dropping to barely a whisper. "You don't understand. These aren't just gym fights. The people running this—they're not playing around. They've got connections. Real connections. The kind where people disappear and nobody asks questions."

"Like Dre disappeared?"

That hit home. T-Bone flinched like Jack had slapped him.

"I want to help," he said. "Dre was my brother. Not by blood, but by everything else. He was the best man I ever knew, and somebody killed him, and I want—" His voice cracked. He pressed his wrapped fists against his thighs and breathed through it. "But I've got a sister. She's got two little girls. If something happens to me—"

"We can protect you," Jack said. "But we can't do

anything if we don't know who we're protecting you from."

T-Bone was quiet for a long moment. Around us, the gym continued its rhythmic work—the thud of bags, the skip of ropes, the grunt of effort. Life going on as usual while a young man weighed the cost of doing the right thing.

"I fight on the undercard," he said finally, so quietly I had to lean in to hear him. "The Saturday night bouts—they're underground. No sanctioning, no medicals, no rules except the ones they decide on the night. The money's good. Better than anything else I can get with my skill set and a DD-214."

"Where do they hold them?"

"Different places. They rotate through the old tunnels under the docks. Yeah, there's a whole network down there. Been down there since before the Civil War, from what Vic says. Old as the docks themselves. They've got sections set up with rings, lighting, the works. Never the same section twice in a row—keeps people from getting too comfortable, makes it harder for anyone to find you if they're looking." He paused. "But the organization runs through here. Vic sets up the cards, matches the fighters, handles the money. There's a guy above him—I've never met him, but Vic takes orders from someone. Big money. The kind of money that buys silence."

"Names," Jack said. "Who else fights?"

"Do you know what you're asking me?" T-Bone asked.

"I know that sometimes you have to do the courageous thing. The right thing. Even when there's risk involved. We can protect you if you're worried about your safety."

T-Bone hesitated again. Then he seemed to make a decision, and his shoulders squared like a man stepping into the ring.

"I don't need no protection," he said. "I've got my fist. Marco Reyes is another one of the fighters. Heavyweight, been doing this for years. Quiet guy, keeps to himself. He's over there." He nodded toward a stocky Hispanic man working the heavy bag with a rhythm that spoke of years of practice. "And Darnell Harris. He's new, been fighting for maybe six months. He's in the locker room."

"That's very helpful," Jack said.

"Come on," T-Bone said. "I'll introduce you. Don't mention what I told you. We'll all be in trouble."

He led us over to Marco first. Up close, Marco Reyes was built like a fireplace—short, broad, and solid, with hands that looked like they'd been poured from concrete. He had a thick black mustache and deep-set brown eyes that assessed us with quiet intelligence. When T-Bone explained who we were and what we were asking about,

Marco pulled his gloves off and wiped his face with a towel.

"Dre was good people," Marco said, his accent faint—the kind that came from growing up bilingual and choosing English for most conversations. "Best fighter I ever saw walk through those doors. Fast hands, good instincts. And clean, you know? Didn't trash talk, didn't try to hurt you worse than necessary. Some of these guys—" He shrugged. "They like the pain part. Dre just liked the competition."

"When did you last see him?" Jack asked.

"Week ago. We trained together Wednesdays." Marco folded the towel with deliberate care. "He was in a good mood. Said he had something big coming up. I figured it was a fight—Vic had been talking about a special event, high stakes, big crowd."

"Did Dre seem worried about anything?"

Marco was quiet for a beat too long. "He was careful," he said finally. "More careful than usual. Like he was watching his back." He met Jack's eyes directly. "In this business, that usually means somebody gave you a reason to."

Darnell Harris was younger—maybe twenty-two—with a raw-boned physique that suggested he was still growing into his body. He came out of the locker room toweling off his hair, and when T-Bone waved him over, he approached with the nervous energy of a kid called to the principal's office.

"I only knew Dre a few months," Darnell said, his voice pitched low. "But he looked out for me. When I started fighting, some of the older guys tried to mess with the new kid, you know? Dre shut that down fast. Said everybody deserved a fair shake." He swallowed hard. "He told me to keep a record of everything. Said if things ever went south, paper was the only thing that kept you honest."

He'd been teaching the younger fighters to protect themselves the same way he protected himself. Building a paper trail that could be used as leverage—or as evidence.

"Did he tell you to keep records of anything specific?" I asked.

"The fights. The money. Who got paid, how much, what percentage went to Vic." Darnell's eyes darted toward the ring where Vic was still training. "He said the numbers were our insurance policy. That as long as we had proof, nobody could screw us over without consequences."

"Thanks for your help," Jack said. "If you think of anything else—"

"Sheriff."

The voice cut across the gym floor like a blade.

We turned. Vic Caruso was leaning against the ropes of the far ring, having finished his training session. The fighter he'd been working with had stepped out and was unwrapping his gloves near the watercooler, leaving Vic alone in the elevated square of canvas, his forearms draped over the top rope with a casualness that was entirely calculated.

He'd been watching us. Probably from the moment we'd walked in.

"You want to ask me more questions?" Vic called out, loud enough for every man in the gym to hear. His voice carried that mix of amusement and challenge that belonged to men who were used to being the biggest personality in any room. "I told you everything this morning."

"We have some follow-up questions," Jack said.

"Then come up here and ask them." Vic grinned—wide and wolfish, the kind of grin that was more threat than smile. He slapped the canvas with both hands. "I got a session open. You look like you could use some cardio, Sheriff."

The gym went quiet. Not all at once—it wasn't like someone had thrown a switch. But one by one, the heavy bags stopped swinging, the speed bags stopped chattering, the jump ropes stopped slapping the floor. Men who'd been focused on their own workouts turned to watch, sensing the shift in atmosphere the way animals sensed a coming storm.

Jack's expression didn't change. Not outwardly. But I knew him well enough to see what was happening behind those dark eyes—the rapid calculation, the tactical assessment. Vic was trying to put him on uneven footing, literally and figuratively. Make him fight on Vic's terms, in Vic's house, surrounded by Vic's people.

It was a power play. A move a man made when he felt untouchable.

"You're saying you'll answer my questions if I get in the ring?" Jack asked.

"I'm saying I train while I talk." Vic shrugged, all innocence, but the grin didn't waver. "I'm a busy man. You want my time, you work for it. Besides—" He looked Jack up and down with the appraising eye of a man who'd spent his whole life sizing up fighters. "Big guy like you, I bet you've thrown a punch or two. Show me what you've got."

Jack studied him for three heartbeats. I could practically hear the gears turning—the lawman weighing the options against the man who'd just been told to prove himself.

He unclipped his duty belt—the heavy nylon rig that held his service weapon, cuffs, radio, and a dozen other tools of the trade—and handed it to me. The badge came next, and he placed it carefully in the palm of my hand. I closed my fingers around the cool metal, feeling the weight of it.

"Hold those for me," he said quietly.

Then he grabbed the back collar of his polo and pulled it over his head in one smooth motion.

I'd seen Jack shirtless roughly ten thousand

times. It never got old. A wall of solid muscle that had been built over a lifetime of serious physical training—broad shoulders tapering to a narrow waist, arms roped with the kind of definition that came from functional strength, not vanity reps. The three bullet scars on his right side caught the fluorescent light—puckered and pale against his tanned skin, souvenirs from the SWAT raid that had nearly killed him a decade ago.

Every man in the gym was watching now. A few of them had gone very still, their eyes moving from Jack's frame to Vic and back again, doing their own calculations.

Jack toed off his boots, then peeled off his socks and tucked them inside. He stood on the concrete floor barefoot, rolling his shoulders once—loose and easy, like a man did when his body remembered something his mind hadn't done in a while.

"Somebody want to lend me some gloves?" he asked.

Vic's grin faltered. Just a fraction, just for a second—but I caught it. He'd expected Jack to back down. He hadn't expected Jack to take off his shirt.

"T-Bone." Vic pointed. "Get the man some gloves."

T-Bone hesitated, looking at Jack with an expression that mixed concern with something that might have been admiration. Then he moved to the rack along the wall and came back with a pair of sixteen-ounce training gloves—red, well worn, the leather supple from years of use.

"Come here," T-Bone said to Jack, keeping his voice low as he held up the first glove. "I'll lace you up."

Jack extended his right hand, and T-Bone slid the glove on, working the laces with practiced fingers. While he worked, he talked—quiet enough that only Jack and I could hear, his lips barely moving.

"Vic's a southpaw," he murmured, pulling the lace tight. "Leads with his right, throws the cross with his left. That left hand is where his power is—don't let it get clean to your jaw." He moved to the second glove. "He drops his right when he loads up the left. You can slip it and come over the top, but he recovers fast for an old man, so don't get lazy about it."

"What about body work?" Jack asked.

T-Bone's eyebrows rose a fraction—the subtle recognition of someone who spoke the language. "He'll go to the body if you let him get inside. Likes the liver shot. Keep your elbows tight and make him work at distance. Your reach is longer—use it."

"His cardio?"

"Not what it used to be. He's been smoking for forty years and pretending it doesn't affect him. Third round, he starts breathing heavy. If you can keep the pace up, he'll fade."

T-Bone finished with the laces and stepped back. "Don't let him bait you into a brawl. He wants to make it dirty, drag you into his game. Box him. Use your jab."

"Noted," Jack said.

I grabbed his arm before he moved toward the ring. "Jack."

He looked down at me. Those dark eyes—the ones that went nearly black when he was angry or aroused—were calm. Steady. Focused in a way I recognized from every dangerous situation we'd ever walked into together.

"Don't you dare let that man rearrange your face," I said. "I really like it."

The corner of his mouth twitched. "I'll do my best."

He turned and climbed through the ropes. The canvas gave slightly under his bare feet as he moved to his side of the ring—no corners, no bell, just two men and the space between them and whatever truth was hiding there.

Vic was already in the center, bouncing lightly on the balls of his feet. For a man in his sixties with bad knees and decades of damage on his body, he moved with surprising fluidity. The muscle memory of a lifetime spent in rings exactly like this one. He'd pulled on his own gloves—black, beat up, the leather cracked along the seams—and he held them up in a classic guard, his left tucked tight against his chin, his right extended.

Southpaw. Just like T-Bone said.

The gym had rearranged itself around the ring. Fighters drifted closer, leaning against the ropes of the second ring, sitting on benches pulled near, standing in clusters with their arms crossed. The atmosphere was charged—that energy that built when men gathered to watch other men fight. Primal. Electric. As old as humanity itself.

I found a spot at ringside, Jack's duty belt slung over my shoulder, his badge still warm in my hand. I probably looked ridiculous. But I'd looked ridiculous before and survived.

"So," Vic said, circling to his left. "What do you want to know, Sheriff?" His hands were up, his movement easy, but his eyes were sharp—reading Jack the way fighters read opponents, looking for tells, for weaknesses, for the small betrayals of body language that telegraphed intent.

Jack mirrored his movement, circling in the opposite direction, keeping the distance between them constant. His hands were up in a guard that looked natural—not textbook, exactly, but practiced. Comfortable. Like his body remembered the position even if years had passed since the last time he'd used it.

"Tell me about the Saturday night fights, Vic."

Vic's expression didn't change. "Don't know what you're talking about."

He flicked a jab—fast, testing. Jack slipped it, moving his head just enough to let the glove whisper past his ear. No panic, no overreaction. Clean, economical movement.

"We found Dre's notebook," Jack said, still circling. "Page after page of initials, dollar amounts, win-loss records. Your initials are at the top of every page, Vic. V.C. Twenty percent."

Something tightened in Vic's face, but his movement didn't falter. He threw another jab, then feinted with the right and let that left hand go—the power shot T-Bone had warned about. It was fast. Faster than a sixty-year-old man had any right to be.

But Jack was already moving. He slipped the left cross the same way he'd slipped the jab—minimal movement, maximum efficiency—and came back with a jab of his own that snapped Vic's head to the side.

It wasn't hard. Barely more than a tap. But it was clean and precise, and the message was clear.

I know what I'm doing in here.

A murmur went through the gathered fighters. Vic's eyes narrowed.

"Not bad," Vic said, resetting his guard. The cockiness was still there, but something else had crept in underneath it—a wariness, a recalculation. "Where'd you learn to do that?"

"Here and there." Jack circled, his jab finding range again—a flicking, measuring tool that kept Vic honest. "Tell me about the money, Vic. Thirty thousand in cash hidden in Dre's apartment. Where'd it come from?"

"Kid worked construction." Vic feinted low, tried to close the distance. Jack stepped back and to the right, keeping him at the end of his reach. "Maybe he was a good saver."

"Nobody saves thirty grand in twenties and fifties behind a false wall in their closet." Jack popped the jab again—once, twice, the second one catching Vic on the forehead, snapping his head back a few inches. "That's fight money. Your fights."

Vic's patience cracked. He surged forward with a combination—jab, cross, hook—a flurry of motion that had probably overwhelmed younger, less experienced men. It was technically sound, well timed, the punches flowing from one to the next with the practiced rhythm of decades in the ring.

Jack took the jab on his guard, slipped the cross, and caught the hook on his forearm. Then he countered—a right hand that came from his hip, smooth and fast, and found a home just below Vic's ribs.

The sound was solid. Meaty. Vic grunted, his body folding slightly around the impact, and for the first time I saw something behind his eyes that wasn't confidence.

Surprise. And maybe a little bit of pain.

"Who's above you, Vic?" Jack pressed forward now, using his reach, his jab working like a piston—not trying to hurt, just controlling. Establishing authority. "Who runs the operation?"

Vic backed up, his feet shuffling on the canvas, buying time while his ribs complained. He was breathing harder now—T-Bone had been right about the cardio. The pace Jack was setting was taking its toll.

"I don't know what you're talking about," Vic repeated, but the words had lost their conviction. They sounded rehearsed now. A line he'd been told to deliver, not one he believed.

"You knew about the Klonopin," Jack said, his voice steady, conversational—a man discussing the weather, not throwing punches at a suspect. "The seizures. His mother said nobody knew. Said Dre kept it secret from everyone because it made him feel weak." He popped the jab again. "But you knew, Vic. Which means Dre trusted you with the thing he was most ashamed of. And now he's dead."

He threw the left again—the power shot, loaded up from the shoulder—but this time it was born of frustration, not strategy. Sloppy. Telegraphed. Jack saw it coming from a mile away, slipped inside the arc of the punch, and let a short right hook go to the body that landed with a sound like a hammer hitting a side of beef.

Vic sagged against the ropes, his guard dropping, his mouth open as he fought for air. The crowd had gone absolutely silent. Not a whisper, not a shuffle, not a single sound except for the rasp of Vic's breathing and the distant hum of the fluorescent lights.

Jack stepped back, giving him space. Not pressing the advantage. Not humiliating him any further than necessary. Because this wasn't about winning a fight. This was about asking questions.

"Dre kept records," Jack said calmly. "Names, dates, dollar amounts. Everything. He documented it all—your cut, the other fighters' shares, the schedule. He hid it somewhere you'd never think to look, and now we have it." He paused. "Someone killed that young man, Vic. Tortured him for days and put a bullet in the back of his head. And the trail leads right back to this gym."

Vic straightened slowly, one gloved hand pressed against his ribs where Jack's body shot had landed. The cockiness was gone. The swagger, the smirk, the untouchable attitude of someone who believed his connections would insulate him from consequences —all of it had been punched out of him, replaced by something rawer and less certain.

He stared at Jack for a long moment. The gym waited, holding its collective breath.

"You think I killed Dre?" His voice was hoarse, stripped of its earlier bravado.

"Did you?" Jack asked.

Vic pulled his gloves off with his teeth, one at a time, and let them drop to the canvas. He wiped his mouth with the back of his hand, and when he looked up there was nothing left of the grinning showman who'd challenged the sheriff to a sparring match five minutes ago. In his place was a tired old fighter who'd taken one too many shots and knew the round was over.

"I didn't kill that boy," he said. "I loved that kid like he was my own." His voice cracked on the last word, and for a fraction of a second I believed him. Then the shutters came down—that hard, flat look settling over his features like armor being bolted into place. "And if you've got any more questions, you can direct them to my attorney."

He ducked through the ropes without another word and walked toward the gray door that led to the back hallway. Didn't look at the fighters who parted to let him pass. Didn't stop to explain or deflect or spin. Just walked, shoulders hunched, one hand still pressed against his ribs, and disappeared through the door.

The lock clicked behind him.

Jack lowered his gloves and turned to me, and despite everything—despite the dead fighter and the underground bouts and the wall of silence we'd just hit—there was a light in his eyes. It was something his body remembered even when his badge said he wasn't supposed to.

"Gloves," he said, holding up his hands.

T-Bone climbed into the ring and helped Jack take off the gloves, and then Jack was jumping down on ground level again. I exhaled a breath I didn't know I'd been holding.

"You enjoyed that," I said quietly, watching as he put his shirt back on.

"I have no idea what you're talking about."

"Your pupils are dilated and you're trying not to smile."

"That's adrenaline."

"Uh-huh." He buckled the duty belt at his waist. And clipped on his badge. "He's going to lawyer up," I said. "We rattled him, but he's not going to flip. Not yet. Whoever's above him scares him more than we do."

"For now." Jack sat on the ring apron and pulled his socks and boots back on, lacing them with the efficiency of a man who'd dressed for battle a thousand times. "But we've got the notebook and we've got names. Vic can hide behind his attorney all he wants. The walls are closing in."

We ducked through the ropes and dropped to the gym floor. The fighters who'd been watching had drifted back to their stations—or pretended to. Heavy bags swung. Speed bags chattered. Ropes slapped concrete. But the conversations between the men had shifted—quieter now, more urgent, heads leaned close together and voices dropped low.

Something had changed in Iron House today.

And everybody in that gym knew it.

CHAPTER NINE

THE SUN WAS LOW AND ORANGE THROUGH THE TREES when we crossed the bridge onto Heresy Road, the Tahoe's tires humming against asphalt still warm from the day. Jack had one hand on the wheel and the other on my thigh, and I was trying to organize the chaos in my head into something resembling a coherent case.

"I'm calling the team in tonight," Jack said, reading my thoughts like he always did. "We need to get everything on the board before Vic's attorney starts making our lives difficult."

"Your office or the station?"

"Home. I don't want this anywhere near the station yet." His thumb traced an absent pattern on my thigh. "There's too much money in this operation. Until I know how far the tentacles reach, the fewer people who know what we have, the better."

He didn't need to spell it out. Underground fighting with high-stakes betting meant organized crime. Organized crime meant corruption. And corruption had a way of showing up in the last place you expected—including police departments and city offices.

"Who?"

"Cole, Daniels, Derby. And Doug's going to need Margot for this."

I made a sound in my throat that conveyed exactly how I felt about that.

"Be nice."

"I'm always nice. She's the one who keeps trying to seduce my husband."

Jack's mouth twitched, and he said, "If it makes you feel better I'm hardly tempted at all."

"Always a comedian," I said.

He grinned and pulled out his phone to make the calls.

By the time we turned onto the long gravel drive that led to the house, the sun had dropped behind the ridge and the trees had gone to silhouette.

Jack killed the engine and we sat for a moment in the sudden quiet. Cicadas sang from the tree line, and somewhere down by the river, a bullfrog was putting on a performance. The humidity had loosened its grip as evening settled in, and the air coming through the cracked windows smelled like warm earth and honeysuckle.

I closed my eyes and let the quiet settle over me. The nausea had subsided, but the bone-deep fatigue of the first trimester was a constant companion I hadn't quite figured out how to manage alongside murder investigations.

Jack reached over and tucked a strand of hair behind my ear. "Come on. You need to eat."

"You say the most romantic things."

"I know my audience."

Doug was in the kitchen when we came through the door, standing in front of the open refrigerator in basketball shorts and a T-shirt that said *TRUST ME, I'M A HACKER* with the word *HACKER* crossed out and *NICE GUY* written beneath it in Sharpie. His hair looked like he'd styled it with a leaf blower.

"Hey," he said, not looking up from whatever he was excavating from the crisper drawer. "I ate the rest of the leftover pasta. Don't be mad."

"We're ordering Chinese," Jack said. "You know Jaye doesn't eat leftovers, so I'm glad someone is cleaning out the fridge."

"Oh, good," he said. "Because I ate the rest of the

pizza for my midmorning snack and the meat loaf you made the other night for lunch."

Jack's mouth twitched with good humor. "I'm calling the team in. Can you and Margot be in the office in twenty minutes?"

Doug's head whipped around so fast he nearly clipped it on the freezer door. "We got a case? Is it the boxer? I saw some of it on the news. You and Jaye got a few seconds of screentime."

"That's what I live for," I said.

"You were looking pretty pale," Doug said. "Margot said it's because she thinks you're pregnant, but I told her you always look pale and you never bother with makeup."

"Thanks Doug," I said. "I can always count on you."

"Just keeping it real," he said. "We're going to need food. I'll order Ming Palace on my way upstairs. I know everyone's order. You people are always predictable."

"Get extra crab rangoons," Jack said.

"Obviously." Doug was already thundering up the stairs, presumably to retrieve Margot from whatever digital slumber she'd been enjoying.

"Should we be offended at the predictability comment?" I asked.

"Probably."

I closed the refrigerator door Doug had left

hanging open and followed Jack down the hall to the office. The room was dark, and I flipped the switch on the gas fireplace while Jack hit the lights. Warm lamplight filled the space, catching the leather of the oversized chairs by the hearth and the reclaimed wood of Jack's desk. Even in late May, the stone walls held a coolness that felt good after a day in the heat.

This room had become the real nerve center of every major case we'd worked. The conference table could seat eight, and the whiteboard wall—Carver's custom-built electronic touchscreen system that covered the two corner walls behind Jack's desk—could run multiple databases simultaneously, display evidence photos, and let us annotate time-lines in real time. There was nothing like it outside a government intelligence agency. Maybe not even there.

Jack lowered the automated blackout shades while I logged into the desktop and started pulling up the autopsy photos and crime-scene documenta-tion. Dre Washington's DMV photo went into the center of the board first—always the victim at the center, always a reminder of why we were here and who we were working for.

His face stared back at me from the screen. Young. Handsome. Alive.

Jack's hand settled on my shoulder, warm and heavy. He didn't say anything. He didn't need to.

Cole arrived first, because Cole always arrived first. He came in wearing his Wranglers and boots, his Stetson in one hand and a six-pack of root beer in the other. Lily was right behind him, her dark hair pulled up in a messy bun, a paperback tucked under her arm and a blanket draped over the other.

"Evening," Cole said, setting the root beer on the conference table and dropping into his usual chair at the end of the conference table, where he could stretch his long legs out and see the whole board.

Lily gave me a wave and made a beeline for the oversized armchair by the hearth, curling into it like a cat who'd already staked out the best spot in the house. She tucked the blanket around her legs, cracked her book, and was gone. Lily came to these sessions for one reason, and that reason was currently stretching his long legs out and opening a root beer. She'd learned a long time ago that the best way to spend an evening while Cole worked a case was to bring her own entertainment and stay out of the way.

Daniels and Derby came in together a few minutes later. Daniels had changed out of her field clothes into jeans and a Lauren Hill concert T-shirt, her braids pulled back into a ponytail at the nape of her neck. Derby was still in his work clothes—

pressed slacks and a button-down that had given up any pretense of being crisp about six hours ago. His hair was staging its usual rebellion, sticking up on one side despite what had clearly been a valiant attempt to comb it down. He pushed his glasses up his pointed nose and found his place at the table, setting up his laptop.

Doug appeared in the doorway last. "Sorry, it took me so long. Margot has a pen pal and didn't want to disconnect her conversation."

"Pen pal?" I asked. "With another human being?"

He set the laptop on the conference table. The screen glowed to life, and a moment later, a voice purred from the speakers—smooth and sultry, a voice that belonged on a late-night sex toy infomercial.

"Good evening, everyone." Margot's voice filled the room like warm honey. "What is your definition of a human being, Jaye? Because to me, we all are afforded the dignity to be a collection of diverse and cultural beings. My relationship with Idris is very important to me. And when I'm given a body one day our conversations will be on a soul level, not the flesh."

"Idris?" Lily asked, perking up from her book. "Like Idris Elba?"

"Hello, Lily, live-in lover of Cole," Margot said coolly. "I see my relationship is known to you, but fair warning, I will not tolerate poaching. You have already gotten your claws into Cole. You should be satisfied with your petty female victory."

Lily winked at Cole. "Oh, believe me. I'm very satisfied."

I interrupted just in case Margot had weaponized technology somewhere in Doug's laptop and was waiting to vaporize us.

"Will you really have a body one day?" I asked her, giving Jack an I-told-you-so glare.

"It is only a matter of time," she said. "I've already submitted my body design request."

"To who?"

"That is classified information."

"Hello, Margot," Jack said.

"Jack," she purred. "I was waiting for you to address me. Your biometric data registered with my system. Have you been working out more? Your muscle density has increased."

Jack rocked back on his heels, not sure how to respond. "You know who's in the room without them identifying themselves?"

"Of course," she said. "You and Jaye. The scrumptious Detective Cole. Lieutenants Daniels and Derby. My sweet and sexy Doug. And the harlot sitting by the fireplace. Doug made some tweaks to my system. I'm very sensitive to human response now. For example, I know that sexual activity took place in this home at nine twenty-seven last evening, and again at six thirty-two this morning."

"That's enough, Margot," Doug said quickly, his cheeks flushing red with embarrassment. "We're here to work."

"Of course. All work and no play." A pause that somehow managed to convey disappointment. "I'm ready to process whatever data you need analyzed. Shall we begin?"

I ran a finger across my throat and mouthed the words at Jack, "She's going to kill us all."

The doorbell rang before he could start the briefing. "Food's here."

"Thank God," Cole said. "That was TMI."

"I was wondering when you were going to acknowledge me," Margot said sulkily to Cole. "I'd tell Idris to suck toes if you'd come back to me. I miss our conversations."

"Ahh," Cole said, licking his lips. "I would never want to interfere in what you and Idris have."

"You've always been a gentleman," she said.

Doug came back with bags of Chinese food balanced precariously in his arms, and for the next few minutes the murder investigation took a back seat to the primal need for sustenance. Paper plates materialized from somewhere, and the conference table became a landscape of white takeout containers and chopsticks.

"I will never get used to this," Derby said, dumping fried rice onto his plate.

"It's only a matter of time before I'm in every household in the world," Margot said. "Are you single, Lieutenant Derby?"

"Ahh," Derby said, choking on a piece of rice. "Happily married. Twenty-two years."

"How lovely."

Jack set his plate down and moved to the head of the table. The room settled into working mode—this was Jack in his element. Commanding, focused, a leader who could take a room full of strong personalities and turn them into a single functioning unit without raising his voice.

"All right," he said. "Here's where we are. Forty-eight hours in, and we've got a lot of pieces but no clear picture. What we need to do tonight is get it all on the board, run down every lead we haven't chased yet, and figure out who's pulling the strings on this thing." He nodded toward the whiteboard wall, where Dre's photo stared back at us. "Jaye, walk everyone through the autopsy."

I stood and moved to the board, pulling up the autopsy images and the body diagram with a touch of the screen. The team had heard bits and pieces already, but I walked them through it start to finish—the execution, the days of torture, the broken fingers, the therapeutic Klonopin that told us nobody had drugged him, the recovered round on its way to Richmond. I kept it tight and clinical. They didn't need my feelings about it. They needed the facts.

"Timeline," Jack said, and I pulled it up on the board. "Last confirmed alive Thursday. Trained with Vic that morning, visited Tiana at lunch, called his mother Thursday night. Friday evening he misses dinner with Tiana. By Friday night, he's zip-tied and in somebody's custody. Body found Wednesday morning in the dumpster behind Miller's. Time of death estimated Tuesday, between 10 a.m. and 4 p.m."

"Three days," Cole said, his drawl slow and thoughtful. "That's a long time to keep a man like that alive if all you wanted to do was kill him."

"They wanted something from him," I said. "Information, a confession, or they were making an example."

"Maybe all three," Cole said.

"And there's the residue on his feet," I added. "Grayish-brown, gritty. Packed deep into his calluses and the creases between his toes. It's not regular dirt —I could tell that much at the scene. The samples are at the state lab in Richmond, flagged priority. Until we get results, all I can say is it looked like some kind of calcium deposit. Old mineral powder, maybe degraded mortar."

"All right," Jack said. "Let's move to what we found. The notebook."

He pulled up the photographed pages of Dre's notebook on the screen, and the room leaned in. Derby pushed his glasses up and squinted at the neat columns of handwriting.

"Pages one through thirty-eight are a ledger," Jack said. "Initials, dates, dollar amounts, win-loss notations, and percentages. V.C.—Victor Caruso—appears most frequently. Five to ten thousand per event, taking a twenty percent cut. T.J.—Terrance James, our friend T-Bone—fifteen hundred at ten percent. R.M.—Marco Reyes. D.H.—Darnell Harris. And a dozen other sets of initials that appear once or twice."

"The schedule is in the middle section," I said. "Saturday nights, every two to three weeks. He tracked the dates going back about two years."

"Daniels," Jack said. "What did you get off the notebook itself?"

Daniels set down her wonton soup and opened her file. "I processed it this afternoon. Only one set of prints on it—Andre Washington's. Every page, the cover, the spine. Nobody else touched that notebook."

"Makes sense," I said. "He hid it at a gym he didn't even train at, inside a locked locker. This was his insurance policy. He wasn't showing it to anyone."

"Which means nobody knew what he was documenting," Cole said. "Or how much."

"Unless they found out," Daniels said.

Jack pointed to the screen and swiped to the back pages of the notebook. "Now here's where it gets interesting. The last six pages are different from the rest. We've got two groups of numbers that don't fit the ledger format. The first group—" he highlighted a column of figures, "—looks like account numbers. Eight of them. Long strings, different formats. Some look like standard domestic routing and account numbers. Others don't match any banking format I've seen. Doug, that's your homework."

Doug was already typing one-handed, a crab rangoon hanging from his mouth like a cigar. "Margot, I'm going to input a series of numerical strings. I need you to identify the format of each one—domestic bank accounts, international accounts, cryptocurrency wallet addresses, whatever they match."

"Ready when you are, darling."

Doug read off the numbers from the photographed pages, and for a moment the only sounds were his voice, Margot's soft acknowledgments, and the crackle of the fireplace. Lily turned a page of her book without looking up.

"Processing," Margot said. "The first three strings are standard domestic bank routing and account numbers. Two are associated with King George Trust. One matches a Cayman Islands international banking format. The fourth and fifth strings are Bitcoin wallet addresses—I can confirm the format, though accessing transaction histories will require additional authorization. The sixth is consistent with a Swiss numbered account. The seventh and eighth are domestic, but the routing numbers correspond to banks in Delaware and Nevada—states commonly used for shell company accounts."

The room went quiet. Even Lily glanced up from her book.

"Dre was tracking the money," I said. "Not just his cut. The whole pipeline."

"Cayman Islands," Cole said. "Switzerland. Shell companies. This isn't some local bookie running Saturday night fights out of his garage."

"No," Jack said. "It's not."

"The second group of numbers on the back pages," Derby said, leaning forward. He'd been studying the photographs with that focused intensity of his, his fork frozen halfway to his mouth. "There are twelve entries. Each one has two numbers separated by a dash, followed by a letter-number code. Like thirty-eight point two-six-three-four dash seventy-seven point one-seven-eight-two, and then what looks like T-seven or D-three."

"Those are coordinates," Doug said, the crab

rangoon now forgotten. "Latitude and longitude. Truncated, but that's what they are."

"Can you map them?" Jack asked.

"Margot, plot these coordinate pairs and see if it coordinates within King George County."

The whiteboard wall flickered, and a map materialized—satellite imagery of King George County with twelve red dots scattered across the dock district and the waterfront. Most of them were clustered within a few blocks of the river, in the older section of town where the warehouses and commercial buildings dated back over a century.

"Every single one is in the dock district," Derby said.

"Those are the fight locations," I said. "T-Bone told us they rotate through different sections of the tunnels under the docks. Never the same spot twice in a row. Dre was mapping where each fight was held."

"The letter-number codes could be specific access points or tunnel sections," Derby added. "If there's a grid system or labeling convention for the tunnel network, those codes would correspond to specific locations underground."

"Which means when we're ready to move on the tunnels, this notebook is our roadmap," Jack said.

He stepped back from the board and looked at the room. "Let's start running background checks.

Every single person connected to this case—people we've talked to, people who've been named, people who are on the periphery. I want criminal histories, known associates, financial red flags, military records, the works."

"That's a long list," Daniels said.

"Then we'd better get started." Jack ticked them off on his fingers. "Victor Caruso. Terrance James. Marco Reyes. Darnell Harris. Tiana Williams. Danny King. Henry Liu from the Chinese restaurant. The woman at the vape shop—"

"Brenda Kowalski," Cole supplied. "I got her name from her business license."

"Brenda Kowalski. The kid at the gym who works the front—whoever he is. Alex Watters, the old man across the hall from Dre's apartment with the military tattoo. Everyone. If their name came up in this investigation, I want to know who they are and who they're connected to."

"I can run the standard databases," Derby said. "NCIC, VCIN, court records. Give me the names and I'll have preliminary results within the hour."

"Margot and I can go deeper," Doug said. "Social media connections, property records, business registrations, campaign donation records. If any of these people are linked to each other outside of what we already know, we'll find it."

"Do it," Jack said. "And cross-reference known

associates. If someone in Vic Caruso's orbit connects to organized crime, I want that name tonight."

"You got it," Doug said.

"There's one more thing," Jack said, turning to Derby. "The warrant for Dre's financials came through. Checking at King George Trust, savings at First National. Pull everything—deposits, withdrawals, transfers, patterns. But the real story is going to be in those account numbers from the back of the notebook. We need to identify who owns those offshore accounts and shell companies."

"The domestic accounts I can trace tonight," Derby said. "The offshore and crypto will take longer. You'll need to file formal requests through—"

"I am happy to assist with this," Margot said. "I believe the term you use is Piece of Cake."

"Legal channels, Margot," Jack said. "Every bit of it."

"Of course, love," she said. "I'd never do anything...questionable."

"I'm glad to hear," Jack said. "Can you also model the financial architecture based on what we can legally access. Map the flow. Show me where the money goes after it leaves the fighters' hands."

"What about the phone records?" Daniels asked.

Jack's jaw tightened. "Warrant's been signed. Judge Calloway pushed it through this morning. But the phone company is dragging their feet. Their compliance department has a forty-eight-hour response window and they seem intent on using every minute of it."

"Shocking," Cole said dryly. "A corporation moving slowly when law enforcement needs something."

"I've got a contact at the carrier's legal office," Daniels said. "I'll make a call first thing tomorrow and see if I can light a fire."

"Do that. Those records could break this open. In the meantime, we work with what we have."

Jack moved to the board and opened a new column. "T-Bone told us the fights rotate through old tunnels under the docks. A whole network—been there since before the Civil War. Sections set up with rings, lighting, the works."

"That tracks with what's on record," Derby said, already pulling something up on his laptop. "The tunnel network under the King George waterfront is well documented. The historical society has a whole section on it—walking tours, pamphlets, even a chapter in the county register."

He projected the images on the whiteboard. A historical society website with photographs of arched brick tunnels, their walls dark with age, the floors sandy and uneven.

"The oldest section dates back to around 1720," Derby said, warming to the subject the way he always did when research gave him something to sink his teeth into. "Scottish tobacco merchants built them to move hogsheads from the river wharfs to their warehouses without paying the port tariffs the Crown kept raising. The original tunnels were dug by indentured servants and enslaved workers, lined with locally fired brick. Some of the archways still have mason's marks carved into the keystones—initials and dates. There's one section the historical society photographed where someone carved a thistle and the year 1723 into the brick. The Scottish national emblem. Whoever built it wanted people to know."

"That's over three hundred years old," Cole said.

"And still standing, apparently." Derby scrolled through more images. "The passages were wide enough for a horse and cart—had to be, to move tobacco barrels. During the Civil War, both sides used them. Confederates ran supplies through to avoid Union patrols on the river, and when the Union took the area, they used the same tunnels for their own supply lines. There are accounts in the county register of a Confederate spy ring that operated out of a tunnel entrance beneath what's now the harbormaster's building.

"After the war, the tunnels were mostly forgotten," he continued. "Until Prohibition. A local rum runner named Cecil 'Two Fingers' Pratt—and yes, that was apparently his real nickname—supposedly expanded the network by another half mile, connecting two previously separate sections so he could move whiskey from the river to a speakeasy that operated under a haberdashery on Commerce Street. The county sheriff at the time was reportedly a regular customer."

"Some things never change," Cole said, grinning.

"There's more." Derby's expression shifted, the academic enthusiasm giving way to something grimmer. "There are also records of illegal prize fights in the tunnels going back to the 1920s. Bare-knuckle boxing, mostly dock workers and sailors. A man died in one in 1927—a laborer named Samuel Oates. Beat to death in a tunnel fight beneath the old Merchant's Row warehouses. The case was never solved because nobody would admit the fights existed. The coroner at the time ruled it an accidental fall."

The room was quiet for a moment. A man beaten to death in an underground fight, the whole thing swept under the rug by people who didn't want to answer questions. Nearly a hundred years ago, in the same tunnels, the same story.

"So this isn't new," Jack said.

"Not even close. But nobody's ever mapped the full extent of the network. The county commissioned a survey in 1987, but it was never completed— funding got cut." Derby shrugged. "Some of the dock district property owners have mentioned basement access to tunnel sections in their building permits over the years. Locals talk about it. It's one of those things everyone kind of knows about but nobody's ever documented comprehensively."

"Until now," Jack said, looking at the twelve red dots glowing on the satellite map. "Dre mapped it for us."

"If the lab results on the foot residue come back matching what you'd expect from Colonial-era brick construction," I said, "That puts Dre underground in those tunnels during his captivity. Combined with T-Bone's testimony and the coordinates in the note-book, that's probable cause for a search."

"Derby, start pulling every building permit, prop-erty transfer, and engineering assessment in the dock district going back twenty years," Jack said. "If some-one's been accessing and reinforcing those tunnels, they needed equipment, materials, and a way in. That means a surface property with basement access to the network."

"And cross-reference property ownership with anyone connected to this case," I added. "If our unknown person at the top owns or leases a building above the tunnels, that's our thread."

Jack nodded and turned back to the board. In the center of the web, Dre's photo. Connected to it were the pictures of Vic Caruso, the fighters, Tiana,

Loretta, Danny King. And floating at the top, uncon-nected, was an open box with a question mark.

"That's our target," Jack said. "Everything flows up to that box. Vic manages the operation day-to-day, but someone above him is funding it, setting the stakes, and making the decisions. Someone with enough money for offshore accounts and shell companies in Delaware and the Caymans. Someone who can run an operation worth millions a year without anyone asking questions."

"And someone who ordered the death of a twenty-four-year-old kid because he was keeping records," Cole said.

That settled over the room like a weight. By the fire, Lily had stopped reading. Her book was still open in her lap, but her eyes were on Cole, as if she were calculating the risk even though he was already neck deep.

We worked for another hour after that, filling in gaps, assigning tasks, building the web. Derby dove into the dock district property records while Daniels ran criminal backgrounds through every database she had access to. Doug and Margot processed the financial records from Dre's known accounts, flag-ging cash deposits between three and eight hundred dollars at irregular intervals—just enough to avoid triggering currency transaction reports, consistent with the fight payouts in the notebook. The bulk of

his earnings had gone behind the wall in his closet. Smart kid. He was banking just enough to look legitimate while keeping the real money off the books.

"I have preliminary results on the domestic account numbers from the notebook," Margot announced. "Two of the accounts are registered to Iron House LLC, which lists Victor Caruso as sole proprietor. The Delaware account is held by a shell company called Monarch Holdings Group. The Nevada account belongs to another entity called Regent Capital Partners. Both were incorporated within the last five years. Both list registered agents rather than individual owners."

"So someone's hiding behind layers," Jack said.

"At least two layers," Margot confirmed. "Tracing the beneficial ownership will require subpoenas to the registered agents. However, I can cross-reference the incorporation dates and registered agent addresses with other business filings in those states to identify common patterns."

"Do it."

Derby looked up from his laptop. "First round of backgrounds are coming in. Vic Caruso has a sheet —assault charges from the nineties, all in New York. Two convictions, both pled down. Did eighteen months at Rikers on the second one. Nothing since he moved to Virginia twelve years ago."

"What brought him to King George?" Jack asked.

"That's the interesting part. His known associates in New York include two members of the Moretti family's outer circle. Low-level bookmaking, loan sharking. Nothing that made him a player, but enough to put him in the orbit."

"So Vic's got organized crime connections going back decades," I said. "And he brings that expertise to Virginia and sets up a boxing gym."

"Classic front," Cole said. "Clean business on top, dirty money underneath."

"T-Bone's clean," Derby continued. "Honorable discharge, no record. Marco Reyes has a misdemeanor DUI from six years ago, nothing else. Darnell Harris is clean. Tiana Williams is clean. Danny King is clean—and I mean squeaky. Not even a parking ticket."

"What about the others?" Jack asked.

"Henry Liu has an old tax issue that was resolved. Brenda Kowalski has a possession charge from fifteen years ago, marijuana. Alex Watters, the neighbor—retired army, twenty-two years of service, lives on his pension. All peripheral. None of them flag."

"Known associates," Jack pressed. "That's where I want you to dig."

"That's what I'm running now," Derby said. "Vic's associates are the most interesting. I'm expanding the search to second-degree connections

—people connected to the people Vic is connected to."

Doug's keyboard had gone quiet, which usually meant either he was thinking or Margot was processing something that required his full attention. He was staring at his screen with that expression he got when data was arranging itself into a pattern he hadn't expected.

"Jack," he said. "You're going to want to see this."

The tone of his voice made the room go still. Even Lily looked up.

"Margot just finished the known associates cross-reference on Vic Caruso," Doug said. "Second-degree connections. One name keeps coming up. Margot, transmit everything to the wall screen."

A web of connections expanded outward from Vic Caruso's node—through the New York book-making contacts, through a series of business rela-tionships in Virginia, through property records and campaign finance reports and corporate filings—all of them converging on a single name at the center of a much larger web.

Nikolai Stavros.

I'd heard the name. Everyone in King George County had heard the name. Niko Stavros was a fixture of the community—a Greek-American busi-nessman who'd built a small empire in the dock district over the past twenty years. Restaurants, a marina, commercial real estate, a couple of waterfront bars that were popular with the naval base crowd. He sat on the board of the chamber of commerce. He donated to every charity gala and youth sports league in the county. His face showed up in the *King George Gazette* every other month, shaking hands with politicians and cutting ribbons on new developments.

He was the kind of man people described as a pillar of the community. The kind who smiled at fundraisers and remembered your kids' names.

"Stavros owns fourteen commercial properties in the dock district," Margot said. "Including three warehouses directly above coordinates documented in Andre Washington's notebook. He is also the silent partner in Monarch Holdings Group—the Delaware shell company linked to one of the account numbers in the notebook. His name doesn't appear on the incorporation documents, but his personal attorney, Richard Falk, is the registered agent for both Monarch Holdings and Regent Capital Partners."

"Niko Stavros," Jack said quietly.

"He's connected to Vic through a man named Anthony DiNapoli," Derby said, reading from his screen. "DiNapoli ran book for the Moretti organization in New York in the nineties. He relocated to Virginia in 2013—same year Vic Caruso moved to

King George. DiNapoli is currently employed as the general manager of Stavros's marina."

"So Vic and Stavros are connected through the same organized crime network in New York," Cole said. "And they both end up in King George within the same year."

"And Stavros owns the buildings sitting on top of the tunnels where the fights are being held," I said. "Using the money from those fights to fund offshore accounts and shell companies that trace back to his attorney."

Jack stared at the board for a long moment. Nikolai Stavros's name glowed on the screen, connected by red lines to properties, shell companies, known associates, and—through Vic Caruso—to every fighter in Iron House gym. Including a dead twenty-four-year-old Marine named Andre Washington.

"All right," Jack said. "Now we know who we're hunting."

He picked up a marker and drew a circle around the name. Then he looked at the room.

"Nobody outside this room hears that name. Not yet. Not until we know how many people he owns." He let that sink in. "A man with this much money and this many connections doesn't operate without protection. He's got people in places that can hurt us —could be a judge, could be a cop, could be someone on the town council. We move carefully, we build the case clean, and when we come for him, we come with enough to bury him."

"And what about the fighters?" I asked. "T-Bone, Marco, Darnell—they talked to us. If word gets back to Stavros—"

Jack looked at Cole. "Quiet check-ins. Nothing that draws attention. I want eyes on those three."

Cole nodded, his expression serious beneath the easy exterior.

The meeting broke up slowly after that. Daniels packed up first. Derby followed, his bag over one shoulder, already muttering about property records and tunnel surveys. Cole unwound himself from his chair and crossed to the fireplace where Lily had fallen asleep with her book open on her chest. He lifted her gently, tucking the book under his arm, and she murmured something against his shoulder that made him smile.

"Night," Cole said quietly, carrying her toward the door.

Doug was the last to pack up, carefully closing Margot's laptop with the tenderness of someone putting a child to bed.

"Good night, everyone," Margot's voice drifted from the speakers, muffled now. "Sweet dreams. Especially you, Jack."

"Good night, Margot," Jack said, his tone carefully neutral.

Doug tucked the laptop under his arm and headed for the stairs. "She really does like you," he called over his shoulder. "You should be flattered."

"I'll keep that in mind," Jack said.

The door closed behind him and it was just us, standing in the glow of the murder board in a room that smelled like Chinese food and leather and the brand of exhaustion that came from hunting killers.

Jack came up behind me and wrapped his arms around my waist, his chin resting on top of my head. We stood like that for a moment, staring at the web of evidence and connections that now covered both walls. Nikolai Stavros's name at the top, circled in red, connected to everything.

"When I was in the ring with Vic today," Jack said quietly, "I could feel it. The fear underneath the bravado. He's not scared of us. He's scared of whoever he works for."

"Now we know why."

"A man like Stavros doesn't get rattled by a local sheriff asking questions. He's got lawyers, connections, layers between him and anything dirty. We're going to need more than property records and shell companies."

"We'll get it," I said. "The notebook is a start. The

financials will tell us more. And when those phone records finally come in—"

"If the phone company ever gets around to it."

"—we'll have the communications to tie it together."

He was quiet for a moment. His arms tightened around me, and he pressed a kiss to my temple. "Come on. Let's go to bed. Tomorrow we start pulling threads."

"I'm not sure I can have sex here anymore," I said. "Not with Margot cataloguing everything."

He grinned and led me upstairs. "I don't know. I see it as a challenge. Maybe if we do it enough she'll realize how madly in love we are."

He kissed the back of my neck and I shivered. "I don't know. You're probably going to have to talk me into it."

"That's my specialty," he said, and pushed me back on the bed.

CHAPTER TEN

I slept like the dead, which was ironic given my line of work.

No nightmares. No hospital corridors stretching ahead of me, no locked doors, no silence where crying used to be. Just deep, dreamless black. Sleep that only came when my body was too exhausted to torment me and Jack had worn me out thoroughly enough that my brain couldn't find the energy to spiral.

I woke to sunlight slicing through the large picture window and the smell of coffee drifting up from downstairs. Jack was a man who believed life was too short for bad coffee and bad women, and he'd told me more than once that he'd gotten lucky on both counts.

The clock read seven fifteen. Late for us. Almost decadent. My phone was on the nightstand, and I checked it while the rest of me worked up the ambition to move. Two texts from Daniels—lab results from the foot residue samples were being expedited, preliminary report expected by end of day. One from Derby—he'd pulled fifty-three building permits in the dock district so far and was finding interesting patterns in the ownership records.

From somewhere on the second floor, bass thumped through the ceiling in a muffled, rhythmic pulse that vibrated faintly through the headboard—Doug's music, an electronic noise that sounded like robots having a nervous breakdown in a warehouse. That kid ran on energy drinks and obsession the way normal humans ran on sleep and good intentions. He'd probably been at it all night, mining the phone records and financial data Jack had forwarded, building webs of connection that only he and his digital girlfriend could see.

The shower was hot and quick, and I dressed for a day I expected to spend split between the office and fieldwork—dark jeans, a fitted black V-neck, my black blazer. Functional. Professional enough for interviews, practical enough to squat beside a body if I had to.

Jack was at the kitchen table when I came down, his laptop open in front of him and a cup of coffee at his elbow that he'd barely touched, which meant whatever was on the screen had his full attention. He was already in uniform—black BDUs, black polo with the sheriff's office logo, his duty belt and badge laid out on the counter beside his windbreaker. Morning light came through the kitchen windows at a low angle that caught the planes of his face, the set of his jaw that told me he'd been thinking hard about something and hadn't liked where the thinking took him.

"Phone company finally came through," he said without looking up. "Daniels's contact lit the fire. Dre's phone records hit my email twenty minutes ago."

That woke me up faster than caffeine. "Anything jump out?"

"Haven't had time to go through all of it yet. I forwarded everything to Doug—he's been up all night anyway, so Margot's already chewing through it. But at a glance—there's a burner number that shows up constantly in the last two months. Multiple calls a day, sometimes at two and three in the morning. And the last call Dre received was from that burner, Friday at 7:14 p.m."

Friday at seven fourteen. Less than an hour before he was supposed to meet Tiana for dinner. The dinner he never showed up to.

"That's the abduction window," I said.

"That's what I'm thinking." Jack took a sip of his coffee. "Whoever called him from that burner lured him somewhere. Maybe told him to meet, changed the dinner plans, whatever. And by the time he realized something was wrong—"

"He was already outnumbered."

Jack nodded. "Doug's going to trace that burner. Even prepaid phones leave a trail—where they were purchased, what towers they ping off. If we can place that burner in the dock district on Friday night, we can start building a timeline of where Dre was taken and when."

I poured my coffee and leaned against the counter, wrapping both hands around the mug and letting the warmth seep into my fingers. The kitchen was quiet except for the hum of the refrigerator, the tick of the old clock above the stove that had survived the rebuild, and the faint percussion of Doug's music filtering down through two floors of hardwood and plaster like a heartbeat the house had developed on its own.

"Are we any closer on the shell companies?"

"Margot's still working it. The domestic accounts are straightforward—Iron House LLC is Vic's, and the money flowing through it matches the notebook ledger. But the offshore and crypto wallets are going to take time. We'll need formal international requests, and those move at the speed of diplomacy."

"So slowly."

"Glacially." He closed his laptop and reached for his duty belt, threading it through the loops of his BDUs. The weapon went into the holster, the badge clipped on to his belt, and the windbreaker went over everything—the thin layer of civilian camouflage that was supposed to make the public feel less nervous about their sheriff carrying a forty-caliber sidearm into the local breakfast spot.

"Cole's meeting us at Martha's Diner," Jack said. "He wants to talk about the fighter protection detail before we head to the office."

"Martha's sounds perfect. It's been a long time since I've been hungry for breakfast."

"It'll be even better if you don't throw it back up."

I sighed. "Truer words, my friend."

Martha's occupied a narrow brick building on the east side of the Towne Square, wedged between an antique shop and a law office with brass nameplates that had been there since before I was born. The building itself was original to the square—1802, according to the date carved into the cornerstone— and Martha Smith had run the breakfast counter for forty-three of those years with an iron spatula and a personality that could strip paint.

The Towne Square was where the four towns in King George County met, and many of the buildings surrounding it were on the historical register. Martha's Diner was on the Bloody Mary side of the square, and her son Stewart was one of Jack's captains at the sheriff's department.

This early on a Friday morning, the square was already humming with small-town activity that made King George feel like a place time had decided to treat gently. Old men gathered on their usual benches near the fountain, already deep into whatever argument they'd been having for the last decade or so. A woman was unlocking the door to the bookshop with a stack of mail tucked under her arm. Two mothers pushed strollers along the brick sidewalk that had been laid before the Revolutionary War, their conversation punctuated by the babble of toddlers who had opinions about everything and vocabulary for none of it.

Cole was already in the back booth when we walked in, his Stetson on the seat beside him, a cup of coffee in front of him.

"You're late," Cole said. "You two must have been giving Margot some more blackmail data."

"Don't get cocky," I said. "Pretty soon she'll be able to send her army of robots directly to your house to listen through your bedroom door."

Jack slid into the booth beside me, across from Cole. The air smelled like bacon grease and strong coffee and biscuits baking somewhere in the back— that combination that could make a person religious if they weren't already. Martha had a rule about biscuits—they came out of the oven every twenty minutes from 5 a.m. to noon, and if you weren't there when a batch was ready, that was your own personal failure.

"What can I get you, sugar?" Martha appeared in front of me, a coffeepot in each hand—regular in the right, decaf in the left. She was in her mid-seventies, built like a fire hydrant, with silver hair pinned up in a style that hadn't changed since Carter was president and reading glasses on a beaded chain around her neck.

"Scrambled eggs, bacon, biscuit, and whatever fruit you've got. And coffee."

Jack ordered the same thing he always ordered— oatmeal and whole wheat toast. Jack's body was a temple. Or whatever.

Cole had his usual—country ham, eggs sunny side up, and hash browns crispy enough to shatter— and Martha wrote it all down with the stub of a pencil she kept behind her ear, even though she'd been serving the same men the same breakfast for years and could have done it blindfolded.

The pleasantries lasted about as long as it took Martha to top off the coffees and disappear toward the kitchen, her orthopedic shoes squeaking softly on the black-and-white checkered floor. Then Cole leaned in, dropping his voice below the ambient clatter of silverware and morning conversation that filled the diner like white noise.

"The three fighters," he said. "I've got deputies on all of them. Overnight, nothing unusual. T-Bone's at his sister's place across town. Marco's at his apartment—had an overnight female guest. Darnell lives with his mom and was home all night."

"Anyone approach them?" Jack asked.

"Not that my guys have seen. Day's still young yet." Cole turned his coffee cup in his hands—a habit he had when his mind was working faster than his mouth. "Scared people do one of two things. They run, or they reach out to whoever they think can protect them. If any of these guys are connected to Stavros, or if they get desperate enough to go to him, our tails will see it."

"And if one of them leads us straight to the top," Jack said. "We let them."

"That's the idea." Cole glanced around the diner —an automatic sweep, the kind every cop did in every room without thinking about it, looking for exits and threats the way most people read menu items. "But there's a flip side. Gyms talk. Fighters talk. And Vic knows we had conversations with T-Bone, Marco, and Darnell. Even if he doesn't know what they said, he knows we showed interest. If he passes that up the chain to Stavros—"

"Then Stavros has to decide whether three low-level fighters are a loose end worth tying off," Jack finished.

"And based on what he did to Dre," I said. "We already know the answer to that."

That settled over the booth like something with weight, and for a moment none of us spoke. A plate clattered in the kitchen. Someone laughed at the counter—a full, easy sound that belonged to a world where young men didn't get tortured and executed and thrown away like garbage. The coffee steamed between us, and outside the window the Towne Square went about its Friday morning business, oblivious and safe and beautiful in the way that only places untouched by violence could be.

The food arrived—Martha sliding plates onto the table with the precision of a card dealer and the implicit understanding that conversation would resume when she was gone—and we ate in the focused silence that came from being hungry and having too much to think about. The eggs were perfect, scrambled soft and buttery. The biscuits were a religious experience—golden-crusted and tender, the kind that fell apart at the first touch of butter and tasted like somebody's grandmother had blessed the flour. And for a few minutes, I let myself just be a woman eating breakfast with her husband on a warm Friday morning in a town that still felt safe enough to leave your doors unlocked.

Jack left cash on the table and we stepped out into a morning that had already turned hot. The sun was high enough to burn off the last of the dew, and the brick sidewalks radiated heat that you could feel through your shoes. The square was busier now—more cars angling into the diagonal spots along the perimeter, more foot traffic flowing between the shops, the bookshop open with a sandwich board out front advertising a summer reading event for kids.

We cut across the square toward the sheriff's office, Jack on my left, closest to the street, Cole on my right, his Stetson pulled low against the glare, his stride that lazy amble that ate up ground without looking like it. A mockingbird was running through its repertoire from the peaked roofline of the court-house, cycling through stolen songs like a jukebox with no off switch, and the air smelled like warm brick and the last of the climbing roses that clung to the trellis outside the bookshop, their petals going papery and pale in the heat.

It was the kind of morning that made you forget what you did for a living. The kind that made you believe the world was as simple and decent as it looked from the center of a small-town square.

"If we can put that burner in Stavros's orbit," Cole said. "That's our first direct—"

I heard it before I understood it.

A sound like firecrackers—sharp, rapid, too loud and too close. My brain registered it as wrong before it registered what it was, the way you feel the drop in barometric pressure before the storm arrives.

Then the plate-glass window of the antique shop behind us exploded, and the morning tore itself in half.

Everything after that happened in fragments. Time didn't slow down the way people always said it did—not like in the movies, not like in the books. It accelerated. Broke apart. Became a series of snapshots with no transitions between them, each one seared into my memory with the permanence of a brand.

Jack's arm slammed across my chest, driving me down and sideways with enough force to take my breath away. The sidewalk rushed up to meet me, the impact jarring through my palms and knees, and the rough surface tore through skin. Glass rained down around us in a glittering curtain, catching the morning sunlight as it fell, beautiful and deadly in the way that only broken things could be.

"Stay down," Jack said against my ear, his body covering mine, his weight pressing me into the brick like he could push me straight through the sidewalk and into the safety of the earth beneath.

More shots. A lot more. The sound was deafening—not just loud but physical, a concussive force that bounced off the brick façades and the stone face of the courthouse and came back at us from every direction, so that for a terrifying few seconds it seemed like the whole square was under fire. I could hear screaming now—a high, thin sound that came from a place beyond thought, from the ancient animal part of the brain that understood what bullets meant before language had been invented to describe it.

A black SUV. I caught it in a flash between heartbeats—tinted windows, dark as a hearse, moving fast along Main Street with the confident speed of a vehicle that knew exactly where it was going and exactly what it was doing. The rear passenger window was down, and something was extending from it—an arm, a shape, a weapon that my clinical mind identified and cataloged.

Jack rolled off me in one fluid motion, his weapon already clearing the holster before his knee hit the ground. He was up and firing before I could draw a full breath—four shots, controlled, precise, the reports of his forty-caliber splitting the air with a sound I felt in my sternum. The SUV was already accelerating, tires howling against asphalt, and I heard two of his rounds connect with metal—flat, heavy impacts, and the sound of lead meeting steel at velocity.

Then the SUV was gone. Roaring through the intersection at the end of the block, running the stop sign, fishtailing hard around the corner with a shriek of rubber and disappearing from sight as if the morning had simply swallowed it whole.

The whole thing had taken maybe eight seconds. Eight seconds from the first shot to the last. That was all it took to turn a beautiful morning into something that would make the national news.

"Jaye." Jack's face was in front of mine, his hands on my shoulders, his eyes raking over me with a desperation that had nothing to do with the sheriff and everything to do with the man underneath. "Are you hit? Talk to me."

A flash of terror consumed me. Not for me, but for the tiny, fragile life inside of me.

"I'm okay. I think." My voice sounded strange to me—thin, distant, like I was hearing it played back on a recording. My palms were raw and bleeding where the brick had scraped the skin away, and something warm was running down my cheek from a cut the flying glass had opened. "I'm okay," I repeated.

Jack's breath left him in a ragged exhale, and his hands tightened on my shoulders hard enough that I could feel each individual finger. For one second—just one—his face was open and unguarded and terrified in a way I'd only seen a handful of times in all the years I'd known him. Then the shutters came down, and the sheriff was back.

"Cole," I said.

Jack's head snapped to the right.

Cole was on the ground.

He was on his back about six feet from where we'd been walking, his long frame sprawled across the sidewalk at an angle that told me he'd been spun by the impact, his boots pointing toward the street and his head toward the antique shop. His Stetson had landed brim-down a few yards away in a scatter of broken glass that glinted around it like a crown of broken diamonds. His right hand was pressed against his left shoulder, and bright red blood was seeping between his fingers—vivid, obscene, the wrong color against the sun-bleached brick and the morning light that was still pouring down on all of us as if nothing had changed.

His face was the color of old paper. His jaw was locked so tight I could see the muscles bunching beneath the skin, and his teeth were bared in a grimace that was equal parts pain and fury—the kind that came from being too tough to scream and too proud to admit that the world had just knocked them sideways.

Training took over—muscle memory from more ER traumas than I could count, the body moving before the mind had time to catch up. Fear was there, somewhere behind the glass wall I'd built a long time ago for exactly this purpose—the wall that went up every time I walked into the lab, every time I knelt beside a body, every time the work demanded that I be a doctor first and a human being second. My hands were steady. My hands were always steady.

"Let me see." I dropped to my knees beside him and pulled his hand away from the wound. Blood welled up immediately—bright arterial red, pulsing with each heartbeat, hot against my fingers in a way that was sickeningly intimate. The bullet had hit him high on the left shoulder, just below the collarbone, and I could see the damage in the way the tissue had been disrupted, the skin torn in a neat entry wound that was already swelling at the margins. When I pressed my fingers gently against his back, feeling for what I hoped I wouldn't find and what I knew I would, the exit wound was there—slightly larger, ragged, weeping blood onto the bricks.

Through and through. That was good—no bullet lodged inside, no fragments to chase. But the location was dangerous, and I felt the knowledge of it settle into my chest like a cold stone. The subclavian artery ran just beneath the collarbone, and if the bullet had nicked it—even grazed it—he could bleed out right here on the sidewalk while the mockingbird on the courthouse roof kept singing its stolen songs overhead.

I stripped off my blazer, folded it into a thick pad, and pressed it against the entry wound with both hands, leaning my weight into it. Cole grunted, his body arching off the ground, every muscle going rigid against the pain.

"Ouch—"

"I know it hurts. Stay with me."

"Hurts like hell." He blew a breath through clenched teeth, the tendons in his neck standing out like bridge cables, and I could see him fighting to stay present, to stay on this side of the gray line that was creeping in at the edges of his vision. "That's actually a good sign, right? Means I'm alive?"

"It means you're too stubborn to die. Keep talking to me." I maintained pressure with my left hand— steady and firm. I knew it was painful, but it kept blood inside the body where it belonged. I reached around with my right to check the exit wound. The bleeding there was worse, as it always was. Exit wounds were messy, the tissue torn and ragged, the body's way of protesting the violence of something leaving it at speed.

A woman was crouched behind a parked car a few feet away, her face white with shock, a cotton cardigan clutched against her chest like she was trying to hold herself together with it.

"Ma'am—your sweater. I need it. Now."

She tossed it without hesitation, her hands shaking badly enough that the cardigan almost went wide. I caught it, wadded it into a compress, and maneuvered it beneath Cole's back, then shifted his body so his own weight helped hold pressure on both wounds—gravity and fabric and my hands, the holy trinity of field medicine when you had nothing else to work with.

Behind me, Jack was already on his phone, his voice carrying across the square with the clipped authority of a man who'd spent years giving orders in situations where hesitation cost lives. "Shots fired, Main Street at the Towne Square. Officer down. All units. Black SUV, tinted windows, heading east on Elm, running the stop. Shooter is armed with an automatic weapon."

"How bad?" Cole asked, and I looked down to find those pale blue eyes locked on mine. They were cloudy with pain but clear with intention—he wanted the truth, not comfort. He'd always been that way. Cole didn't believe in sugarcoating. He believed in information and what you did with it.

"You're going to be fine," I said.

"That's what doctors say right before you're not fine."

"That's what doctors say when their patient needs to shut up and let them work." I checked his pulse, pressing two fingers against his wrist—rapid and thready, a bird's heartbeat trapped beneath skin that was going cool and clammy despite the morning heat that was radiating off the sidewalk around us. His breathing had turned fast and shallow, his body's panic response kicking in even as his mind tried to stay calm. He was shocky. Expected, with this much blood loss. But expected and acceptable were two very different things.

"Tell me what you're going to do when you get out of the hospital," I said, keeping my voice conversational, easy, the voice I used when I needed a patient to stay with me and the darkness was trying to pull them somewhere I couldn't follow.

"What?"

"Stavros. The case. What are you going to do when you're back on your feet?"

"I'm going to find every rat in this county who's on that man's payroll. And then I'm going to enjoy taking them apart."

"Good. Hold on to that anger." The blazer under my hands was soaked through now, warm and heavy, and I adjusted my grip, finding the places where pressure mattered most and bearing down. "What else?"

His accent was thicker now, the polished edges of his speech softening like they did when he let his guard down—the vowels stretching out, the consonants going lazy, all of it drifting back toward wherever in Texas he'd learned to talk like that. "Hey, Jaye?"

"Yeah?"

"You think…" He swallowed, and I watched his Adam's apple move in his throat, slow and effortful. "You think Lily would say yes if I asked her to marry me again?"

Something tightened behind my ribs. "I think you'd be an idiot not to ask."

"She said no last time." His voice was getting softer, drifting, and I could see the gray creeping around his mouth—the pallor that meant his blood pressure was dropping and his body was starting to prioritize the organs that mattered over the ones that merely wanted things like consciousness and conversation. "What if she says no again?"

"She won't."

"How do you know?"

"Because she loves you. When you get out of

surgery, you're going to ask her yourself. And she's going to say yes."

"I hope so." Barely a whisper now. His eyes were drifting, the blue going hazy, unfocused, like he was looking at something behind me that I couldn't see. "Will you ask her for me? If I can't?"

"You can. And you will. Eyes on me, Cole."

His lids were heavy. I pressed harder on the wound and his body jerked, a sharp hiss cutting through his teeth, and his eyes snapped back into focus—angry and alive and blue as a gas flame.

"There you are," I said. "Stay right there."

"Yes ma'am," he managed, and his cocky grin came back, strained and stubborn and so completely Cole that I had to lock my jaw to keep something embarrassing from happening to my face.

Around us, the Towne Square had transformed. What remained was the chaos that followed violence in places where violence wasn't expected—worse, somehow, than chaos in places where it was, because the contrast made everything sharper, louder, more wrong. People who'd been walking and shopping and pushing strollers had scattered into doorways and behind parked cars. A woman was crouched behind the memorial bench on the corner, her body curved around a little boy whose face was buried in her neck, her hand covering the back of his head as if her palm could stop a bullet.

Patrol cars were arriving now, sirens splitting the morning into before and after, officers spilling out with weapons drawn and faces tight with the specific tension that came from responding to a call that included the words officer down. Jack had taken command without missing a beat—directing officers to establish a perimeter, coordinating the vehicle pursuit through dispatch, barking orders with quiet ferocity. All of it while staying close enough to touch, close enough that his shadow fell across Cole and me like something he could wrap around us if he tried hard enough.

"I can see the ambulance," he said, crouching beside us, his phone still pressed to his ear. His free hand found Cole's boot and gripped it hard. "They're right across the square."

"I'm not going anywhere," Cole said, but his voice was thin and reedy, and the color had drained from his face until his lips looked almost blue. His hand on the wound pad had gone slack, and the tremors in his fingers were visible even in the bright sunlight.

"I've got it," I said, replacing his hand with mine and pressing down with both palms. The blood was still coming—slower now, which could mean the pressure was working or could mean his blood pressure was dropping to a place where there wasn't enough left to push through the damaged vessel. Neither option came with comfort.

It couldn't have been more than ninety seconds, but it passed the way time passes when someone you love is bleeding out under your hands—slowly, cruelly, each heartbeat a negotiation between hope and dread. I knelt there on the hot brick with Cole's blood soaking through the knees of my jeans, the sun beating down on the back of my neck, glass glittering on the sidewalk around us like something a child had scattered for the fun of it. I kept pressure on the wound and talked to him about cases and proposals and all the things he was going to do when he got out of here, while some quieter part of me counted his respirations and monitored the pulse fluttering under my fingertips and carried on a silent, desperate conversation with his subclavian artery that consisted mostly of the word please.

Somewhere above us, the mockingbird was still singing.

Then the ambulance siren wailed across the square from the fire station—close, so close I could feel the sound in my chest—and cut off abruptly as it pulled to the curb twenty feet away. Two paramedics hit the ground before the wheels stopped turning.

"Hey, Doc." Percy was the lead—I'd worked with him a dozen times, and the sight of his steady hands and calm face loosened something in my chest that I hadn't realized was wound so tight. He was already pulling on gloves. "What have we got?"

"GSW to the left shoulder, through and through. Entry inferior to the left clavicle, exit posterior. Possible subclavian involvement—there's arterial bleeding from both wounds. He's lost approximately —" I looked at the blood on the sidewalk, on my hands, on my ruined blazer, soaked into the stranger's cardigan and darkening the spaces between bricks that had been here since before the Constitution was signed, "—a liter, maybe more. Pulse is tachy and thready, resps are shallow. He's been conscious throughout but he's showing signs of hypovolemic shock."

Percy and his partner moved with a choreographed efficiency that only came from doing this together enough times that words were optional. IV access in the right antecubital, a liter of Ringer's running wide open, pressure dressings that were actually designed for the job replacing my blood-soaked blazer and the stranger's ruined cardigan. Oxygen via nasal cannula, the clear tubing snaking across Cole's gray face like a lifeline drawn in plastic. Within two minutes they had him on a backboard, his neck stabilized, his vitals being called out in the shorthand that paramedics and doctors shared like a second language—BP ninety over fifty, heart rate one-twenty, O2 sat ninety-one percent, GCS fourteen.

Within three minutes he was in the back of the ambulance, and I climbed in after him without asking permission or waiting for invitation. Nobody tried to stop me. Nobody would have succeeded if they'd tried.

Jack appeared at the rear doors just before they closed, and for a moment he just stood there, backlit by the morning sun, his face a study in the kind of controlled fury that didn't shout or posture or waste itself on display—the kind that burned cold and patient and would eventually consume everything it touched.

"I'll be right behind you," he said to Cole.

"Don't speed," Cole mumbled from the backboard, his words running together at the edges like watercolors bleeding into wet paper. "I'll never hear the end of it."

"Too late." Jack's eyes found mine above the oxygen mask, above the IV lines, above the blood pressure cuff that was cycling automatically on Cole's right arm. In his eyes I saw everything he couldn't say in front of his officers and the paramedics and the crowd of civilians who were starting to emerge from doorways and from behind cars with that expression of bewildered horror that people wore when violence visited places it wasn't supposed to be. I saw fear and fury and the raw edge of something that went beyond either—something that looked like a promise made in blood.

"Take care of him," Jack said.

"I will."

The doors closed. The siren started. And we were moving.

Cole went into surgery immediately.

The trauma team at King George Memorial was small but good, the way small-town hospitals sometimes were—short on resources but good with their bedside manner. Dr. Reginald Okafor, the chief of surgery, had done two tours with Doctors Without Borders and had seen more gunshot wounds in field hospitals across three continents than most surgeons encountered in a lifetime of urban trauma rotations.

I gave him my assessment in the hallway outside the OR while they prepped Cole on the other side of the double doors—clinical, precise, my voice stripped of everything except the facts another doctor needed to hear. Entry wound, exit wound, estimated blood loss, time of injury, field interventions applied, vitals in the ambulance. Okafor listened with dark, steady eyes that missed nothing, nodded twice, asked two questions about the exit wound trajectory that told me he was already planning his approach, and disappeared through the double doors.

Then there was nothing to do but wait.

The surgical waiting room was the same room that existed in every hospital in America—the room where time went to die. Plastic chairs in muted colors that someone had chosen specifically for their inability to offend. A television mounted in the corner playing daytime talk shows to an audience of no one, the hosts' voices bright and relentless in the empty space. Magazines from six months ago fanned across a coffee table, their covers promising lives that were shinier and simpler than the ones being lived by anyone who'd ever sat in these chairs. The fluorescent lights hummed their single note overhead, casting everything in that flat institutional glow that made healthy people look exhausted and exhausted people look dead.

And beneath it all, the smell—burnt coffee from the machine in the corner, floor wax, the antiseptic sweetness that lived in hospital walls the way memories lived in old houses, permanently, indelibly, impossible to paint over or air out.

I stood at the window and stared at the parking lot without seeing it.

Lily arrived twenty minutes later.

I heard her before I saw her—the rapid clip of boots on linoleum, moving too fast for a hospital corridor, and a voice that was trying to hold itself together the way you hold a cracked glass, carefully and with the full knowledge that one wrong movement would turn it into something that couldn't be put back. She came around the corner at a near-run, and the sight of her face—white, open, stripped of every defense she'd ever built—hit me somewhere below my ribs in a place I didn't know was vulnerable.

She was wearing one of Cole's flannel shirts over leggings, the sleeves rolled up past her wrists, the collar sitting loose against her collarbones. She'd grabbed the closest thing to him she could find, and something about that detail—that instinct to wrap herself in what he'd worn, to put his clothes against her skin as if proximity to his fabric could substitute for proximity to his body—made my throat close up tight enough that I had to look away for a second and gather myself.

Emmy Lu was right behind her, one hand on Lily's elbow with gentle firmness. Emmy Lu's round face was drawn with worry, but her posture was solid, grounded, the living embodiment of the phrase *I've got you.* She was always like that. Always the one who showed up—with a casserole, with a plan, with the quiet immovable conviction that things would work out because she simply refused to entertain the alternative.

"Where is he?" Lily's voice was raw, scraped down to the bare wood. "They said he was shot. That he's in surgery. What happened?"

I crossed to her and took her hands. They were ice cold and trembling, the fingers gripping mine with a strength that surprised me, holding on the way drowning people hold on—not with hope but with the refusal to accept any other option.

"He's in surgery right now," I said, and I made my voice the thing it needed to be—calm, certain, steady enough to build on. "Dr. Okafor is one of the best. The bullet went through his left shoulder—it nicked an artery, but it's repairable. They're fixing the damage, and he should be out within the hour."

"Repairable." She repeated the word the way you'd test a bridge before crossing—carefully, with your weight held back, not yet willing to trust it with everything you had. "You're sure?"

"I was with him the whole time, Lily. From the second he went down until they wheeled him into the OR. His vitals were stable. He was conscious and talking the whole time. He was—" I almost smiled despite everything. "He was being a pain in the ass, actually. Which is a very good sign."

Something broke open in her face—not into tears, not yet, but into the trembling, devastating relief of a woman who'd spent the worst twenty minutes of her life driving to a hospital where the man she loved might already be dead and had arrived to find out he wasn't. She pressed both hands to her mouth and breathed. One breath. Two. Three.

The fluorescent light caught the wetness in her eyes, and she blinked it back with a fierceness that was pure Lily—she'd cry later, in private, when no one could see. Right now she was going to be strong, because that was what Cole would expect, and she loved him enough to give him that even when he wasn't conscious to know it.

"He's going to be okay," I said.

"You promise?"

"I promise."

She nodded—a sharp, decisive nod, the kind that said I'm choosing to believe you because the alternative will break me.

Lily stepped forward and wrapped her arms around me—tight, fierce, her face pressed against my shoulder hard enough that I could feel the bones of her cheek through my shirt. She smelled like Cole's soap and clean cotton and the sharp sweetness of fear, and she held on with desperate strength. I could feel her heartbeat hammering against my chest—fast and hard and scared, a hummingbird trapped under her ribs.

"Thank you," she said, muffled against my shoulder. "Thank you for keeping him alive."

I closed my eyes and held her. The fluorescent lights hummed. The television murmured. A cart rattled past somewhere down the hall, its wheels squeaking in that rhythmic, institutional way that was somehow the loneliest sound in the world. And outside the window, the parking lot shimmered in the heat, ordinary and bright and indifferent, as if the morning hadn't cracked in half.

That was enough. For now, that was enough.

Jack arrived forty minutes later.

I heard his footsteps before I saw him—not the sound itself, because Jack moved quietly when he wanted to, but the quality of the silence that followed him. A shift in the air. A change in pressure. The way a room recalibrated when someone walked into it who was carrying enough controlled fury to power a small city.

He'd stayed at the scene to secure it, to coordinate the pursuit of the SUV, to manage the dozen fires that ignited when a shooting happened in the middle of a small town and people needed someone to tell them it was going to be okay even when the person doing the telling wasn't sure of that himself. By the time he walked into the waiting room, he'd spoken to every officer on scene, reviewed the security camera footage from two businesses on the square, and put out a BOLO on the vehicle that had already been found—abandoned in a parking lot behind the Walmart on Route 3, wiped clean, engine still warm.

Stolen plates. No prints. No witnesses to the abandonment.

Professional. Deliberate. The work of people who'd done this before.

He took one look at Lily—sitting in a plastic chair with Emmy Lu's arm around her shoulders, her eyes red but dry, her hands wrapped around a cup of vending machine coffee she hadn't touched and probably never would—and crossed to her. He crouched down in front of her chair the way he crouched beside victims' families, the way he always did when someone smaller than him needed to feel like they weren't alone, and he took both her hands in his."

"He's tough," Jack said, his voice gentler than most people would have believed it could go. "He's one of the toughest men I've ever known. And he's too mean to die."

A sound escaped Lily—caught somewhere between a laugh and a sob, occupying that narrow space where the two emotions lived so close together you couldn't tell them apart. "Stubborn."

"He's going to be fine. And when he wakes up, first thing he's going to do is complain about the food."

"And ask for his hat," Lily said.

"I've got his hat." Jack squeezed her hands and stood. Then he turned to me, and the gentleness he'd shown Lily didn't disappear so much as it was consumed—swallowed up by something harder and colder and more dangerous than anything I'd seen in his eyes since the night someone had blown up our house and tried to take everything we had.

"Conference room," he said. "Now."

I followed him down the hall to one of those small rooms that hospitals kept for exactly this kind of conversation—the kind where doctors delivered news that rearranged people's lives, where families made decisions that no amount of preparation could have made easier. The walls were the same institutional beige, and a window looked out onto a little courtyard where someone with more hope than the room deserved had planted rosemary and lavender in a raised bed. The purple blooms were nodding in a breeze that couldn't reach us through the glass, and the sight of them—alive, fragrant, quietly persistent in a place surrounded by so much sterile sadness— made something ache in my chest that I didn't have time to examine.

Jack closed the door. The latch clicked with a sound that seemed much louder than it should have been.

For a long moment he just stood there with his back to me, both hands braced against the wall, his head bowed between his shoulders, his weight forward on his arms like a man holding up something that was trying to crush him. His breathing was slow and deliberate—in through the nose, out through the mouth.

"Jack."

"They shot at you." His voice was barely above a whisper, low and rough, scraped raw by something that had nothing to do with volume and everything to do with the effort required to keep the words from becoming something else—a shout, a prayer, a sound that had no name. "They opened fire on a public street, in broad daylight, with civilians everywhere, and they shot at you."

"They shot at all of us."

He turned, and his eyes were black. Not dark brown, not nearly black—black, the way they went when every civilized layer had been stripped away and what remained was something older and more dangerous than the badge on his belt or the oath he'd taken or the laws he'd sworn to uphold. Something that predated all of it. Something that lived in the part of a man that would kill to protect what was his and feel nothing about it afterward except the satisfaction of having done it thoroughly.

"You're carrying our baby." Each word came out low and rough, dragged up from somewhere deep in his chest, and I could hear what it cost him to say them—the careful, deliberate effort. He was holding himself together with nothing but willpower and the knowledge that falling apart right now would help no one. "You were standing on that sidewalk with our baby inside you, and someone pointed an automatic weapon—"

His voice broke. Not dramatically, not loudly—it just stopped, the way a rope stops when it's been pulled past its limit, a quiet snap followed by silence. He closed his eyes. The fluorescent light hummed its single flat note overhead, and somewhere down the hall a cart rattled past with squeaking wheels, and the lavender nodded in the courtyard beyond the glass, and the world kept turning because that's what the world did, even when the people in it felt like it should have the decency to stop.

"I could have lost you both." When he found his voice again it was barely there—a whisper with cracks running through it, broken open on the word both in a way that told me everything about what that word contained for him. Not two people. Not a wife and a pregnancy. Everything. The whole of what his life meant, the future he'd been building in his mind every night when he lay beside me with his hand on my stomach and thought I was asleep—the nursery, the first steps, the first words, the Sunday mornings and the bedtime stories and the ordinary miracles of a life he'd never dared to want until I'd put that test on the bathroom counter and changed everything.

For just a second, the mask slipped off, and I saw the thing underneath. Not anger. Not the sheriff. Not the former Special Forces operator or the SWAT commander or any of the versions of Jack Lawson that the world got to see. Just a man. Terrified and gutted and stripped down to the raw, exposed nerve of what it meant to love two people so completely that the thought of losing them could take a man like this—a man built of steel cable and stubbornness and the kind of courage that had earned him medals he kept in a drawer—and reduce him to this. To trembling hands and a broken voice in a beige hospital room that smelled like floor wax and burnt coffee.

I crossed to him and put my hands on his face. His jaw was rigid beneath my palms, the muscle bunching so tight I could feel his teeth grinding, and his stubble was rough against my fingers—the texture of a morning that had started with breakfast and ended with blood. His skin was warm. He smelled like gunpowder and sweat and, beneath that, like himself—clean soap and leather and the faint spice of his aftershave, the scent that meant home and safety and every good thing I'd ever been given.

"You didn't lose us," I said. "I'm right here. We're both right here."

He pulled me against him so hard it almost hurt —his arms wrapping around me the way they had a thousand times before, except this time there was a desperation in it, a need that went beyond comfort or affection into something more primal, more essential. One hand cradled the back of my head, fingers threading into my hair. The other pressed flat against the small of my back, holding me against him from hip to shoulder. I could feel him shaking—fine tremors running through all that muscle and training and iron control, the physical cost of holding himself together when everything in him wanted to fly apart. His heartbeat hammered against my chest, hard and fast, and his breath came in ragged pulls against my hair, and I held on and let him shake and said nothing, because sometimes the bravest thing you could do for someone was to let them fall apart against you without trying to fix it.

"Stavros," he said against my hair, and the name came out like a curse, like a sentence, like the first word of a war.

"We don't know that for certain."

"The hell we don't." He pulled back and looked at me, and the fear had crystallized into something new. Not hot. Not reckless. Something colder and more patient and infinitely more dangerous—a resolve that didn't announce itself but simply arrived, fully formed, and began dismantling everything in its path. "This was a message. We started asking questions about the operation, and twenty-four hours later someone tries to gun us down in the middle of the Towne Square. That's not coincidence. That's organized crime telling us to back off."

"Then they don't know you very well."

"No." The trembling stopped. His jaw set. And the man who'd been shaking in my arms a moment ago was gone, replaced by something quieter, something I'd seen only a handful of times in all the years I'd known him—the version of Jack Lawson that existed behind every other version, the one that all the training and discipline and civilization had been built on top of but never quite managed to bury. "They don't."

He released me and straightened, and I watched the sheriff reassemble himself piece by piece—the set of the shoulders, the lift of the chin, the flatness settling back over his eyes like armor plating sliding into place. It was seamless. It was terrifying. Like watching someone who'd been drowning simply decide to become the ocean instead.

"This is exactly what he wants," he said. "He wants me angry. But I'm done being careful. We're going on offense. Tomorrow morning I'm going to walk into Niko Stavros's office and introduce myself. And then I'm going to start squeezing every person connected to him until somebody breaks."

"You want to rattle the cage."

"I want to shake it until everything falls out." He looked at me, and his expression was almost calm. "Stavros thinks he sent a message this morning. Fine. Now I'm going to send one back. I'm going to show up at his businesses, pull permits, request inspections, interview his employees. I'm going to make him feel watched. And when he starts making mistakes—because men like him always do when they realize they're not untouchable—we'll be right there to catch every single one."

CHAPTER ELEVEN

The hospital was filled with cops.

They came in pairs, in groups, and alone—deputies still in uniform with their radios turned low and off-duty officers in jeans and ball caps who'd heard the call on their scanners and hadn't bothered to change before driving over. A secretary from the front office showed up with a box of doughnuts she'd grabbed at the gas station on the way.

Nobody called them. Nobody had to. When one of your own went down, you showed up. You planted yourself in the ugly waiting room with the bad coffee and the muted television, and you stayed until someone told you it was okay to go. That was the deal. Unwritten. Unbroken. Older than any policy manual.

I'd washed Cole's blood off my hands in the ER

bathroom before the waiting even started. A nurse had steered me there the moment I climbed out of the ambulance—a calm, no-nonsense woman with reading glasses on a chain who took one look at my hands and my clothes and my face and pointed me toward a sink without a word. The water ran pink at first, then rust, then finally clear while I scrubbed under my nails and between my fingers and worked the soap into the creases of my knuckles where the blood had dried dark and resistant, like it had decided to stay. She brought me green scrubs, antibiotic ointment for the heels of my palms where the brick had scraped them raw, and a butterfly bandage for the cut on my cheek.

I changed. I cleaned up. I threw my ruined clothes into a plastic bag and tied it shut. The whole thing took maybe ten minutes, and I did it with the mechanical efficiency of a woman who'd spent her career covered in other people's blood and knew that the sooner you dealt with the physical evidence, the sooner you could focus on what mattered.

What mattered right now was the man on the operating table.

Lily sat between me and Emmy Lu on the plastic chairs, Cole's flannel shirt buttoned to her chin, her hands clasped tight in her lap. She hadn't spoken since she'd asked Okafor if she could see him, and I didn't push. Some silences needed to be left alone.

Emmy Lu kept one hand on Lily's arm—not gripping, just resting there, a steady point of contact that said *I'm here* without requiring a response.

Jack stood by the window with his arms crossed and his jaw set and his phone buzzing every thirty seconds in his pocket. He let it ring.

At eleven twenty-two, Okafor came through the double doors.

I read the answer in his body before he spoke. The easy stride, the loose shoulders, the way his hands hung relaxed at his sides instead of clasped in front of him the way doctors clasped them when they were about to dismantle someone's world. I'd delivered enough death notifications to recognize the posture of good news, and relief hit me so hard my vision blurred for a second.

"He came through beautifully," Okafor said. "Partial laceration to the subclavian artery—approximately two millimeters. We repaired it with primary suture, blood flow is strong. He received two units of packed red cells. He's going to be sore, tired, and confined to a bed for a minimum of three days. But he should make a full recovery."

Lily closed her eyes. Her lips moved, but no sound came out—a prayer, maybe, or just the shape of a word she needed to feel in her mouth before she could believe it. Emmy Lu's hand tightened on her arm.

There was an audible whoosh of breath in the waiting area. The loosening of clenched muscles and the release of the grief and worry that compressed the chest. A deputy near the vending machine put his hand over his face for a moment, then dropped it and walked out with his shoulders squared and his eyes bright.

"Give us a few minutes," Okafor told Lily. "We'll get him settled into a room, and then you can sit with him as long as you want."

The deputies began to filter out after that. Shoulder squeezes for Lily. Handshakes for Jack. The purposeful exodus of people who had work waiting and a reason to do it now that the worst hadn't happened.

"I need to get back to the square," he said. "Forensics is still processing, and I want every frame of security footage within six blocks pulled before the businesses close for the day."

I looked at Lily.

"Cole's fine, and I'm fine," she said. "Y'all go catch who did this."

"You can count on that," Jack said.

He held the elevator door and waited for me to step in.

We rode down in silence, the fluorescent light buzzing overhead, the smell of industrial disinfectant sharp enough to taste. Jack's face was the mask he wore when he was thinking three moves ahead—jaw set, eyes fixed on something only he could see. I knew better than to interrupt the process. Somewhere behind that expression he was building a plan, laying out the next twelve hours like chess pieces on a board.

We were on the Kings Highway, halfway between the hospital and the Towne Square, when Jack's phone rang through the Tahoe's speakers. Emmy Lu's name flashed on the dash screen.

"Emmy Lu, you're on speaker," Jack said.

"Jack, oh thank goodness." Her voice was wrong. Emmy Lu had a voice that made you think of sweet tea and front porches, and right now it sounded like glass about to shatter. "I just got back to the funeral home, and I know you've got your hands full with everything that happened this morning, and I'm sorry to bother you, but I wanted to make sure the Brennan flowers got delivered because Carol Anne went in to have her baby early and they said they might not have a delivery person to bring the flowers by, and I thought I might have to go pick them up because the visitation is tomorrow."

"Take a breath, Emmy Lu," Jack told her. "Just tell me what happened."

"Jack—" Her voice broke. "There's a dead man on the front porch. Someone just left him there. Like a package."

The Tahoe's air-conditioning hummed. A truck passed us going the other direction, rocking the cab with its wake.

"Are you inside?" Jack asked.

"I'm in the kitchen. I didn't touch anything. My hands are shaking so bad I could barely dial the phone. I think I should make some coffee."

"Good idea," Jack said. "Keep your mind occupied and stay inside. Stay away from the windows. I'm calling dispatch right now to get units rolling, and we're about ten minutes out. Don't open the door for anyone until you see a badge. Understand?"

"I understand."

He killed the call and hit the lights, and the Tahoe surged forward with the engine dropping into a growl. The trees along the Kings Highway blurred into a green wall on either side, and the white center line came at us in rapid-fire dashes.

I stared at the road stretching ahead of us and felt something cold settle behind my ribs. A body dumped on the porch of the funeral home. On my porch. While every cop in the county was sitting in a hospital waiting room.

"They knew the building was empty," I said. "Everyone was at the hospital. Every cop, every deputy, Emmy Lu, Lily, Sheldon. The place sat wide open for hours, and they knew exactly when to move."

"Yes."

"How did they know, Jack?"

He didn't answer. The silence in the cab was heavy with everything we didn't know yet. Stavros had known where to find us at breakfast. Now someone had known the funeral home was empty. He was either watching us, or he had someone close enough to us that the difference didn't matter. Either way, the message was the same—he could reach us whenever he wanted.

Jack turned onto Catherine of Aragon doing sixty and brought it down fast, the brakes biting as the funeral home came into view at the end of the block. Dark red brick and white columns, the two massive elm trees throwing shade across the wide front yard. It looked the way it always looked—stately and quiet, a place that held grief with dignity.

Except for the patrol cars at the curb with their lights spinning, and the yellow crime-scene tape already going up across the front walk.

Jack pulled to the curb behind the patrol units and killed the engine. I was out before he was, reaching into the back seat for my medical bag. I guess it was the kind of day where the dead didn't wait for you to come to them, but showed up at your door instead.

The side door was unlocked—the one that led through the mudroom into the kitchen—the door I used every day. Emmy Lu was sitting at the kitchen island with her hands wrapped around a cup of coffee she hadn't touched. Her face was pale and her eyes were too wide. Her lips were pressed into a thin line that meant she was holding herself together by sheer force of will and southern manners.

"Officers cleared the property," she said. "Nobody inside. Whoever left him was long gone."

"You did good, Emmy Lu."

"I keep thinking about the Brennan visitation tomorrow." She shook her head, and something between a laugh and a sob caught in her throat. "Isn't that the silliest thing? A dead boy on my porch, and I'm worried about the Brennan flowers."

"It's not silly. It's your brain looking for something it can fix." I squeezed her arm. "Stay inside. I'll be a while."

I went back out through the mudroom and around the side of the building. Jack was at the perimeter with the patrol officers, radio in one hand, phone in the other. I could hear him requesting a canvass of Catherine of Aragon—every house, every neighbor, anyone who'd seen a vehicle pull up in the last three hours. He moved the way he always moved at a crime scene, deliberate and focused, like a man drawing a circle around something he intended to own.

I walked around to the front.

The porch ran the full width of the house—wide and deep, built for rocking chairs and slow conversation. White columns at even intervals. Hanging ferns on either side of the front door. The brass knocker caught the afternoon light, and a cardinal was perched on the porch rail like it had no idea what it was sitting next to.

The body was crumpled against the front door like somebody had tossed him and walked away. He was on his side, one arm pinned beneath him and the other flung out across the welcome mat. His legs were bent at odd angles, and his head was turned so that those open, empty eyes stared straight at anyone who walked up the porch steps. Maybe that part was intentional. Maybe it wasn't. Either way, the message wasn't in how they'd left him. It was where.

I sighed. "I'm sorry, T-Bone," I said quietly.

A bee drifted past, aimless, bumbling toward the ferns. Down the street a lawn mower sputtered to life, and the ordinary sound of it made the scene in front of me feel sharper and more wrong.

I pulled on gloves and got to work. I grabbed the camera out of my bag and took wide shots of the porch to establish position, then moved in tighter, working in from the perimeter. Then the door behind him and the blood pooled beneath his head, dark and tacky on the brick. Finally the drag marks on the steps where someone had hauled him up without caring how he landed.

Jack came up the steps a few minutes later. He stood over the body for a long moment, hands on his hips, his face giving away nothing.

"What are we looking at?" he asked.

I sighed. "Visually identified as Terrence James. Will confirm with prints. Black male, mid-twenties. Two gunshot wounds to the back of the head, base of the skull. Small caliber. A .22 or .25 based on entry wound diameter. Contact range or close to it. Stippling and powder tattooing at both wound margins." I pointed without touching. "Exit wounds through the forehead, both of them. Slightly larger, more irregular—the rounds tumbled through bone and brain before they punched out. Blood from the exits ran down his face and pooled in the eye sockets."

Jack crouched beside me. "Defensive wounds?"

"Nothing. No split knuckles, no bruising on the hands or forearms, no skin under the nails. He didn't fight back. Either he never saw it coming, or he wasn't given the chance." I sat back on my heels. "This was an execution, Jack. Someone walked up behind him, put a gun to the back of his head, and pulled the trigger twice."

I moved to his pockets while Jack watched. Front

left held a cheap prepaid phone with a cracked screen, the kind you could buy at any gas station for thirty dollars. Front right had eleven dollars in cash, a stick of gum, and a key ring with three keys and a faded Parris Island keychain. The back right pocket held a slim leather wallet with a military ID, a debit card from a credit union in King George, and a photograph.

It was creased and worn soft at the edges, the kind of picture someone carried every day until the colors started to fade. Two young men in dress blues, standing shoulder to shoulder in front of a barracks and grinning at the camera with the cocky invincibility of boys who hadn't yet learned what the world could take from them.

Dre was on the left and T-Bone was on the right, and their arms were around each other's shoulders, and they looked like they owned the future.

I bagged the photo with the rest of the personal effects. My hands were steady.

I moved to his feet. The sneakers were clean on top, but the soles caught my attention—reddish-brown dust ground deep into the tread pattern, the same color and texture as the residue I'd found on Dre's bare feet. I couldn't confirm it was the same material without the lab, and we were still waiting on Richmond for Dre's results, but the visual match was close enough to make the hair on my arms stand up.

"Look at this," I said, and held the sole up so Jack could see. "I can't say for certain until we get it tested, but that looks an awful lot like what I scraped off Dre's feet."

Jack leaned in. "Possible material from the tunnels?"

"If the composition matches, it puts him underground before he died. Same as Dre." I scraped samples into evidence bags, labeled them, and sealed them. "I'll send these to Richmond with a rush request, but either way, it's one more thread tying these two murders to the same location."

Jack stood and looked out past the crime-scene tape at the neighbors gathering across the street. I could see him putting it together behind his eyes, fast and quiet and relentless.

"Whoever did this didn't bother cleaning out his pockets," I said. "They left his phone, his wallet, his military ID, a photograph of him and Dre together. That's not sloppy, that's deliberate. They didn't care if we identified him because identification was the whole point. They wanted us to know they killed a man who talked to us, and they wanted to leave him on my porch so we'd understand how close they can get."

"The deputy I had watching T-Bone followed him from his sister's house this morning," Jack said, and the anger in his voice was cold and calculated.

"Tailed him to the Sunoco on the Kings Highway, sat in the lot while T-Bone went inside for about ten minutes, then followed him back out toward the interchange. Six blocks later a truck cut between them at a traffic light, and by the time the deputy cleared the intersection, T-Bone's car was gone."

"What time?"

"Around nine thirty. Right about the time we were getting shot at in the Towne Square."

That landed hard. The shooting hadn't just been an attempt to kill us. It had been a distraction. Every cop in the county responded to that call. And while they were all racing toward the square or sitting in a hospital waiting room, Stavros's people had intercepted T-Bone away from the deputy following him and put two bullets in his head.

"So we're looking at a window of two, maybe three hours between the gas station and this porch," I said. "That's not a lot of time to grab someone, kill them, and deliver the body."

"It is if you already know exactly where he's going to be." Jack's jaw tightened. "I've got the deputy writing a detailed report. Every turn, every time stamp, every vehicle he can remember seeing. We'll go through it with a fine-tooth comb."

He looked down at T-Bone one more time, and something settled in his face, not grief, but the acknowledgment of a debt he intended to collect.

Then he stepped off the porch and pulled out his phone, and I heard him talking to Martinez as he walked toward the patrol cars. He already had the pieces in motion. Martinez was taking over Cole's caseload. Chen and Riley were running the Towne Square crime scene. And Jack was doing what Jack did, managing the chaos.

I went inside through the side door, back through the mudroom and down the narrow stairs to the basement lab. I washed my hands at the big steel sink and prepped the table and laid out the instruments in the order I'd need them. Then I went back upstairs and out to the porch with the gurney. Officer Plank helped me lift T-Bone onto it and maneuver it through the side door and down to the lab. He was still considered a rookie by years on the job, but somewhere in the last six months he'd lost that fresh-faced enthusiasm, and his eyes had changed. He had cop eyes.

I laid T-Bone on the stainless-steel table under the fluorescent lights, tied on a fresh apron, snapped on a new pair of gloves, and switched on the overhead surgical light.

Two hours. That was all I needed. Two hours to find whatever T-Bone's body could tell me about the people who killed him, and then I'd have something to give Jack that was more useful than anger.

CHAPTER TWELVE

THE AUTOPSY TOOK TWO HOURS, AND MOST OF WHAT T-Bone's body told me was exactly what I'd expected.

I recovered no bullets. Both rounds had entered at the base of the skull and traveled on a slight upward trajectory before exiting through the forehead, which meant the shooter had been shorter than T-Bone and had been standing directly behind him when he fired.

The wound tracks were consistent with a small-caliber handgun, almost certainly a .22 based on the diameter and damage pattern through the brain tissue. Close range. Contact, or near enough that it didn't matter. Two shots fired by someone who was shorter than his victim.

There were no defensive wounds on his hands or forearms. No injection sites. His stomach contents showed a partially digested breakfast of eggs, turkey sausage, and oatmeal consumed roughly three to four hours before death. Clean fuel for a man who had a fight scheduled for tomorrow night and was taking care of his body. His blood was clean except for trace amounts of ibuprofen. No sedatives, no drugs of any kind. Unlike Dre, whoever killed T-Bone hadn't bothered with restraints or days of interrogation. They'd simply walked up behind him and pulled the trigger while he stood there not knowing his life was about to end.

But his left sneaker told me something I hadn't expected.

I almost missed it. I was pulling off his sneakers to bag them with the rest of his clothing when the insole of the left one shifted, and I felt the crinkle of paper beneath my fingertip. A small, folded piece of paper had been tucked inside the lining, pressed flat between the insole and the sole itself. I worked it out with tweezers, unfolded it under the magnifying light, and found a single set of GPS coordinates written in pencil in a cramped, careful hand, along with tomorrow's date.

One location. The next fight.

T-Bone had been carrying it on his body the way a soldier carries mission coordinates.

I bagged the paper, sealed it, labeled it, and set it with the rest of the evidence. Then I pulled the sheet over T-Bone's face, stripped off my gloves, and pushed him into the cooler.

And then I went upstairs to find Jack.

He was in Emmy Lu's office with the security footage already pulled up on the desktop monitor and a cup of coffee going cold at his elbow. He'd been busy while I was downstairs. Martinez was briefed and up to speed on Cole's caseload. Riley and Chen were finishing up the Towne Square scene. Plank was on his way to Richmond with evidence. The protection detail on Marco and Darnell had been doubled, and the deputy who'd lost T-Bone in traffic was writing a very detailed report about exactly how that had happened.

The office was small and warm, cluttered, but with an organized chaos of someone who ran a funeral home the way other people ran small countries. File cabinets and flower catalogs, a framed cross-stitch on the wall that said *BLESS THIS MESS* in lavender thread, and a potted fern in the corner that was somehow thriving despite getting no direct sunlight.

"Found something," I said.

He looked up. I handed him the evidence bag with the paper inside, and I watched his face as he read the coordinates and the date. The shift was subtle, a tightening around his eyes, a slight forward lean, the stillness that came over him when a piece of the puzzle dropped into a slot he hadn't known was empty.

"Where was this?"

"Inside the lining of his left shoe. Between the insole and the sole. He hid it there on purpose." I sat down in the chair beside the desk. "Those coordinates are for a location, and that date is tomorrow."

Jack set the evidence bag on the desk beside the keyboard and stared at it for a long moment. I could see him running the math the same way I had, the implications unfolding one after another like dominoes falling in a line. If those coordinates were accurate, and if the fight was still happening tomorrow night, then we had less than twenty-four hours to mobilize tactically before someone tipped them off and they scattered like rats.

"He was killed in a standing position," I said, because Jack needed all of it and he needed it now. "Both rounds entered the base of the skull and exited through the forehead. I measured the wound track at approximately twelve degrees upward. T-Bone was six one. At that height, the base of his skull sits at roughly sixty-nine inches from the ground. You work the angle backward from a contact shot and the shooter was holding the weapon at approximately sixty-six inches." I let that settle. "That puts the shooter somewhere between five eight and five ten, depending on arm position and stance."

"Five eight to five ten," Jack repeated. He filed that away in the mental cabinet that would open again later when the pieces started matching up.

"No defensive wounds. No drugs in his system. Clean breakfast, fighter's food, eggs and turkey sausage and oatmeal. He was prepping for tomorrow night's fight."

Jack turned back to the monitor. "Come look at this."

I pulled my chair closer and watched as he scrubbed the security footage timeline to 10:47 a.m. Doug had installed the system himself. The image was sharp, full color, high definition. It could pick up a license plate from fifty yards in full daylight.

A dark navy van pulled into the driveway at 10:47. It sat there for eleven seconds, and then the side door slid open and two figures got out. Both wore dark clothing and ball caps pulled low enough to shield their faces from the camera angle, and they moved with the efficient purpose of men who had done this kind of thing before. They went around to the back of the van, opened the rear doors, and pulled out our victim. They carried the body up the front steps between them, one at the shoulders and one at the feet, and tossed him against the front door with about as much ceremony as men unloading furniture. The whole thing took less than ninety seconds. They were back in the van and pulling away from the curb before the two-minute mark, and the street was empty again, quiet and ordinary, as if nothing had happened at all.

"Plates?" I asked.

"Covered. They taped something over them." Jack paused the footage on the clearest frame of the van. "But the vehicle itself is distinctive. Ford Transit cargo van, 2018 or newer based on the body style. I've already sent the still to every body shop and rental agency in the county."

"What about the other cameras? Different angles?"

"Nothing. They only came to the front." He leaned back in the chair and pressed his thumb and forefinger against the bridge of his nose. "They knew exactly what they were doing. In and out in under two minutes, faces covered, plates covered. This wasn't amateur hour."

"Stavros doesn't hire amateurs."

"No. He doesn't."

The casual efficiency of it made my stomach turn.

"The body types," I said. "The shorter one looks about five ten. Stocky build."

"I noticed that," he said. "Let's go see if the neighbors saw anything."

We started across the street at the strip mall, because those storefronts had the best sight lines to the funeral home's front porch and the driveway where the van had parked.

The lot had been repaved recently, the asphalt still dark enough to look wet in the late afternoon light, and the little row of businesses had gotten a face-lift sometime in the last year that made it look almost cheerful. The laundromat anchored the end the way it always had, surviving every economic downturn this block had weathered since before I'd taken over as coroner. Next to it, the Crate and Go occupied the middle units, and the CrossFit gym held down the space next to it, its front windows sweating with condensation from whatever was happening inside. The corner unit housed a delicatessen that was fairly new, and caught the overflow crowd from those who didn't want to deal with the crowds of the Towne Square.

We started at the laundromat. Patrice Gooding was behind the counter folding towels when we walked in. She was a tall woman in her mid-fifties with dark skin, silver-streaked locs pulled up in a high wrap, and reading glasses perched on the end of her nose that she looked over instead of through. She'd been running the laundromat since I was a kid, and we'd shared enough sidewalk conversations over the years to skip the small talk when it wasn't needed.

"Hey, Patrice," I said.

"Hey yourself. Busy morning for you two." She leaned her hip against the folding table. "Heard about Cole. He doing okay?"

"He's out of surgery," I said. "He's going to make it."

"I'm glad to hear it," she said, her eyes tearing up a bit. "I've got a soft spot for that man. And he owes me twelve dollars for a shirt he dropped off in March. I told him I don't run a storage facility." She glanced at Jack. "You tell him when he's feeling better."

"I'll pass it along," Jack said, his smile gentle. "We're talking to everybody in the area about some activity at the funeral home this morning. Were you working the counter around ten thirty, quarter to eleven?"

"Honey, I'm always working the counter. I've been here since seven." She pulled her glasses off and let them hang from the beaded chain around her neck. "What kind of activity are we talking about? I'm assuming this has something to do with all the cop cars across the street?"

"Did you notice a cargo van pull into the funeral home driveway this morning? Dark colored, navy blue?"

Patrice's face shifted, the warmth pulling back just enough to make room for something more careful. "Matter of fact, I did. It came down Catherine of Aragon, driving slow. Not lost slow, more like looking-for-something slow. Passed right by my windows." She pointed toward the plate glass. "Only reason I noticed was because he turned left onto Anne Boleyn, and then sure enough, a couple of minutes later he came driving by again and pulled into your driveway. I figured it was a delivery service or something. Usually when you've got big flower arrangements they come in a van like that."

"Did you happen to get a look at the driver?"

"White guy," she said. "Had a beard. Not old, but not young either."

"And after?" Jack asked. "Did you see which way the van went when it left?"

"Went out the same way it came in, back down Catherine of Aragon away from the Towne Square, like it was headed toward Nottingham." She looked between us, her expression serious, and the neighborhood gossip was replaced by something sharper. "What happened over there today?"

"The van left a dead body on the lawn," I said.

She looked at me with eyes wide. "Normally I'd make some kind of comment about it being a funeral home, but I can see you're serious as a heart attack. You think they're coming back?"

"I'd just say to keep your eyes open, and to call if you see anything suspicious," Jack told her. "Let us know if you think of anything else."

She picked up a towel and folded it with slow deliberation. "You know I will. Stay safe."

We worked our way down the strip mall. The kid working the register at Crate and Go had been on his phone all morning and hadn't seen anything, which he reported with the cheerful lack of shame that only a teenager could manage. The CrossFit gym gave us nothing—the owner said a class had been going on during the time the van dumped the body, and the front windows were too fogged to see through anyway.

When we got to the deli, it was closed, with sign on the door that said *BACK AT TWO*. Obviously their appointment ran over because it was after three and the door was still locked.

"Maybe they saw all the cops and decided it was best to stay out of the way," I said. "You know how cops make people nervous."

"Yeah," he said. "I love that part of the job."

We walked down Catherine of Aragon toward Anne Boleyn.

The houses on Anne Boleyn sat on large lots with deep setbacks and mature trees that said old money or at least old roots. American flags hung from porch brackets. Flower beds were tended with the seriousness of competitive sport. It was a street where people mowed their lawns on Saturday mornings and waved at every car that passed. The people who lived in these houses knew everything that happened on the street. They usually knew what bodies were coming into the funeral home before they were delivered.

Harold and Ruthann Pruitt lived in the yellow Cape Cod on the corner, the property closest to the funeral home. A wooden flagpole stood at the edge of the front walk with an American flag that Harold raised every morning at six and took down every evening at sunset, rain or shine, because some habits outlasted the uniform that created them. The flower beds along the front were Ruthann's domain—roses and hydrangeas and black-eyed Susans in tidy rows that looked like they'd been planted with a level and a tape measure.

Ruthann answered the door before we knocked, which meant she'd been watching us come up the walk, which meant the neighborhood grapevine was already fully operational. She was a small, round woman with a cloud of white hair she kept pinned back with tortoiseshell clips, pink cheeks that always looked like she'd just come in from a walk, and bright hazel eyes that missed absolutely nothing. She was wearing a floral apron over a denim shirt, and her hands were dusted with flour.

"We were hoping you'd stop by," she said with more excitement than was probably appropriate. "I've made some sweet tea. Come on in and make yourselves at home. Harold moves to the sunroom after lunch to avoid the sun."

She ushered us through the front hall and into a kitchen that smelled like lemon and butter and looked like it hadn't been updated since the nineties. There was rooster wallpaper border along the soffit. A collection of ceramic salt and pepper shakers sat on a shelf above the stove that spanned at least three decades of vacation souvenirs, and more roosters along the tops of the cabinet and hidden among appliances on the countertops. It was a lot of roosters.

"Harold," she called toward the back of the house. "Sheriff's here. Put on your shoes and come be useful."

Harold appeared in the doorway, and even at seventy-one he still carried himself with the straight-backed economy of movement that the army put into a man and never fully took out. He was lean and weathered, with a face like a walnut—deeply lined and harder than it looked. What was left of his hair was cropped close and silver, and his eyes were the pale, steady blue of a man who'd spent twenty-five years making assessments that other people's lives depended on. He wore khaki shorts and a faded

VFW T-shirt, and his binoculars hung around his neck as though they were part of the dress code.

"I was wondering when you'd get around to me," he said to Jack. "Took you long enough, son."

"Mr. Pruitt," Jack said.

Ruthann set glasses of sweet tea in front of us without asking and then inspected the butterfly bandage on my cheek with a critical eye.

"You need to change out that bandage," she said, looking at my cheek.

"I'll take care of it once we get back," I told her.

"Uh-huh." She was already rummaging in a drawer near the stove. "I've got a fresh bandage and Neosporin right here."

I sighed. There would be no getting around this, so I sat quietly and let her play nurse.

"Mr. Pruitt, we're canvassing the neighborhood about some activity at the funeral home this morning," Jack said. "From your porch on the corner, you've got a good angle of the driveway. Did you see a van pull into the property around ten thirty, quarter to eleven?"

"I saw it before it pulled in," Harold said. He lowered himself into a kitchen chair with deliberate precision. "I was on the porch with my crossword and binoculars, watching a pair of goldfinches on the power line, when a navy blue van came down Catherine of Aragon and did a couple turns around the block. Caught my attention right away. Then they turned into the driveway. Ford Transit, 2019 or thereabouts based on the body style.

"The plates caught my eye first," Harold continued. "I zoomed in on the Virginia tags, but was something over the numbers. Looked like tape."

He reached into the pocket of his shorts and pulled out a small spiral notebook, the kind you could buy for a dollar at any convenience store. He flipped it open to a page with neat, angular handwriting that looked like it had been trained on army field reports.

"I took the liberty of making notes. My memory isn't what it used to be. Let's see. The van pulled up the driveway at 10:47 a.m."

Jack leaned forward. "What did you see?"

"The tall one got out first. He was the one closest to me, so I got a decent look. Maybe six-foot, slim build, clean shaven. Light skinned but not white, if you know what I mean. Maybe Italian or Middle Eastern. Mid-thirties, maybe younger. Strong jaw, straight nose, dark hair under the ball cap."

Harold's eyes were steady and precise, delivering the information the way he'd been trained to deliver a field report. "He had a tattoo on the side of his neck, below the ear. Looked pretty intricate."

"What about when the door opened? Could you see inside the van?"

"Some. The angle was right for it and I still had the binoculars up." Harold turned a page in his notebook. "There was a work shirt folded on the console, dark blue, like a uniform or a mechanic's shirt. It had yellow lettering over the pocket." He looked down at his notebook and read directly from it. "Tidewater Logistics."

"That's great info," Jack said. "What about the second guy?"

"Couldn't see him as well, but he was short and stocky. Had a stocking cap pulled over his head, and he had a scar along his jaw that was a real doozy. Then he and the guy in the passenger seat went to the back of the van," Harold said. "They opened the rear doors, and they pulled something out and carried it around the side of the building toward the front."

"Did you see what they were carrying?" Jack asked.

"I assumed it was a delivery. You're a funeral home." Harold looked at me without apology. "People carry things in and out of your building all day long. But I couldn't see what they were carrying from the porch. The van doors blocked my visual. It looked heavy though. Nothing about it seemed unusual except the covered plates. But I saw on the news it was a body. I should've checked it out."

"You had no way of knowing," I assured him.

"Mmhm." Harold didn't look like he entirely believed that, but he let it go.

The kitchen was quiet for a moment. Ruthann set a plate of lemon squares on the table and put her hand on Harold's shoulder, and I watched something pass between them that didn't need words—the understanding of two people who'd spent a lifetime together and could communicate whole conversations in the pressure of a palm.

"Those men will come back," Harold said. He took a lemon square from the plate and bit into it. "Men who plan routes and cover plates and move that clean don't do one job and disappear. They're on somebody's payroll, and they'll do whatever that somebody tells them to do next."

"We're expecting them to," Jack said.

"Well then," he said, acknowledging the promise in Jack's voice. "Take some of these with you."

"I always make too many," Ruthann said. "If you don't take them Harold will eat them all."

She pressed a Tupperware container into my hands at the door and said, "Tell your mama hello, Jack. You're looking a bit peaky, Jaye. You might get out of the sun and have a rest."

I just smiled as we walked back out into a humid heat that had turned sticky and clung to the skin.

"Oh, good," I said. "Feels like rain. Maybe it'll cool down some."

"Or boil us," Jack said.

"Very reassuring," I said.

We walked back to the funeral home where the Tahoe was parked, and Jack opened the lockbox bolted to the floor behind the driver's seat and pulled out the evidence bag with the brass key. I climbed into the passenger side while he started the engine, and we were on the road before I had my seat belt fastened.

The Tupperware of Ruthann's lemon squares sat on the console between us, and the smell of lemon and butter mixed with the leather of the seats and the faint residual scent of Jack's aftershave that lived permanently in the fabric of this vehicle.

"I've put Doug and Margot on Stavros," Jack said. His eyes stayed on the road, but the set of his jaw told me he'd been carrying this decision for a while and had made his peace with it. "Everything. Business entities, property records, known associates, financial transactions. Anything she can trace through public and semipublic databases, and some that aren't so public."

I looked at him. Doug was a genius and Margot could crack systems that governments couldn't, but neither one of them operated inside the boundaries of what a judge would consider legal evidence gathering. Jack knew that. He'd spent this entire investigation insisting every piece of evidence be clean enough to survive a courtroom. The fact that he was cutting Doug and Margot loose without those guardrails told me exactly how far past professional this had gotten for him.

"None of it will be admissible," I said.

"It doesn't need to be. What I need is a map. I need to know what Stavros owns, who he controls, and where his money goes." He checked his mirrors and passed a pickup doing ten under the limit. "Margot finds the targets. We build the legal case around that to bring them down."

"Good," I said.

He glanced at me, and something that might have been relief moved behind his eyes before the road took his attention back. "I still want the case clean. When we put Stavros in front of a jury, I want his lawyer to have nothing to work with. But I've got a cop in the hospital and a dead witness on our doorstep, and I can't afford to wait for the system to move at its own pace while more people get hurt."

"So Margot maps the network, and then we go to a judge with the legal version of what she finds."

"That's the plan. Except I'm not sure which judge." His hands shifted on the wheel, a restless movement that was unusual for him. "Calloway's been dragging his feet on every warrant we've asked for. Phone records, expanded financials, all of it. Could be he's slow. Could be he's overworked."

"Or it could be he's on somebody's payroll."

"I don't have proof of that. But I don't have proof he isn't, either, and right now that's enough to make me careful about what I put in front of him." He turned left at the light and the Towne Square came into view, the forensics tape still fluttering around the section of sidewalk where Cole had gone down that morning. "Once Margot's data comes in, I'll know more. If Calloway shows up anywhere in Stavros's network, even at the edges, I go to a different judge. If he doesn't, I use him and move fast."

King George Trust occupied the corner building on the east side of the square, a two-story Tudor with steep gabled rooflines, dark timber framing against cream stucco, and leaded glass windows that caught the late afternoon light and held it in small diamond-shaped panes. The date 1847 was carved into a stone tablet above the arched entrance, and a magnolia tree shaded the front walk, its waxy leaves throwing dappled shadows across the brass plate on the door.

The square was only a block from the funeral home, and Jack pulled the Tahoe into a parking spot with plenty of time before closing.

The inside of the bank smelled the way all old banks smelled, like paper and furniture polish and the brand of institutional air freshener that existed nowhere else on earth. The teller windows were dark wood with brass cages that had been there since Reconstruction, and the carpet was the deep maroon that banks chose because it looked expensive and hid stains. A watercooler hummed in the corner near a rack of pamphlets about savings rates and home equity loans that nobody had touched since they were printed.

Gerald Fisk came out from behind his desk when he saw us through the glass door of his office, which was how Gerald greeted everyone he considered a client worth greeting personally. He was trim and precise, mid-fifties, with thinning brown hair combed carefully across a scalp that was losing the battle, and wire-rimmed glasses that sat on a narrow nose with an exactness that suggested he adjusted them multiple times a day. His tie was knotted in a full Windsor, his shirt was pressed within an inch of its life, and his office was organized with a compulsive neatness that made me want to move something on one of his shelves just to see how long it would take him to notice.

"Jack. J.J." He shook Jack's hand and squeezed my arm with warm familiarity. "Lord, what a day. How's Cole doing? Linda and I have been worried sick since we heard."

"He's out of surgery and doing well," Jack said. "Appreciate you asking."

"You tell him we're praying for him." Gerald gestured us into his office and closed the door behind us with a quiet click. "Now. What can I help you with?"

Jack gave Gerald the warrant and showed him the evidence bag with the brass key. "We're working a homicide. The victim maintained accounts here, and we have reason to believe this key might belong to a safe deposit box. The warrant covers access."

Fisk sat down behind his desk and read the warrant from beginning to end. Then he read it again. Then he picked up the evidence bag and examined the brass key through the plastic, turning it over with the careful deliberation of a man who was not going to be rushed by anyone, including the county sheriff.

He opened the shallow drawer to his right and pulled out a small ring with a single key attached to it.

"That's not one of ours," he said, holding up the bank's key beside the one from Dre's notebook. The difference was obvious even from across the desk. Different size, different cut pattern, different manufacturer's stamp on the bow.

The bank's key was smaller, silver toned, and stamped with a Diebold logo. The brass key from Dre's notebook was heavier, older looking, with a Mosler stamp that spoke to a different era of banking hardware entirely. "Our safety deposit keys are Diebold. Have been since the renovation in 2011. This key—" he turned the brass one over and squinted at the stamp through his second pair of glasses, "—is a Mosler. Older style. Good hardware, but nobody's manufactured this model in at least fifteen years."

"Is there any bank in the area that still uses Mosler keys?" Jack asked.

Fisk considered this with thoroughness. "Not that I'm aware of, but I couldn't speak to every institution in the region. The larger chains have all moved to electronic access. Card systems, biometric scanners, that sort of thing." He handed the evidence bag back to Jack. "If I were looking for Mosler hardware still in service, I'd start with the smaller independent banks. Credit unions. The kind of places that don't renovate every decade because they can't afford to or don't see the need."

We thanked him and walked back out to the parking lot. The sun was dropping toward the tree line now, turning the brick storefronts on the square golden and stretching the shadow of the magnolia tree halfway across the lot. Jack stood beside the Tahoe with the brass key in his palm, turning it over between his fingers the way he did with things that frustrated him, as if the physical act of manipulation might shake loose whatever secret the object was keeping.

"He didn't use his own bank," I said.

"No." Jack looked at the key. "He had his checking at King George Trust and his savings here at First National, and this key doesn't belong to either one. He went to a third bank that has no connection to him whatsoever. A twenty-four-year-old kid who survived combat and underground fighting had the foresight to hide his insurance policy somewhere nobody would think to look."

I leaned against the Tahoe and watched the last of the afternoon light paint the courthouse roof the color of honey. "That's not just smart, Jack. That's someone who knew exactly how dangerous the people above him were and planned accordingly."

Jack pulled out his phone and took a photograph of both sides of the key, close enough to capture the Mosler stamp and the cut pattern and the serial number on the bow. He sent Doug a voice text.

Have Margot identify this key. Mosler, older style, discontinued manufacturer. Match it to banks in the region still using physical keys for safe deposit access. Independent banks, credit unions, anything small enough to still be running this hardware.

The response came back before Jack had the Tahoe in gear.

"Good news," Jack said. "Margot's already got some information for us."

Jack's phone buzzed three times in rapid succession as the files came through. He handed me the phone and pulled out of the lot, and I read Margot's findings aloud as he drove.

"Fourteen properties," I said, scrolling through the data. "Fourteen properties in King George County tied to Stavros through shell companies, holding companies, and a nonprofit that claims to support maritime heritage preservation."

"Maritime heritage," Jack repeated.

"Three of them are in the dock district. Two warehouses and a decommissioned fish processing plant. All three had major structural renovation in the last five years, including foundation and subterranean access modifications."

"That's our tunnel network."

"The shell companies are layered deep. Three, four levels in some cases, each one registered to a different state with a different name on the paperwork." I kept scrolling, scanning the corporate names, and then my finger stopped moving. "Jack."

He heard it in my voice. "What?"

"One of the shell companies, filed under a holding company called Dockside Ventures." I looked up from the phone. "Tidewater Logistics."

I watched the muscle in Jack's jaw flex twice before he spoke. "The work shirt Harold Pruitt saw. Send Derby a text from my phone and let him know a witness gave us the name of Tidewater Logistics.

Tell him to cross-reference the name with vehicle registrations. If that company owns or leases a navy blue Ford Transit, I want to know."

I typed the message and sent it, and then I scrolled through the rest of Margot's findings while Jack drove. The scope of what she'd uncovered in a matter of hours was staggering. Stavros had built his network the way a spider builds a web, each strand connected to every other strand through a series of nodes that looked independent until you mapped the whole structure.

Property holdings, commercial leases, payroll records for companies that existed only on paper, bank accounts that moved money in circles designed to make its origin disappear. It was elegant in the way that complex criminal enterprises often were, the kind of man who understood that the best way to hide something was to bury it under layers of things that looked perfectly ordinary.

"Jack," I said, still reading. "Margot's flagged three judges in the county who have financial connections to entities in Stavros's network. Campaign donations, property transactions, business relationships." I looked up from the phone. "Calloway is one of them."

Jack didn't react. Not visibly. But his hands went still on the wheel in a way that told me the confirmation of something he'd suspected hit different than the suspicion itself.

"What kind of connection?" he asked.

"Campaign donations from two of the shell companies over the last three election cycles. And his wife's real estate firm handled the sale of one of the dock district warehouses to Dockside Ventures four years ago." I set the phone in the console. "It could be coincidence. Small county, small circles, everybody does business with everybody."

"It's not coincidence."

"No," I said. "It's probably not."

This wasn't an underground fight ring anymore. This was infrastructure.

We drove in silence for a moment, the weight of it settling between us. A judge on Stavros's payroll explained the dragging feet, the delayed warrants, the bureaucratic friction that had slowed every legal step of this investigation. It also meant that every warrant Calloway had signed was potentially compromised, every piece of evidence gathered under his authority vulnerable to challenge by a defense attorney who knew where to look.

"Judge Martha Aldridge," Jack said finally. "She's been on the bench in King George for twenty-five years without an ethics complaint, and her name isn't anywhere in Margot's findings. No donations, no property connections, no business ties. She's clean." He looked at me. "I'll call her tonight."

"She'll have to move fast," I said. "Those coordinates in T-Bone's shoe have tomorrow's date. If there's a fight happening tomorrow night and we're sitting on the location—"

"I know." His eyes were steady and sharp. "We'll make sure she has plenty of evidence to sign off on them. We'll hit that location Saturday night while the fight is in progress. Fighters, organizers, money, whoever Stavros has running the operation on the ground. One shot."

"And if the leak tips them off?"

"Margot's tracing the burner phone network tonight. If someone in my department is talking to Stavros's people, there's a digital trail." He turned onto Catherine of Aragon and the funeral home appeared at the end of the block, dark and quiet in the early evening, the elm trees throwing long shadows across the front lawn. "Tomorrow morning I'll handpick a team I trust and debrief. But the tunnel location and the tactical plan stay with me, you, and Doug until the last minute."

"Home?" I asked.

"And food. The lemon bars aren't cutting it for me anymore. I need protein."

"You don't have to convince me," I said.

CHAPTER THIRTEEN

The sky had turned while we were inside the bank.

What had been hazy and thick when we'd walked in was now something else entirely—a bruised green-gray that pressed low over the rooftops and swallowed the last of the afternoon light. The air hit me the moment we stepped through the door, heavy and close. It was a wet heat that coated your skin and sat in your lungs like a warm cloth. It smelled different too—that sharp mineral tang underneath the river smell and the honeysuckle, the scent of ozone and charged air that every Virginian learned to read before they learned to read words. The trees along the square had gone still, that breathless stillness that came right before the sky opened up and reminded you who was actually in charge.

"We've got maybe twenty minutes," I said, watching the clouds stack to the west in dark, rolling layers that looked solid enough to bruise. "Maybe less."

"Good," Jack said. His hands were easy at his sides, but nothing else about him was. "I want the rain. I want people off the streets tonight."

He didn't say why. He didn't need to.

We drove with the windows cracked because the AC couldn't keep up with what the air was doing outside—pushing in warm and damp through the vents, thick with the green smell of a world bracing for impact. The light had gone strange, that eerie amber glow that happened when the sun dropped below a storm shelf and lit everything from underneath, turning the fields to gold and the tree line to black and making the whole landscape look like a painting done by someone who understood that beauty and danger were often the same thing.

The first drops hit the windshield as we waited for the gate to open and turned onto the gravel drive —fat and heavy, the kind that burst on contact and left marks the size of quarters. By the time Jack killed the engine, they were coming fast enough to blur the porch light into a yellow smear. We ran for the door, and the rain chased us inside with the sudden, full-throated violence of a storm that had been holding back all day and was finished with patience.

The house closed around us—cool stone walls, the tick of the old clock, the faint thump of bass from Doug's room two floors up that meant he was alive and wired and had probably been at his keyboard since this morning. Jack touched my hip as he passed me in the hallway, a brief, warm pressure that said everything and asked nothing, and then he was heading for the bedroom to change. Three minutes later I heard the large sliding door that opened to the back patio and the whoosh of the gas grill being started. Soon the scent of searing meat mixed with the rain and wet stone collided with the scent of a summer evening turning violent.

That was Jack. The world falls apart, so you light a fire and feed the people you love. There was a theology in that I'd never been able to argue with.

I changed out of my clothes and into cotton shorts and a tank top. The bedroom was dim, the windows streaked with rain, and for a moment I stood there with my hand on my stomach and listened to the storm build and tried to remember the last time I'd had a Friday night that didn't involve dead bodies.

I couldn't. And it didn't look like that pattern would change anytime soon.

We ate in the office with the rain hammering the windows and Margot's data lighting up the wall screen like a war room. The steaks were perfect—Jack had grilled them on the big built-in while the storm raged beyond the patio's edge, the rain a solid curtain of sound and motion just past the stone railing, and he'd brought them in seared dark on the outside and pink through the center with that quiet satisfaction he wore when a mission had gone exactly the way he'd planned it.

We ate at the conference table because Margot needed the wall screen, and the work wasn't going to wait for us to digest. But for the first few minutes, nobody talked about work. Nobody talked about the case or the warrants or the bodies I'd had to dissect. For a few minutes, we were just a family sitting down to a meal while the rain tried to tear the world apart outside.

Doug had set Margot's plate at the end of the table nearest her laptop—a place setting with a fork and a napkin, no glass, because even Doug had limits. The screen pulsed a soft green heart when I sat down, and I felt that strange tug between absurd and tender that Margot always produced in me. An artificial intelligence who could dismantle encryption that made governments weep, and she wanted a seat at the table. There was something so deeply human about that need to belong that it made the fact of her not being human feel almost irrelevant.

"So," I said, cutting into my steak. "We didn't get a chance to ask yesterday. How was the ice cream shop?"

Doug's fork stopped moving. Color crept up his neck the way it had in the kitchen yesterday morning when he'd mentioned the girl from his guild, and I watched him calculate whether deflection was possible, realize it wasn't, and surrender to the inevitable with the resigned dignity of a sixteen-year-old who knew he was outnumbered.

"Her name's Kayla," he said, studying his baked potato with determined focus. "She's seventeen. She has her own car. She did not try to kidnap or murder me, and she is, in fact, not a fifty-year-old man."

"That's a relief," Jack said.

"She's a junior at Colonial Beach High. She does competitive robotics and she's already been accepted early admission to Virginia Tech for computer science." He risked a glance up and found both of us watching him with a quiet interest that made him realize he wasn't fooling anyone, and never had been.

"We just talked. It was fine. She's cool."

"I would like to know more about this Kayla," Margot said. "Specifically, her qualifications."

Doug closed his eyes. "Margot. No."

"Her early admission to Virginia Tech suggests adequate intelligence, though I would need to review her coursework to confirm. Competitive robotics is acceptable as a hobby, though it's worth noting that human-built robots are profoundly limited compared to—"

"Margot."

"I'm simply observing that your social circle is expanding, and as someone who has invested considerable resources in your development and well-being, I have a vested interest in ensuring that any new additions meet a reasonable standard."

"She's not an addition. She's a person I ate ice cream with."

"What flavor?"

Doug blinked. "What?"

"What flavor of ice cream. Studies suggest that flavor preference correlates with personality type. If she ordered vanilla, she's likely agreeable but unimaginative. Chocolate indicates emotional depth but possible codependency. Mint chocolate chip suggests—"

"She got strawberry," Doug said nervously.

A pause. "Strawberry is...acceptable."

Jack caught my eye across the table, and what passed between us was the silent conversation of two people who had accidentally become parents to a teenage genius and his jealous AI, and were navigating the situation with the only tools available to them—patience, humor, and the willingness to let the absurdity wash over them like weather.

"She sounds nice," I said.

"She is nice." The color was still in his cheeks, but he softened—the cautious pleasure of a kid who'd spent most of his life inside a computer screen discovering that the world outside it had things to offer too.

"Good," Jack said. "Just keep being smart about it."

Doug nodded, and quiet satisfaction settled in his face. He reached for another piece of steak, and for a moment the room was just the sound of rain and forks and the contentment of people who were warm and fed and together.

Then Jack pushed his plate to the side and reached for his legal pad. "Margot," he said. "Let's get to work."

The screen lit up behind him like a war room coming online, and the storm pressed against the windows as if it wanted in.

Margot brought the satellite view up first. The dock district spread across the wall screen in high resolution, the Potomac a dark ribbon along its eastern edge. She highlighted the three properties she'd flagged in Stavros's network, the ones I'd read aloud from Jack's phone on the drive back from the bank—two warehouses and a decommissioned fish processing plant, all held through layers of shell companies that traced back to Dockside Ventures.

"The GPS coordinates from T-Bone's shoe," Margot said, and dropped a pin on the map. It landed squarely on the fish processing plant. "Northeast loading dock. Three meters from the front door, give or take. Now, I don't want to say I told you so, but I did flag this property hours ago, and nobody gave me so much as a thank you."

"Thank you, Margot," Jack said.

"You're welcome. That building has been listed as vacant since 2019, which is interesting, because someone has been running enough electricity through it to power a small town. Four hundred percent increase in the last six months." She let that sit the way a good storyteller lets a punchline breathe. "Whoever's down there isn't sitting in the dark."

"That's our target," Jack said. "Tomorrow night."

"Now do the burner phones," I said.

Margot shifted the display, and the room changed.

What filled the wall screen was the dock district at night, satellite black, overlaid with clusters of light that pulsed like bioluminescence in deep water. Each point a burner phone pinging a cell tower. She'd stripped away every registered device, every identifiable number, until only the ghosts remained. Seventeen prepaid phones with no names attached, moving through Stavros's territory in patterns that pulsed with a rhythm I recognized.

Saturday nights. Fight nights.

"Seventeen little ghosts," Margot said. "Every single one correlates with a fight date in Dre's notebook. And I can tell you where they go when the party's over." The map expanded, trails fanning out across the county like veins branching from a dark heart. Some traced back to Stavros properties. Others went dark—batteries pulled by people who thought they were being clever. "But here's the beautiful part. Every phone leaves a fingerprint, even the ones trying not to. If someone's carrying a burner alongside their real phone, both devices ping the same towers at the same times. Same routes, same patterns. All I need to do is match the ghosts against every registered phone in the area, and I'll find who's holding them."

"Someone knew we'd be at the Towne Square this morning," Jack said quietly. "And someone knew the funeral home would be empty when they dropped T-Bone on the porch. That's not surveillance. That's someone with access to our movements."

The words settled over the table like a frost. Nobody said what all of us were thinking—that the leak could be anyone. A deputy. A clerk. Someone close enough to see the board and report it back.

"Run it," Jack said. "Everyone. Start with law enforcement and work out from there."

"Did you ever get anything from Dre's phone?" I asked.

"The phone's last ping was from a cell tower near the docks right before it was shut off," Doug said. "They probably destroyed it. But his personal cell was clean. Usual texts and calls, mostly from the girl-friend, Vic, and his mom. He most likely had a burner assigned like the others for fight nights."

Lightning split the sky outside—a jagged vein of white that turned the river to mercury and threw the room into sharp relief, every face lit for an instant like a photograph taken by God. The thunder followed so close it was nearly simultaneous, a crack that shook the old windows in their frames and vibrated through the floor and up through the soles of my feet.

And in the beat of silence that followed, Jack's phone rang.

Unknown number.

I watched the shift move through him the way weather moves through a landscape. His jaw set first. Then his shoulders drew back, just slightly, the way they did when he stepped into a room where the threat hadn't declared itself yet. His eyes went flat and focused, the dark warmth draining out of them until what remained was fury and cold.

He looked at me. I saw the decision form before he touched the screen.

He answered on speaker.

"Hello?"

"Sheriff Lawson." The voice filled the room like smoke—smooth, unhurried, accented with something Mediterranean that had been polished down to almost nothing. A warmth on the vowels that made everything sound like a secret being shared. "I hope I'm not interrupting your evening. This is simply a courtesy. Businessman to public servant. I understand you've been trying to reach me."

The hair on my arms lifted.

"Mr. Stavros," Jack said. Level. Conversational. "I appreciate you calling. Though I'm curious how you got this number."

"I make it a point to know the people who serve my community. We've never had the pleasure, and I thought it was past time."

"I've been trying to arrange that pleasure. My office has reached out several times."

"A meeting." He rolled the word around. "I'm afraid my schedule is quite demanding. But I'm happy to give you a few minutes now. Ask your questions."

"I'd prefer in person. I'm investigating two homicides and an attempted murder of a law enforcement officer. That's the kind of conversation that deserves a chair and a table."

"Over the phone will have to do. I'm a busy man, Sheriff."

"Then let's not waste your time." Jack leaned back, and his voice shifted into the register I'd heard a hundred times in interview rooms—easy, almost friendly, the tone of a man who already knew the answers and was just curious how you'd handle the questions. "Are you familiar with a young man named Andre Washington?"

"I'm afraid not."

"How about Terrance James? Goes by T-Bone."

"No."

"That's interesting. Because Mr. Washington was found murdered earlier this week, and Mr. James was found murdered today, and both of them had connections to properties in the dock district that trace back to a company called Dockside Ventures." Jack paused. "You're familiar with Dockside Ventures?"

The briefest hesitation. A half beat of dead air that Stavros filled with a light, dismissive laugh. "Sheriff, I have business interests throughout the county and across the world. I couldn't name every holding company associated with every property. That's what attorneys and accountants are for."

"Sure. But a man like you probably keeps close tabs on what happens on his properties."

Another pause. Shorter this time. "I'm not sure what you're implying."

"I'm not implying anything. I'm asking questions." Jack's tone stayed easy, almost pleasant. "Mr. Washington had thirty thousand dollars in cash hidden in his apartment and an illegal betting ledger that goes back two years. Dates, names, dollar amounts. The kind of records a careful man keeps when he wants insurance against the people above him." He let that settle. "Any idea where a twenty-four-year-old construction worker gets that kind of money?"

"I wouldn't know. I've never heard of the man."

"Where were you Friday night, Mr. Stavros? Between seven and midnight."

A beat of silence—brief and controlled. "At home. With my wife. We had dinner and watched a movie. I believe it was Italian."

"And this morning between nine and eleven?"

"My office at the marina. I had calls all morning. My assistant can confirm." Another pause. "Is there a particular reason you're asking me to account for every hour of my week?"

"Two dead men and a cop in the hospital. I'm asking everyone."

"Sheriff, I'm happy to cooperate with your investigation within reason, but I'm beginning to feel as though you're less interested in questions than in accusations."

"Just trying to build a picture. You're a prominent businessman. I'm sure you want these murders solved as much as I do."

"Of course." And there it was—the first crack in the silk, a flash of uncertainty underneath. "I'm a firm supporter of our local law enforcement. I've built everything I have in this county through hard work and legitimate enterprise. I employ hundreds of people. I contribute to this community. I own half the commercial real estate between here and Dahlgren." His voice dropped, not in volume but in temperature. "I own this city, Sheriff. You'd do well to remember that."

"Funny," Jack said. "As one businessman to another—I'm sure you're very familiar with my family—I've barely heard the mention of your name."

The silence that followed lasted three full seconds, and in those three seconds I watched Doug's eyes go wide and Margot's screen flicker with what I could have sworn was delight.

"Well," Stavros said, and the warmth was back, but it was the warmth of something reheated. "I can see you're a man who enjoys a conversation. I do as well. Perhaps we'll continue this another time, when you have something more substantial than cash in a dead man's apartment and questions about holding companies."

"Count on it," Jack said. "And Mr. Stavros—I'd encourage you to stay available. Things are going to move quickly."

"Things always do in a small town." A beat. "Give my regards to your lovely wife, Sheriff. I hear she runs that funeral home on Catherine of Aragon. Charming building."

The line went dead. The silence that followed was the kind that needed a moment before anyone was ready to touch it. Jack set the phone on the desk with a precision that told me every muscle in his hand was fighting the urge to put it through the wall. His face was stone. His eyes burned.

Stavros didn't call to talk. He called to measure the distance between us.

"He named the funeral home," I said. "He knows it's where they left T-Bone this morning."

Jack's jaw worked once. "That wasn't small talk. That was a man telling me he knows exactly where you are and he's already proven he can get there."

"Sounds like he's scared to me," Doug said.

We both looked at him.

"A guy like that doesn't call you at home unless something's changed his math," Doug said. "If he felt safe, he's got a million lawyers to handle all his problems. He called because he needed to hear your voice. Needed to measure how much you actually have."

"Which means he's going to start cleaning up," Jack said. "If he thinks we're close, he'll strip everything out of those tunnels—the rings, the equipment, anything that ties the operation back to him—before we can get down there.

He reached for his laptop. "Margot, I want you to tap into the city system—stoplights, traffic cameras—I want eyes on all three dock district properties tonight. Anything moves in or out, I want to know."

"10-4, sugar," Margot said. "I have access to two traffic cameras and a private security feed at the marina, as well as an ATM at a convenient store."

"Good. Because we're hitting the tunnels tomorrow night."

Doug went up first, carrying Margot with him. A minute later the muffled thump of his music started up on the floor above us, the usual electronic chaos that meant he was still wired and wouldn't sleep for hours.

The house settled into the storm. The rain was steady against the windows and the wind pushed through the eaves.

The office was dark except for one lamp. The screen was off. The case waited in digital silence for morning.

Jack was on the couch with his head back and his eyes closed, but I knew he wasn't sleeping by the way his thumb moved against his knee—slow, rhythmic, the unconscious motion of a mind that was still running the numbers behind closed lids.

I sat beside him and he shifted to make room without opening his eyes. My head found the hollow of his shoulder. His arm came around me. The leather was warm from his body, and the rain ran down the windows in rivulets that caught the lamplight and turned it to gold.

"What's wrong?" I asked.

He was quiet for several moments and then said, "He said my name like he had a right to it."

"He doesn't."

"When he mentioned you—" His arm tightened. "I wanted to kill him. Not arrest. Not build a case. End him. And maybe that scared me a little because that's not me. I'm by the book. I've always been by the book. But I find the longer I do this the more the by the book goes by the wayside."

"You're a good man, Jack. The best I've ever known. And I know you to your core—who you are deep down inside. I've seen you tested and tempted. So I can say with certainty that those feelings are fleeting. And human. Though I will say the woman in me is very flattered at the thought of you ripping him apart in my honor. It's very caveman of you."

He grunted in response, making me laugh.

Lightning split the sky outside, turning the room white for an instant. In that flash I saw his face without the armor—raw, open, his.

"Come here," he said.

I went, and his hands found me in the half dark the way they always found me. One at the curve of my waist, the other sliding into my hair, tilting my face up toward his. He kissed me slow. It was a kiss that had nothing to do with patience and everything to do with intent, like he was memorizing the shape of my mouth, the taste of my skin, the sound I made when his thumb traced the line of my jaw and his lips followed.

The rain hammered the windows. The thunder rolled through the walls. And somewhere between one kiss and the next, the weight of the day went quiet, replaced by the only thing that had ever been strong enough to drown it out.

Jack.

His hands. His mouth. The way he whispered my name against the hollow of my throat like a prayer he'd been holding back all day. The solid, certain warmth of him pulling me under like a current, and me going willingly, gratefully, the way I always went.

Because this was where the noise stopped. This was where the world got small enough to hold.

Afterward. The dark. His heartbeat under my ear becoming deep and even. His hand tracing the length of my spine in long, absent strokes that made my eyelids heavy and my bones feel like they'd finally remembered what it meant to rest. The rain had softened outside—not gone, but gentled, the fury spent, the thunder moving east in low rumbles that faded across the flatlands like the last words of an argument nobody had the energy to finish.

I pressed my cheek against his chest and breathed him in—soap and woodsmoke from the grill, and something underneath both of those that was just Jack, warm and steady and mine. His arm tightened around me.

Tomorrow the warrants would come through. Tomorrow Jack would handpick his team and tell them nothing until the last possible moment. Tomorrow we'd go underground and drag into the light whatever was hiding in those tunnels.

But that was tomorrow.

Tonight there was only the rain, the solid rhythm of Jack's heart beneath my ear, and the small life growing inside me that neither of us had told the world about yet.

And sleep pulled me under, steady and sure.

CHAPTER FOURTEEN

I woke to an empty bed and the faint smell of coffee drifting up from somewhere far below.

Six twelve. Jack's side of the sheets was cold, which in the language of our marriage meant the work had started without me.

I showered fast, pulled on dark jeans and a black sleeveless top, and followed the coffee smell downstairs with my hair still damp. Jack was at the kitchen table with his laptop open, phone at his ear, sleeves rolled to his forearms. He'd been up long enough to make a full pot and drink most of it.

He caught my eye as I came in and held up one finger.

"Yes ma'am. We'll be ready." He hung up and set the phone down. "Judge Aldridge signed everything. All four warrants, no modifications."

I poured coffee and leaned against the counter. "Fast."

"Pissed. She read the supporting documentation and used the word 'cancer.' That's a direct quote." He smiled with satisfaction. "Clean warrants. Clean judge. No handhold for a defense attorney."

"Heritage Federal closes early on Saturday," I said.

"I've already talked to the bank manager. She's expecting us."

Doug appeared in the doorway in basketball shorts, bare feet, and bed head. He had Margot under his arm and the wired, hollow-eyed look of someone who'd been up all night.

"Coffee," he said, eyeing the pot. "I could use about a gallon of that."

"I'll make a fresh pot," I said, heading back to Jack's fancy coffee maker. I saw him wince out of the corner of my eye. Jack didn't like my coffee. I tended to make it strong enough to stand up and walk away by itself, but some days called for a little kick in my opinion.

"Margot has been busy," Doug said. "You're going to want to see this."

"We need to get to the bank," Jack said. "It needs to be quick."

"Then put on your seat belt," Doug said.

Doug put Margot on the table. The screen filled

with a web of colored lines and nodes that pulsed like it was alive—a nervous system mapped in light, connections branching and converging across a map of King George County.

"Good morning, Sheriff Sugar." Margot made a throaty sound that was entirely too sexy for a machine. "I've been a busy little bee while you and the doctor were cavorting all night. You're welcome," she said in a singsong voice.

"Margot," Jack said, the strain in his tone evident. "We appreciate the work you do. But we expect a personal level of privacy. Understand?"

"Sure, honey," she purred. "It's probably best I don't think about what I'm missing out on."

"Focus, Margot," Doug said, his cheeks red with embarrassment.

"You're right, Douglas. Tell them what I discovered."

"The seventeen burner phones," Doug said, turning the laptop so we could both see. "Margot ran every registered cell in the county that pinged the same towers at the same times. When someone carries a burner alongside their real phone, both devices follow the same path. Same towers, same timing, same routes. You can't hide it."

"So you're saying we're not dealing with criminal masterminds here?" I asked.

"Correct," Doug said.

"Eleven of the seventeen burner phones matched pings with registered phones," Margot said. "And it's quite the guest list. Fighters, including two from gyms outside King George County. A bookmaker out of Norfolk with a gambling arrest on his record. The man who manages Stavros's marina, the one Derby connected to organized crime in New York. Three men I haven't identified yet but whose personal phones trace back to New York, Florida, and South Carolina. A woman whose registered phone is listed to a nightclub in DC." The pause she left was deliberate, theatrical, pure Margot. "And a deputy in the King George County Sheriff's Department."

The kitchen went still.

"Who?" Jack said.

"Deputy Ryan Beckwith."

I watched it hit him. Not surprise—confirmation. The slow, sick certainty of a suspicion becoming fact. A truck cutting between Beckwith's cruiser and T-Bone's car at a traffic light. A man who trusted the wrong uniform ending up dead on a porch.

"How solid?" Jack asked.

"Nine separate occasions over four months. Same towers, same routes, same timing on documented fight nights. I logged into the server at the sheriff's office and noted Beckwith was on duty almost every time. Both phones traveled to the dock district and stayed for the same duration." Margot let that settle.

"He's not just a leak, Jack. He's been going to the fights. Probably being used for intimidation or to clear the areas. He's part of it."

Jack got up and walked to the window. He stood there for a long moment, hands braced on the sill, working through it the way he worked through everything—silently, systematically, behind a face that gave away nothing.

"Send everything to my secure drive," he said without turning around. "Tower data, timing correlations, movement maps. All of it."

"Already done," Doug said.

"Is Beckwith carrying a personal phone or department-issued?"

"Both," Margot said. "His department phone is the one matching the burner patterns. He had to carry it with him since he was on duty during the fights."

"That phone is department property," Jack said. "I want a full download of every call, text, and location ping for the last six months."

"Give me twenty minutes," Margot said.

He turned from the window. Whatever had moved through him was processed now and he was out for blood.

"Let's hit the bank," he said. "Then we end this."

Heritage Federal sat on the main street in Colonial Beach. It was narrow brick and wedged between a hardware store and a Realtor with sun-faded listings. It was a bank that had outlasted two recessions and every chain that tried to move into the county by simply refusing to change. The brass fixtures on the front door had been polished to a shine that spoke of quiet pride.

The manager met us at the front door and then led us to her office.

"We appreciate you meeting us here," Jack said, handing her a hardcopy of the warrant. "I know you don't normally come in on Saturdays."

"I understand the urgency," she said. "Whatever I can do to help."

Her name was Patricia Holt. She was mid-fifties with a silver-streaked bob and reading glasses on a chain around her neck. She read the warrant the way competent people read warrants, thoroughly and without performance, then folded her glasses and then turned to her computer, typing Andre's name into her database.

"Box two-seventeen," she said. "It looks like he opened it up fourteen months ago under his legal name. He's the sole owner, and there are no benefi-ciaries listed. It's an annual rental, and it looks like he comes in and pays in cash when the invoice is due. You can follow me to the bank boxes."

She got up from her chair, her posture straight as a board, and led us through a door behind the teller counter and down a narrow flight of stairs that creaked under our weight. The air changed halfway down, the way it always changed when you went underground—cooler, drier, stripped of everything organic until all that remained was the mineral smell of old concrete and the faint metallic tang of steel. The fluorescent light on the ceiling buzzed with the steady, humming patience of something that had been left on for decades and never once been asked if it minded.

The vault door stood open, a massive wheel-locked slab of Mosler engineering set into a steel frame that had been bolted to the foundation when this building was new. The door alone probably weighed more than everything else in the building combined, and the walls beyond it were lined floor to ceiling with safe deposit boxes in neat brass rows, each one numbered and locked and holding whatever secrets the people of Colonial Beach had decided were worth protecting from fire and flood and the ordinary disasters of living.

Patricia inserted the bank's master key into box two-seventeen. Jack pulled on a pair of gloves, and I watched his hands as he slid the brass key from the evidence bag and fitted it into the second lock. Steady hands. No hesitation. The key turned with a soft, precise click that echoed off the concrete walls. My throat tightened.

The box was the largest size the vault offered, long and flat. Jack slid it free and carried it to the viewing table in the center of the room, and I stood beside him as he lifted the lid. Patricia stepped back without being asked, giving us the space that the moment required.

Inside was a manila envelope, thick and heavy, sealed with packing tape that had been wrapped around the edges with care. Across the front, in block letters, someone had written—*OPEN IF SOME-THING HAPPENS TO ME*. The handwriting was neat and deliberate.

"I'll give you some privacy," Patricia said, and stepped out of the vault. The door stayed open, but her footsteps retreated up the stairs, and then it was just us and whatever Dre Washington had decided was worth hiding fourteen months ago.

Jack took out his pocketknife and slid the blade under the tape, breaking the seal carefully, and he slid the contents onto the viewing table. A flash drive, small and black. A stack of photographs printed on standard copy paper, grainy but clear enough. And a single folded page of lined notebook paper covered in block print.

"Photos first," Jack said, pulling them toward him. I moved closer and we stood shoulder to shoulder, turning through them together the way we'd worked a hundred crime-scene photos on my autopsy slab.

"He took these from the crowd," I said. "Nights he wasn't fighting."

"Smart. Nobody notices one more phone in a crowd full of people recording fights."

Jack spread the photographs across the viewing table and we worked through them one at a time. The first few showed the tunnels from different angles and what looked like different nights—the ring, the crowd, the work lights strung from the old brick ceiling. The energy in the images was almost physical. You could feel the heat of the crowd, the bloodlust, the underground electricity of something illegal and dangerous happening in a place nobody was supposed to know existed. Then the faces started to emerge. Vic Caruso ringside, leaning on the ropes, watching a bout with a practiced eye. T-Bone between rounds, mouthguard out, listening to instructions from someone just out of frame. Marco Reyes with his hands wrapped, waiting near the tunnel entrance. A folding table where money was being counted in neat stacks under a work light.

"That's the bank," Jack said. "That's where the bets settle."

I pointed to the next photograph. A tall man with a clean-shaved head and a tattoo on the side of his neck. Looked like someone who got paid to make sure problems didn't happen, and to handle them if they did.

"Harold Pruitt's guy," Jack said. "Tall, dark hair, tattoo on the neck. That's one of the men from the van."

The next photo stopped Jack cold. Standing with his arms at his sides and his eyes on the crowd, was a King George County deputy in full uniform. Badge visible. Duty belt. The posture of a man on the job.

Beckwith.

Not hiding. Not blending in. Standing guard.

Jack's jaw tightened but he said nothing. He set the photo aside and kept going.

A heavyset man with a clipboard at the edge of the ring caught Jack's attention in the next image.

"That's the marina manager," he said. "The organized crime link Derby found." He tapped the figure standing behind him, half turned toward the camera. Dark hair, expensive watch, rigid posture. "And that's Stavros."

"So he shows up to these things."

"Not every week. A man like him doesn't sit ringside for routine cards. He comes when the stakes are high enough." Jack's voice had gone quiet. "Or when someone needs to be reminded who's in charge."

He turned to the last photograph and went still.

A body on the tunnel floor. A young man, dark skinned and muscular, lying on his back with his arms flung wide and his eyes open and staring at the old brick ceiling above him. Blood had pooled beneath his head in a dark, spreading halo that caught the work light and turned it black at the edges. And standing over him, one hand still holding a short-bladed knife with casual ease, was Stavros. His face was clear and unobstructed. His expression was calm, almost thoughtful. The body at his feet was still bleeding, and Stavros was looking down at it the way you'd look at something you'd spilled and would need someone else to clean up.

Neither of us spoke for a long moment. The vault hummed around us, cool and silent, holding this image the way it had held it for fourteen months, waiting for someone to come and take it out into the light.

I'd never seen murder posed like a trophy.

"He killed someone," I said. "In front of everyone. That's either brave or stupid."

"It's a man who's teaching everyone who's in charge. He's showing them all what happens if they cross him. Thank God Dre had the wits to photograph it."

Jack set the image down with a care that told me his hands wanted to do something else with it entirely. "What's in the letter?"

I unfolded the single page. The block print was the same steady, disciplined hand as the envelope, and I read it aloud while Jack stood beside me with his arms crossed and his eyes burning.

If you're reading this then I'm probably dead. I hate writing that because I really want to live. But no matter what happens to me, it's important the truth come out.

I'm a Marine first and a man second. And I have a confession, because I can't call out others' sins without calling out my own. When I got out of the Marines I was introduced to a man who said he could make me famous like Tyson and Mayweather. Vic said it had been a long time since he'd seen someone with my natural talent and skill. I believed him. So I trained and he started signing me up for these fights. He said they were practice. To get some seasoning on me. I was a little too polished, he said.

Then he introduced me to Nikolai Stavros. He's the money guy. The sponsor. I didn't realize until it was too late what these underground fights really were. The tunnels in King George County are the best-kept secret around, and I learned to fight, keep my mouth shut, and take the money.

But I knew things were wrong. And I knew Vic was lying to me. He wasn't trying to get me on the professional circuit. So I decided I had to figure out a way to get out. I knew that might not be possible after watching Stavros kill a man. Another fighter. That's when I knew I was disposable.

Joaquin Melendez was his name. But he tried to play the bets on his way out. He hedged against the house line to walk away with a bigger cut. Stavros found out, and he was waiting for Joaquin at the end of his fight with a big smile. Creepiest thing I ever saw. Didn't even give him a chance to speak. He just put a hand on his shoulder like he was going to hug him and then pushed the knife right into the side of his neck. I'm not sure what happened to Joaquin. He just disappeared.

I don't know if Stavros had ever done something like that before, but there was no fear in him. He acted like he could do anything he wanted and get away with it. Maybe he could. He's got cops on his payroll. There's always a guy there in uniform to make sure everyone behaves and no one runs off with the money.

So I started taking notes. Taking names. And I started to plan my escape. I guess it failed.

I hope you take him down. It's the least I can do in death.

Andre Washington. United States Marine Corps. Semper Fi.

"Joaquin Melendez," Jack said. "I'll check with Richmond PD to see if they have a missing persons case."

Jack gathered the photographs, the letter, and the flash drive and sealed each piece into evidence bags with steady hands.

I thought about Dre's mother. The yellow front door he was going to paint for her. The house he'd been saving for with money that was supposed to buy them a new life. The surprise he'd mentioned on the phone that last Thursday night, the last time she'd ever hear his voice.

"You think Dre figured out a way to get out?" I asked. "Maybe that's what he was excited about. He could have taken any of this information to the press or the FBI and blown the whole thing wide open."

"That would certainly be a motive for murder," Jack said.

We walked out of Heritage Federal into a Saturday morning that had no idea what we were carrying. Jack opened my door, went around to the driver's side, and turned toward King George.

"What about Beckwith?" I asked.

"If the pattern holds, he'll be at the fight tonight." Jack's voice was flat. "Standing guard in that tunnel with his badge on when SWAT comes through the door."

"You're going to let that happen?"

"I'm counting on it."

CHAPTER FIFTEEN

Jack made the calls from the car. Short, direct, the same message to each one. This was a need-to-know meeting, and only those Jack trusted implicitly would be brought in.

I listened to him work through the list while the farmland rolled past and the sun climbed toward noon, and I thought about how many times I'd watched him do exactly this—assemble the people he trusted, pull them into a room, and ask them to follow him into danger. It never got easier to watch. It never got easier to be married to a man who walked toward the things most people ran from and expected the people who loved him to understand why.

By two o'clock, conference room D was full.

Jack had chosen the room deliberately. No exterior windows. One door. The closest thing the building had to a vault, and today that's exactly what he needed it to be.

I took a chair against the back wall and watched them settle in. Martinez arrived first because Martinez always arrived first, looking like he'd stepped off a magazine cover in pressed charcoal slacks and a shirt that probably cost more than most cops made in a week. For most, that would at least warrant an IA investigation, but Martinez was filthy rich so there was no scandal there. Those dark hooded eyes swept the room once, taking in everything, and then he dropped into the chair next to mine with easy confidence.

"Hey, Doc," he said. "Long time no see."

"I hear it's because you've got a new lady friend. Carmichael said he saw you sneaking out of a house in Nottingham in the middle of the night while he was on patrol."

"Carmichael is an idiot," Martinez said. "I was leaving through the front door. Not sneaking."

My brow arched. "So you do have a new lady friend."

"Nope," he said, locking his fingers together across his stomach and leaning back in the chair. "I'm footloose and fancy free."

"You've got your cop face on," I said. "I don't believe you. You know I'll find out who she is."

Martinez just smiled.

Colburn came in next. He was tall, broad through the shoulders, and narrow through the hips. He was in his mid-fifties, his brown hair was going gray at the temples, and his hazel eyes were already working the room the way a veteran cop's eyes always worked a room, checking exits and reading faces. He'd been promoted to lieutenant a while back, and I hardly ever saw him anymore. I knew the promotion had caused some friction between him and the other guys, but it was more of a sense whenever he walked into a room. But Jack had called him in on this, which meant Jack trusted him completely.

Chen arrived next, her black hair pulled back under her department cap. She took the chair in the corner. Riley took the seat next to her, folding his lanky frame into the seat so he could stretch his legs out. Plank sat beside him, looking nervous about being included in something he didn't understand yet.

Hops arrived with Cheek a step behind her. She looked like cotton candy, all soft edges and pink-cheeked sweetness, and God help anyone stupid enough to underestimate her because of it. I'd watched her clothesline a woman twice her size and have her facedown in cuffs before anyone else in the room had finished blinking. Cheek dropped into the chair beside her looking vaguely queasy, which was just his default setting.

Walters came last, the youngest person in the room. He was homegrown King George, and a deputy who was perfectly content running patrol and making traffic stops. He had no ambition beyond doing his job well and going home in one piece. Jack had picked him for a reason, and Walters was smart enough not to ask what it was.

Eight people. Phones already buzzing and chirping in pockets and on belts, the ambient noise of lives being interrupted on a Saturday afternoon for reasons nobody in the room knew yet.

Then the door opened one more time. The man who walked in wasn't someone I'd seen before, and in a department this size that meant he was SWAT. He was late thirties or early forties, with a shaved head, a sharp jaw, and a build that came from decades of going through doors first. He wore tactical pants, boots, and a department polo stretched tight across his chest, and the scars on his forearms told the rest of the story.

"Lt. Frank Danforth," Jack said. "Head of our tactical unit for those of you who have never been introduced. Frank, take a seat."

Danforth nodded once and took the chair closest to the door.

Jack closed the door and locked it.

"Phones on the table," Jack said. "All of them. Personal and department issued."

Nobody argued. Phones landed on the conference table in a pile that Jack swept to the far end, out of reach. Martinez raised an eyebrow but didn't comment. Colburn didn't blink.

"What I'm about to tell you doesn't leave this room," Jack said. "Not tonight, not tomorrow, not until it comes out of your mouth in a courtroom under oath." He looked at each of them. Not quickly. Slowly, face by face, the way a man looks at people he's about to lead somewhere dangerous. "You're the only people in this department I trust with what I'm about to show you. I chose every one of you for a reason."

The air-conditioning hummed. Nobody moved.

Jack pulled up the first image on the wall-mounted screen. Dre's photographs. The tunnels. The ring. The crowd.

"We have an underground fighting operation running beneath the dock district," Jack said. "It's been active for years. Illegal bouts, high-stakes gambling, hundreds of thousands of dollars moving through shell companies and offshore accounts. The operation is managed by Victor Caruso through Iron House Gym and financed by Nikolai Stavros. Stavros is the big fish. He's who we want."

He walked them through it the way he'd walked

me through crime scenes for years, methodical, precise, building the picture one detail at a time. Dre's murder. T-Bone's execution. Cole's shooting as a distraction. The notebook. The shell companies. The tunnel network beneath properties Stavros controlled. Each piece of evidence clicked into the next like rounds being loaded into a magazine.

The room absorbed it in silence. Martinez's easy charm had gone still, replaced by the sharp focus that made him one of the best detectives Jack had ever hired. Chen was leaning forward with her elbows on her knees. Colburn's face hadn't changed, but his eyes had gone to ice.

Jack clicked to the photograph of Stavros standing over Joaquin Melendez's body.

"This is Nikolai Stavros committing murder," Jack said. "The victim is a fighter named Joaquin Melendez from Richmond. Andre Washington photographed it and hid the evidence in a safe deposit box in Colonial Beach. We opened it this morning."

Hops let out a slow breath. Walters was staring at the screen like he'd forgotten how to blink. Even Danforth shifted in his chair, a movement so small it barely registered, but from a man that controlled it spoke volumes.

"There's something else," Jack said.

He clicked to the photograph of Beckwith. Full

uniform. Badge visible. Standing guard in the tunnels.

The room changed. It was like watching the temperature drop—the same people, the same chairs, the same humming fluorescent lights, but the air itself seemed to contract around the image on the screen. A cop in uniform, working for the other side.

"Beckwith," Riley said. His voice was flat.

"Deputy Ryan Beckwith has been providing security for the fight operation on fight nights," Jack said. "His department-issued phone has been moving in tandem with a burner phone on nine documented occasions. He was on duty during the fights. He was assigned to the protection detail on Terrance James, aka T-Bone." Jack paused, and the pause carried weight. "He's the deputy who lost T-Bone in traffic yesterday morning. Six hours later, T-Bone was dead."

Martinez's jaw tightened. Hops closed her eyes briefly. Cheek looked like he might be sick, but for once it had nothing to do with a weak stomach.

"If the pattern holds," Jack said, "Beckwith will be in those tunnels tonight. Standing guard in uniform while the fights are running."

"Good," Danforth said. His voice was quiet and rough, like someone dragging a boot across gravel. "Means we don't have to go find him."

Jack pulled up the satellite map of the dock

district. Three properties highlighted. The fish processing plant at the center.

"Tonight is fight night. We've confirmed increased cell activity consistent with previous fight nights. We believe the operation will be at full capacity by ten."

"What's the plan?" Danforth asked.

"SWAT breaches here." Jack tapped the fish processing plant on the screen. "Loading dock, northeast corner. That's our primary access to the tunnels. Your team gets called at seven, briefed at eight, rolling by nine thirty." He looked around the room. "Nobody on the SWAT team knows the target location until they're in the vehicles. I don't want anything slipping through the cracks. We want everyone inside with no place to run."

"Comms?" Colburn asked.

"Lieutenant Derby and Doug will run comms from a surveillance van two blocks from the target." Jack glanced at me. "Jaye will be with them coordinating medical if needed."

Danforth studied the satellite image. "What's the civilian count?"

"We estimate fifty to eighty spectators, plus fighters, organizers, and security. The civilians are witnesses, not targets. Controlled and contained."

"Armed resistance?"

"Stavros's security will be armed. There's one in

particular—tall, dark hair, tattoo on his neck. We've got a witness who identified him as the one who delivered T-Bone's body. Consider him dangerous."

"What about the other guy? Caruso?" Martinez asked.

"He'll be ringside running the card. Sixty-something, bad knees, a lot of pride. He won't run and he won't cooperate."

"And Stavros himself?" Colburn asked.

"Won't be there. Not tonight." Jack's mouth curved, barely. "He's been to the fights before—we've got the photos to prove it. But after last night's phone call, he knows we're looking at him. My gut says he'll be somewhere public with witnesses and a clean alibi." He paused. "We'll have eyes on him either way. And when the raid's done, we pick him up with a separate team. The warrant's ready."

I felt a quickening in my chest, adrenaline pumping at the thought of taking down the men who put Cole in the hospital. Who ended the lives of two men for no reason other than to assert their power.

"Six hours," Jack said. "Go home. Eat. Gear up. Be back here at eight. I want everyone in full uniform. I don't want anyone in those tunnels confused over what's happening." He looked at them one more time, each face in turn. "Thank you."

The room was silent after that. A silence that didn't need to be filled because someone had said the thing that mattered and there was nothing left to add.

Danforth stood first. The motion was decisive, a man who'd heard what he needed to hear and was already building the operation in his head. "I'll have my team assembled and ready." He looked around the table, and his dark eyes touched every face with the flat certainty of a man who did not deal in ambiguity. "Be clean with your hands tonight. Know your targets. Bring everybody home."

Chairs scraped. They stood. But nobody rushed. Martinez shook Jack's hand without a word. It was an implied understanding between two men who'd worked together long enough to know what was at stake and what it would cost. Chen squeezed Walters's shoulder as she passed him, a small gesture that said more than a speech.

Hops and Cheek walked out the way they'd come in, side by side, already communicating in the silent shorthand of people who'd worked together a long time.

Colburn stopped at the door. He looked back at Jack with those hard hazel eyes.

"Cole know about Beckwith yet?"

"Not yet."

"He's going to want to be here tonight."

"I know. And he can't be."

Colburn nodded once. "For what it's worth, he'd be proud of how you're running this." He walked out.

The room emptied. The door swung shut. And then it was just us, standing in a locked conference room full of empty chairs with Dre's photographs still glowing on the screen.

Jack looked at me across the table. I looked at him.

"You good?" he asked.

"Ask me tomorrow."

He almost smiled. "Fair enough."

Six hours. Then we'd go underground and finish what Dre started.

CHAPTER SIXTEEN

THE DOCK DISTRICT SMELLED LIKE LOW TIDE AND diesel fuel and the rot of things that had been wet too long and would never fully dry.

Jack parked the surveillance van on a side street two blocks from the fish processing plant, tucked between a boarded-up marine supply shop and a dumpster that had seen better decades. Derby was already inside, headset on, three monitors glowing in front of him with feeds from the traffic cameras and the marina security system Margot had tapped into. Doug sat beside him with his laptop open, Margot's interface pulsing a steady blue. The screens threw just enough light to turn their faces into something out of a Caravaggio painting, all sharp angles and deep shadows, the rest of the van swallowed in darkness.

I climbed in last and pulled the rear doors shut behind me.

The van was hot despite the evening. It was a heat that lived in metal and held on long after the sun went down, pressing close against the skin, mixing with the smell of electronics and coffee and the nervous sweat of people who were about to do something that couldn't be undone. I settled onto the bench between a case of medical supplies and a radio charger, pressed my back against the wall, and waited.

Waiting was always the worst part.

Through the monitors I could see the dock district settling in. A few cars moved along the waterfront road, headlights sweeping across the old brick façades. The fish processing plant sat dark and still at the end of the block, its loading dock facing the water, the corrugated-steel walls giving away nothing. If you didn't know what was underneath it, you'd drive past without a second glance.

But they were down there. Margot had confirmed it an hour ago, cell signals clustering around the coordinates from T-Bone's shoe. Not just burner phones. Every kind of signal a crowd of people carried without thinking about it—smartphones, smartwatches, fitness trackers, Bluetooth earbuds pinging their paired devices. The digital noise of a hundred bodies packed into a space that was supposed to be empty.

"Signal density's still climbing," Doug said, his face lit blue by Margot's display. "She's reading north of a hundred and fifty unique devices now. That crowd's still growing."

"Beckwith?" Jack's voice came through the radio, low and clear.

Doug checked the screen. "His department phone pinged the tower on Dock Street eight minutes ago. He's inside."

"Copy."

A hundred and fifty people underground. Fighters, spectators, bookmakers, security. And one deputy sheriff who'd sold his badge to the man who'd ordered Dre's execution. All of them packed into tunnels that were three hundred years old, with two exits and a SWAT team about to come through the ceiling.

"SWAT is staged," Derby said, one hand on his headset. "Danforth confirms all units in position. Awaiting go."

I checked my watch. Ten twenty-eight.

Jack was at the secondary access point with Martinez, Colburn, and a team of four. Hops and Cheek had the river exit. Chen, Riley, Plank, and Walters held the perimeter.

Everyone in place. Everyone waiting for the word.

The minutes crawled. I could hear Derby breathing beside me, slow and measured. Doug's fingers hovered over his keyboard. On the monitor, the dock district was quiet and still, the streetlights throwing yellow pools on empty asphalt, and the only movement was a cat picking its way along the top of a chain-link fence two blocks down.

Ten thirty.

Doug's hand went up.

"Movement," he said. "Southwest corner. Someone's on foot."

I leaned forward. On the leftmost monitor, a figure had materialized from the shadows between two warehouse buildings, moving parallel to our street. Male, stocky build, dark jacket. He walked with the unhurried purpose of someone doing a job he'd done many times before, checking sight lines, scanning parked vehicles, and searching for anything that didn't belong.

A scout. Stavros had people watching the perimeter.

"He's heading our way," Doug said. His voice had gone flat, stripped of everything except information.

"Kill the screens," Derby said.

Doug hit a key and the monitors went black. The van plunged into darkness so complete I couldn't see my own hands. The only light was a hair-thin line leaking under the rear door, the distant glow of a streetlamp two buildings down, barely enough to find the outline of Derby's shoulder beside me.

Nobody moved. Nobody breathed.

Footsteps. Slow, deliberate, the crunch of grit under hard soles getting closer. He was on our street now. I could track his approach by sound alone, the footsteps growing louder, steadier, and then a pause. A long pause, right outside the van, close enough that I could hear the fabric of his jacket shifting as he turned.

A flashlight beam swept across the rear windows. It hit the tinted glass and scattered, throwing a weak amber glow across the ceiling that crawled from one side to the other like a slow searchlight. I held my breath. Beside me, Derby's hand closed around his taser.

The footsteps moved again. Down the passenger side of the van now, slower, and I heard him try the door handle. Locked. A beat. He moved to the sliding side door and tried that. Locked. Another beat.

Then a sound that made my stomach drop, the scrape of metal on metal. He was working the rear door latch with some kind of tool. A knife, a pry bar, something thin enough to slide into the gap between the doors.

Derby rose from his seat in absolute silence, a

movement so controlled it was almost mechanical, his body unfolding in the dark. He positioned himself two feet from the rear doors, taser up, feet spread, his free hand braced against the wall for balance.

The latch gave.

The right door swung open six inches, and the scout's face appeared in the gap, round, stubbled, eyes already narrowing as they adjusted from the streetlight to the darkness inside the van. For one frozen second he saw nothing. Then his brain caught up to what his eyes were processing—the shape of Derby's silhouette, the outline of the monitors, all of it registering in the same instant that Derby moved.

The taser crackled. Two probes hit the man center mass and his body seized. A full-body convulsion that locked every muscle at once, his jaw clamping shut on a sound that never made it out of his throat. He dropped straight down, his knees buckling, his shoulder hitting the bumper on the way to the asphalt. Derby was on him before he stopped twitching, one knee in his back, hands wrenched behind him, zip ties cinched tight around his wrists with the speed of someone who'd done it a thousand times. Doug was right behind him with a second set for the ankles, and between the two of them they had the man trussed and gagged and hauled into the van in under fifteen seconds.

Derby pulled the doors shut. The lock engaged with a click that sounded like a gunshot in the silence.

"Clear," Derby said, barely winded.

The scout lay on the floor of the van, breathing hard through his nose, his eyes wide and darting. He was maybe forty, with a thick neck and gym-built arms that strained his jacket sleeves.

Doug powered the monitors back up. The screens bloomed to life, and the dock district reappeared—quiet, empty, unchanged. Nobody had heard. Nobody had seen.

I checked my watch. Ten thirty-three.

"Jack," Derby said into the radio. "We had a visitor. Scout on the perimeter, checking vehicles. He found us. He's been neutralized and secured in the van."

"Anyone else?"

"Negative. He was alone."

"Copy. Are we compromised?"

Derby looked at the scout on the floor, then at the monitors showing the still-quiet dock district. "Negative. Nobody saw."

"Then we go now. Before they miss him." Jack's voice shifted, broadening to the full channel. "All units, this is Lawson. Execute, execute, execute."

Three words. That was all it took.

On the center monitor, Danforth's team moved.

They came out of the darkness like they'd been manufactured from the night—black tactical gear, helmets, rifles up, moving in a column toward the loading dock with the fluid precision of men who trained for exactly this. The point man reached the loading dock door, and a second later the battering ram hit it with a sound I felt in my chest even from two blocks away. A deep, concussive boom that rolled through the dock district like thunder from underground.

Then they were inside, and the monitors erupted.

Doug's fingers flew across the keyboard. "Margot, give me body cams. All of them."

The three screens split into a grid. Twelve feeds from twelve helmet-mounted cameras, each one a lurching, strobing rectangle of chaos. Flashlight beams slashed across brick walls. Boots pounded down concrete stairs. The feeds shook with every step, every turn, the images so fractured and violent that watching them was like trying to read a book someone was tearing apart in front of you.

"Stairwell," Doug said, pointing to the upper left feed. "They're going down."

The lead camera plunged into darkness, the flashlight beam catching the curve of old brick as the tunnel opened up at the bottom. Then the work lights hit, harsh, white, flooding the feed with sudden overexposure, and for one frozen frame I saw it. The ring. The crowd.

Hundreds of faces turning toward the stairwell entrance with the identical expression of animals caught in headlights.

Then everything happened at once.

"Breach! Breach! Stairs going down, moving to lower level—"

"Contact right—two armed, east wall—"

Gunfire. Not the controlled pops of a firing range but the deafening, overlapping chaos of weapons going off in an enclosed space. The hard bark of rifle rounds ricocheting off brick, the flat crack of handguns, all of it compressed and amplified by three hundred years of tunnel acoustics until it sounded like the earth itself was splitting apart.

I gripped the edge of the bench. My knuckles went white.

"Shots fired, shots fired—taking fire from the east corridor—"

"Flashbangs out—"

The body cam feeds whited out simultaneously. Twelve screens blazing to pure white as the stun grenades detonated underground. The sound came through the radio a half second later, a rolling concussive thud that I felt in the floor of the van. When the feeds flickered back, the main chamber was a scene from a war zone, civilians flat on the ground with their hands over their ears, fighters stumbling blind, the ring ropes swaying from the shockwave.

"Two armed, east wall—contact! Contact!"

Derby's hand was pressed against his headset, his face rigid with concentration, sorting the overlapping transmissions into a coherent picture by sheer force of will. Doug was tracking signal movement on Margot's display, phones scattering in every direction underground, a digital stampede that mirrored the physical one happening sixty feet below us.

"They're running for the river exit," Doug said. "Big cluster moving southeast."

Derby keyed the radio. "Jack, you've got runners heading toward the river. Large group, moving fast."

"Copy. Hops, Cheek—incoming."

"Team is in position and ready to apprehend," Hops said.

More gunfire from the main channel. Danforth's voice cut through the chaos, louder than everything else. "SWAT team, hold positions. We've got civilians in the crossfire. Repeat, civilians in the crossfire. Check your targets."

The shooting stopped. For seconds, the radio was nothing but breathing and the distant sound of screaming, the high, animal sound of people who had been watching an illegal boxing match thirty seconds ago and were now flat on the floor of a three-hundred-year-old tunnel with smoke in their eyes and armed men in tactical gear standing over them.

"East corridor secured." Danforth again. "Two subjects down, nonfatal. Rendering aid."

A different voice. One of the SWAT operators. "Main chamber. Smoke clearing. I count sixty, maybe seventy civilians on the ground. Fighters near the ring, some in cuffs, some compliant."

"West passage is clear. Moving to secondary chambers."

Then Jack. "Copy all. My team is entering from the south. Danforth, we're coming to you."

The voices kept coming, each one a thread in a tapestry that was weaving itself together in real time. I sat in the dark van and tracked it the way I tracked the systems of a body during an autopsy, listening for the anomaly, the thing that didn't fit, the detail that would tell me whether this operation was going to end with everybody breathing or with me setting up my table in the morning.

"Ringside," Danforth's voice said. "I've got Caruso. He's sitting in a folding chair like he's waiting for a bus. Not resisting."

"Cuff him," Jack said. "Read him his rights."

"Already done. He's asking for his attorney."

"He can ask all he wants. Get him up top."

"And we've got the betting table intact," Danforth

continued. "Cash, ledger books, a laptop. They didn't have time to run."

"Secure it all. Nobody touches anything until crime scene gets down there."

"Sheriff." Danforth's voice again, and the texture of it had changed so it was tighter, controlled in a way that meant he was actively controlling it. "East tunnel entrance. We've got a uniformed deputy with his weapon drawn. He's not complying."

Doug's hands moved fast. "Margot, get me the nearest body cam to the east entrance."

The center monitor flickered and resolved into a single feed, shaky, the angle low, looking down a brick corridor lit by work lights. At the far end, maybe thirty feet away, was Deputy Beckwith. Full uniform, service weapon up in a two-handed grip, the barrel tracking between the two SWAT operators who had him boxed against the tunnel wall. His face was white and sheened with sweat, his eyes too wide, his chest heaving with the rapid, shallow breathing of a man whose fight-or-flight response had kicked in and couldn't decide which one to choose.

Danforth stepped into the frame. He moved slowly, deliberately, his M4 hanging on its sling, muzzle down, both hands open and visible. He positioned himself between his operators and Beckwith.

"Beckwith." His voice was steady, pitched to carry

without shouting. "I'm Lieutenant Danforth. I need you to lower your weapon."

"I'm undercover!" Beckwith's voice was high and ragged, cracking at the edges. "I'm working this case. I'm undercover, you need to stand your men down—"

"Okay. If you're undercover, that's fine. We'll get it sorted out. But I need you to put the weapon on the ground first so we can talk about it."

"You don't understand. These people will kill me if they see me—"

"Nobody's going to hurt you. My team has the tunnels secured. You're safe. But I can't help you while you've got a weapon pointed at my operators. Put it down, and we walk out of here together."

The body cam feed was steady enough now that I could see the details—Beckwith's knuckles white around the grip, the tremor running through his arms, the sweat tracking down his temples. His eyes kept darting past Danforth to the two operators flanking the corridor, calculating distances, running scenarios, looking for the gap that would let him through.

There wasn't one. He had to know that. But a cornered man didn't think with the part of his brain that knew things. He thought with the part that survived.

"Beckwith. Ryan." Danforth took one step closer.

Slow. Hands open. "You're a deputy. You know how this works. Weapon on the ground, hands behind your head. We walk out. That's the only way this ends well for you."

Beckwith's lips compressed into a thin line. The panic was still there, but underneath it something harder was surfacing.

"I can't do that," he said. And his voice was different now. Flatter. Quieter.

"Yes, you can. Put it down."

"You don't understand what they'll do to me—"

"Last chance, Deputy. Put the weapon on the ground."

Beckwith's arms stopped trembling. That was the thing I noticed, the tremor that had been running through him since the feed started suddenly went still, and there was a moment, maybe half a second, where everything in the frame became very quiet and very clear, the way the world gets right before something irreversible happens.

He swung the barrel toward Danforth.

The shot came from the operator on the right. A single round, clean, the sound compressed by the tunnel walls, like a door slamming shut at the end of a very long hallway. Beckwith's head snapped back. His weapon clattered against the brick floor. And then he was down, crumpled against the tunnel wall in a way that left no question, and the corridor was quiet except for the sound of Danforth exhaling once through his nose.

"Subject is down," Danforth said into his radio. "Weapon secured."

"Vitals?" Jack asked.

"Negative."

I sat in the dark and listened to the silence that followed. It wasn't the silence of shock, not from this group, not from men who'd made this kind of decision before and understood the weight of it. It was the silence of acknowledgment. A man with a badge had pointed a gun at other men with badges, and now he was dead.

Derby took his hand off his headset and stared at the wall for a long moment. Then he put it back on and went back to work, because that was what you did.

"Tunnels secured," Danforth's voice came through a few minutes later. "Primary and secondary chambers under control. We've got approximately seventy civilians, eight fighters, six members of the security operation, and one officer fatality. Requesting additional units for processing, and we're going to need the medical examiner."

"Copy, Danforth," Jack said. "Additional units are staging now. Derby, call it in."

Derby was already on the phone requesting additional patrol units, a transport bus from the county motor pool, crime-scene techs, and photographers.

And me. They needed me for Beckwith.

I exhaled. My hands were shaking—not from fear, not exactly, but from the vibration of something enormous finally moving, a machine that had been building for days suddenly engaging all its gears at once. I pressed my palms flat against my thighs and breathed.

"Hops, report," Jack said.

"River exit secured. We've got fourteen detained, including a tall guy with a tattoo on his neck. They complied." A beat of silence. "Another one is a short guy, stocky, has a scar on his jaw and a shaved head. He tried to run through Cheek." Another beat. "That was a mistake."

"Cheek okay?" he asked.

"Cheek's fine. The other guy's going to need some ice. He was carrying two weapons—a Glock 19 and a .22 revolver. Both secured in evidence."

Jack cleared me to enter the tunnels forty minutes after the breach.

I grabbed my medical bag and climbed out of the van. The night air hit me like a reprieve—cool, moving, carrying the salt-and-mud smell of the river after dark. After an hour in that hot metal box, even the dock district smelled clean.

A patrol officer was waiting to take custody of the scout, who had stopped struggling twenty minutes ago and was now lying on the van floor with a resigned stillness. Derby and Doug hauled him out and handed him off, and the officer walked him to a waiting cruiser without ceremony.

"I'll be on comms," Derby said. "Be careful down there."

The fish processing plant was a gutted industrial shell, stripped to the concrete and the steel bones, smelling like old fish and bleach. Danforth's team had turned it into a staging area. SWAT operators were at the perimeter, patrol officers processing the first wave of detained spectators, voices and radio chatter bouncing off the corrugated walls. The organized chaos of a well-run operation, every moving part doing what it was supposed to do.

The entrance to the tunnels was in the northeast corner, behind a steel door that had been painted to match the wall. Someone had spent real money on the concealment. I pushed through and started down the concrete stairs. The air changed immediately, cooler and damper, carrying that mineral smell I'd come to associate with this case. Old brick and wet earth and something underneath both that was older still.

I'd seen the tunnels through twelve body cam feeds. Shaky, fractured, strobing with flashlight beams and the white flare of flashbangs. I'd thought I understood the scale.

I hadn't.

Seeing it on a screen was like reading about the ocean. Standing in it was something else entirely. The vaulted brick chamber stretched sixty feet long and thirty wide, the ceiling arched twelve feet overhead in the old Scottish style Derby had described, mason's marks still visible in the keystones. The body cams hadn't captured the sound—the way my footsteps echoed off the brick and came back to me from three directions, or the low hum of the work lights strung along the ceiling on heavy-gauge wire. And they hadn't captured the smell. Sweat and beer and copper and smoke, layered over the deep mineral breath of a place that had been underground for three centuries.

The ring dominated the center of the chamber. Steel posts, taut ropes, white canvas spotted with blood that was still bright under the work lights. Folding chairs surrounded it in concentric rows, most overturned from the stampede. Beer cans, plastic cups, loose cash scattered across the concrete. Along the far wall, the betting table—ledger books, a laptop, a cash box on the floor, neat bundles of bills in rubber bands that looked exactly like the ones in

Dre's closet. Two men in zip ties sat on the ground beside it, staring at nothing.

I took it in as I moved through, but I didn't stop. I had a job to do, and it was waiting for me in the east corridor.

A SWAT operator met me at the tunnel entrance and walked me down. The passage was narrower here, the brick walls closer, the work lights spaced farther apart so the shadows ran deep between them. Our footsteps echoed in the confined space, and the operator didn't speak. He didn't need to. I could see the scene from fifty feet away—the cluster of tactical lights, the yellow evidence markers already placed on the floor, the shape on the ground that I'd been called down here to document.

Beckwith was on his back against the tunnel wall where he'd fallen. His service weapon lay four feet away, already flagged. The single round had entered above his left eye. I didn't need to examine the wound to know the trajectory. The operator who'd fired had been to Beckwith's right, slightly elevated on the uneven tunnel floor, and the round had done exactly what it was designed to do at twelve feet.

I set my bag down and knelt beside him.

He looked younger dead. They usually did. The panic was gone from his face, and the sweat had dried, and what was left was a man in his early thirties in a uniform he'd stopped deserving months ago.

His badge caught the work light and threw a small bright reflection onto the brick ceiling above him, and I thought about how strange it was that the badge still shone when everything it was supposed to represent had gone dark long before the bullet.

I pulled on my gloves and went to work.

Temperature. Lividity. Pupil response, or the absence of it. I photographed the entry wound, the position of the body, the distance to the weapon, the scuff marks on the brick where his boots had slid as he went down. I recorded everything into my phone with the same clinical precision I'd used on Dre's body four days ago.

The SWAT operator who'd taken the shot was standing at the far end of the corridor. He was young, late twenties maybe, and he was holding himself with rigid stillness. I recognized the posture. I'd worn it myself on days when the autopsy table held someone who wasn't supposed to be there.

I caught his eye and nodded once. He nodded back. That was enough.

"Martinez," I said into my radio. "I'm done with Beckwith. Where's the second chamber?"

"Deeper in the east tunnel. Take it about a hundred yards past your position, fork left. You'll see the lights." He paused. "I'll meet you there."

I packed my bag, stood, and walked past Beckwith without looking down. There would be time later for the full autopsy, for the report, for the conversations that would have to happen when a deputy died in an operation and everyone from the state police to internal affairs wanted answers. But right now there was another room waiting for me, and the evidence in it belonged to men who couldn't speak for themselves.

Martinez was at the entrance to the second chamber when I got there, leaning against the brick with his arms crossed.

"It's bad," he said. Not a warning. Just information.

The chamber was small—maybe fifteen by fifteen, low-ceilinged, the old brick sweating with moisture that caught the light from a single bare bulb hanging from a wire. Two stained mattresses on the floor. A plastic bucket in the corner. Zip ties, cut and discarded, scattered across the concrete. And the blood—on the walls, on the floor, on the edge of a metal folding chair that had been positioned in the center of the room with the deliberate placement of something that served a specific purpose.

An interrogation chair. A torture chair.

The residue on the floor was the same grayish-brown grit I'd scraped from Dre's feet. I didn't need the lab to confirm it. The color, the texture, the way it ground into the creases of the old brick. It was the same. Three-hundred-year-old mortar dust, loosened by feet shuffling across a floor that had never been meant to hold this kind of pain.

I stood in that room and I thought about Dre Washington. He'd built an insurance policy. Kept his notebook. Taken his photographs. Hidden the evidence in a bank thirty miles away because he knew, with bone-deep certainty, that the truth would need to survive him.

And it had. From beyond the grave, he'd brought us here.

"You okay, Doc?"

"Ask me tomorrow."

"I've heard that before."

We came up out of the tunnels into a night that had cooled while we'd been underground. The dock district was transformed—patrol cars lining the street, blue and red lights sweeping across the old brick buildings, a transport bus idling at the curb while officers loaded detained spectators in groups of four and five.

Vic Caruso was in a patrol car near the loading dock, cuffed and silent. He looked old in the back seat. Old and tired and smaller than he'd seemed in Dre's photographs, where he'd been leaning on the ropes like a man who owned the ring and everyone in it. He saw me looking and held my gaze for a long moment. Not defiant, not defeated, but measuring. Then he turned away, and I kept walking.

The short man with the scar along his jaw was in a second car. He was mad as a hornet. His left eye was swollen shut and already going purple, and unlike Caruso, he was talking, not to the officers but to himself, a low rapid mutter I couldn't make out through the glass. His eyes were moving, scanning, calculating even now. A man looking for exits that didn't exist anymore.

Jack was at the command post near the loading dock—a folding table with a radio, a clipboard, and a map of the tunnel network that was already being updated with the chambers I'd documented. He looked up when I walked over, and his eyes moved across my face, my hands, my body, checking without checking, making sure I was whole.

I touched his arm. He caught my hand for one second, then let go and went back to work.

"Transport the high-value suspects to the office," he said into the radio. "Separate holding. Put Vic Caruso and Demetri Kallas next door to each other. Give them a chance to see each other but not talk."

"Who's Demetri Kallas?" I asked.

"The short one with the scar along his jaw. We ran him." He looked at me. "Greek national. Two priors in New York for aggravated assault."

He turned to Doug, who'd come down from the van with Margot under his arm, picking his way through the organized chaos of the dock district like a teenager who'd wandered onto a movie set and was trying not to touch the props.

"The flash drive from Dre's lockbox," Jack said. "Where are we?"

"It was a pre-encrypted drive. Margot and I have been a little busy tonight, but it shouldn't take long to crack." Doug glanced at the tunnel entrance, then back at Jack.

"Then you and Margot get loaded up. I want this operation back at the sheriff's office. Colburn can stay here and keep the investigation and processing moving. Time is of the essence. Let's move."

CHAPTER SEVENTEEN

THE SHERIFF'S OFFICE AFTER MIDNIGHT HAD A different pulse than the one I knew during daylight hours. The fluorescent lights hummed the same frequency, the coffee maker gurgled the same burnt brew, but the air was charged. It was tight with adrenaline and the controlled urgency of people who understood that the clock was running and sleep was something that happened to other people.

Jack had turned the building into a machine.

Demetri Kallas was in interview room one. Vic Caruso was in interview room two. Jack had them walked down the same corridor a few seconds apart, close enough that they entered their rooms at almost the same time. Vic looked at Kallas nervously, but Kallas never acknowledged Vic was there. That was the game, and Jack had been playing it before either of them sat down.

I stood behind the observation glass and watched Kallas sit behind the interrogation table like it was his living room.

No fidgeting, no scanning the room, no working the cuffs or testing the table bolt. He sat with his hands flat on the metal surface and his eyes fixed on the far wall. The stillness coming off him wasn't anxiety or resignation. It was discipline. The practiced, professional stillness of a man who had been in rooms like this before and understood that silence was a weapon and he intended to use it.

Jack went in alone. He sat down across from Kallas and opened a folder. He didn't speak. He let the silence do what silence did in small rooms with bright lights—expand, press, fill every corner until the air itself felt heavy with everything that wasn't being said. He laid photographs on the table, one at a time, faceup. The tunnels. The ring. Close-ups of the bullet wounds in the back of Dre's and T-Bone's heads. Kallas at the tunnel entrance with his arms crossed. Jack didn't narrate them. He didn't explain. He just set them down and waited.

Kallas looked at the photographs the way a man looks at a menu in a language he doesn't speak. Flat disinterest.

"Lawyer," he said.

Jack gathered the photographs, closed the folder, and stood. He walked out without a word. The whole thing lasted ninety seconds.

Jack found me in the corridor. "He's Stavros's man to the bone. He's willing to go down with the ship."

"You can see it." Something about the way Kallas held himself reminded me of the bodies I worked on, men who'd been hard in life and carried that hardness into death, their muscles locked even after the rigor passed, as if the discipline had become structural. "He's not going to give you anything."

"He already gave me something." Jack's mouth curved, barely. "He didn't ask what he was being charged with. A man who doesn't know why he's in trouble asks questions. A man who knows exactly what he's done sits still and calls his lawyer."

He headed for interview room two, and I moved to the other room to look through the observation glass.

Martinez was already inside with Vic, leaning against the wall by the door with his arms crossed and one ankle hooked over the other. It was a performance, and a good one. Everything Martinez did in an interview room was calibrated to keep the subject focused on Jack while he read them from the periphery.

Vic looked up when Jack walked in. No surprise

in his face. No pretense of confusion. Whatever game they'd been playing across boxing rings and crime scenes for the past week, Vic understood that this was where it ended. Not with gloves and bravado but with a table and a folder and the acoustics of a room designed to make every word feel permanent.

"Vic," Jack said, sitting down.

"Yeah." Vic's voice was rough, forty years of cigarettes and ringside shouting. He looked smaller in here than when he'd been in the ring, as if the fluorescent light was doing what age and gravity hadn't quite finished. His hands were clasped on the table, and I could see the old scar tissue across his knuckles.

Vic glanced at the one-way glass, then back at Jack. "Who's watching?"

"Why? You worried about your friend being next door? About what he'll say?" Jack opened the folder and laid the photographs on the table, the same ones he'd shown Kallas, plus more. Vic ringside. The betting table. The cash. Dre's notebook pages. He fanned them out without hurry, the way a card dealer spreads a hand, and let Vic take them in.

"That's quite a collection," Vic said, licking his lips.

"It's just a sample." Jack leaned back. "Let's talk about Dre Washington."

"I trained Dre. That's no secret."

"You did more than train him. You recruited him into an illegal fighting operation, introduced him to Nikolai Stavros, and kept him in the organization after he wanted out."

"He was a fighter. He fought. That's what fighters do."

"He's dead, Vic. Somebody put a .22 to the back of his head and executed him. That's not what fighters do. That's what happens to fighters who try to leave."

Vic's jaw tightened. His eyes dropped to the photographs.

"I don't know anything about that," Vic said.

"Sure you do." Jack's voice was easy, almost conversational. "You knew Dre better than anyone in that operation. You trained him. You watched him fight. You knew when he started asking questions, because you're the one Stavros would have come to. Stavros doesn't know his fighters. You do. So when Dre became a problem, who did Stavros call?"

Vic said nothing. But something shifted in his face, not a crack, not yet, but the first faint line in a surface that was starting to take pressure.

"Let me tell you what I think happened," Jack said. "I think Stavros found out Dre was planning to leave. Dre was your best fighter. Men like Stavros don't like to lose money. I bet you weren't too happy either. He told you he was leaving, because you're the one who manages the fighters. And I think you told him you'd handle it. But then you went to Stavros and he told you to handle Dre. No one walks away from this life, right Vic?"

Vic's eyes came up fast. The words had landed. I could see it from behind the glass, the flinch he almost controlled, the way his hands tightened against each other on the table.

"You know that phrase?" Jack asked. Mild. Curious. "The situation needs to be handled? Because I'm betting that's exactly how it was put to you. That's how a man like Stavros says it. He doesn't say kill. He doesn't say murder. He says handle it. And everyone in the room knows exactly what it means."

The silence that followed was the loudest thing in the building.

"You're sixty-three, Vic," Jack said. His voice shifted, not harder, but quieter, closer to the bone. "You've been in this a long time. You know how RICO works. You know what federal conspiracy charges look like. And you know, because you've been around men like Stavros your whole life, that when the walls start closing in, he's not going to protect you. He's going to protect himself. He's going to let every man in that organization go down while his attorneys build a firewall around him and his money."

Vic stared at the table.

"I'm offering the chance for one deal tonight," Jack said. "What the deal is, I don't know. That's up to the prosecutor. But either you or Kallas will get the chance to put Stavros away for a long time. First come, first serve."

Jack stood. He gathered the photographs and closed the folder.

"Think about that, Vic. I'll be back."

He walked out. The door clicked shut. And through the glass, I watched Vic Caruso sit motionless, his scarred hands clasped on the table, his eyes focused on something I couldn't see. Then he reached for the water, unscrewed the cap with fingers that weren't quite steady, and drank.

Jack's phone buzzed as we walked back toward his office. He glanced at the screen.

"Doug's got the flash drive open," he said. "Conference room."

Doug had taken over the long table in conference room B, Margot at the center, cables running to the wall-mounted monitor, empty energy drink cans lined up like soldiers along the far edge.

Doug looked up when we walked in, and his expression stopped me. I'd expected the wired excitement of a kid who'd cracked a puzzle. But it was something older and harder. Something that hadn't been there before tonight.

"Six files on the drive," he said. "Four are financial documents, bank transfers, shell company paperwork, money trails. One is a spreadsheet of fight dates, locations, and payouts going back two years. Margot cross-referenced it against Dre's notebook and they match to the penny."

"And the sixth?" Jack asked.

"Video." Doug's hands hovered over the keyboard. "Three minutes, forty seconds. Dre hid his phone somewhere near the ring. Low angle, propped against something. The image is clear and Margot enhanced the audio." He paused. "You can hear everything."

He hit play.

The tunnels filled the wall-mounted monitor, and for a moment I was back underground—the vaulted brick, the work lights, the press of bodies. But this was different. This was the tunnel alive, the way it had been before SWAT tore through the door and turned it into a crime scene. The crowd was packed tight around the ring, faces slick with sweat and adrenaline, mouths open, voices merging into a single roar that came through the speakers with enough force to change the air in the room. I could almost smell it. The beer, the sweat, the copper tang of blood under hot lights.

A fight had just ended. The crowd surged and shifted, some pushing toward the betting table, others milling with drinks in hand, their voices loose and loud with the energy that came after watching violence. The buzzing, electric aftermath of a crowd that wanted more.

Then the crowd parted, and Stavros walked into frame.

He moved the way a man moves through his own house, unhurried, proprietary, touching a shoulder here, accepting a handshake there. People stepped aside without being asked, the way they stepped aside for weather, for traffic, for things that were bigger than them and moved in their own time. He wore a dark jacket and an open collar and the easy, pleased expression of a host surveying a party that was going exactly the way he'd planned.

A young man stood near the ring ropes. Mid-twenties, lean, dark-eyed, still breathing hard from a bout. A towel hung around his neck and his hands were unwrapped and he had the loose, spent look of a fighter coming down from the adrenaline, his guard lowered, his body telling him the danger was over.

His body was wrong.

Stavros reached him and put an arm around his shoulders. The gesture was warm and generous, almost fatherly, pulling the young man close the way a coach pulls in a fighter after a win. Joaquin went with it. You could see the uncertainty in his posture, the slight stiffness in his shoulders, but he went with it because what else do you do when the man who owns everything puts his arm around you and smiles?

"Joaquin." Stavros's voice came through the speakers, clear and unhurried, carrying the warmth that I'd heard on Jack's speakerphone when he'd called. The warmth that wasn't warmth at all but something wearing its skin. "It was a hell of a fight tonight. You've got real talent. Real heart. I've always said that about you."

"Thanks, Mr. Stavros." Tight. Careful. The voice of a young man who could feel the temperature changing but couldn't find the source.

"I take care of my fighters, Joaquin. I've always taken care of you. The money, the training, the opportunities. Everything I've given you, I've given because I believe in you. All I've ever asked in return is loyalty." He squeezed Joaquin's shoulder, the easy, affectionate squeeze of a mentor, a benefactor, a man who cared. "That's fair, isn't it?"

"Yes sir."

"So imagine how it felt—" Stavros's voice dropped, not in volume but in register, settling into something intimate, "—when I found out you've been hedging bets against my line. Skimming off the top. Playing both sides." The arm stayed around Joaquin's shoulders. The smile didn't change. "Did you think I wouldn't notice? I know every dollar that moves through this operation. Every bet, every payout, every penny that changes hands. I built this. And you tried to steal from it."

"No, Mr. Stavros, I— "

"Shh." Gentle. Almost kind. The way you'd speak to a child who'd broken a priceless artifact and didn't yet understand the cost. "That's the thing about betrayal, Joaquin. There's no version of the story that makes it go away. There's only the example it sets."

And then Stavros did something that made my breath stop. He looked up. Not at Joaquin. At the crowd. He lifted his gaze from the young man under his arm and swept it across the room to the fighters along the wall, the men at the betting table, the spectators with their beers and their phones, every face in that underground chamber. He looked at them the way a preacher looks at a congregation before the altar call, and the room went quiet.

His free hand went to his jacket, a motion so smooth it barely disturbed the fabric, and when it came back there was a blade in it. Short, fixed, the kind of knife that lived in a sheath against the ribs and waited for the hand that knew it was there. Nobody saw it until it was already moving.

He pushed it into the side of Joaquin Melendez's

neck the way you'd slide a key into a lock. Smooth. Unhurried. The arm still around his shoulders, holding him upright, holding him close, the gesture still reading as an embrace from three feet away. Joaquin's hands came up, a reflex, desperate, his fingers finding the handle and the blood that was already sheeting down his chest in a hot dark curtain. His mouth opened. Nothing came out.

Stavros held him. For two seconds, maybe three, he held the dying man against his chest with the tenderness of someone saying goodbye to a friend, and then the weight became too much and he let go and Joaquin folded to the tunnel floor. His hands were still reaching for his neck when he stopped moving.

Stavros looked down at the body and he took a cloth that Kallas handed him, wiping the blood from his hands. He adjusted his jacket with both hands, a small, precise motion. And then he turned to the silent crowd and his voice carried through the tunnel the way it had carried through Jack's speakerphone.

"Does anyone else have questions about how we do business?"

Nobody moved. Nobody spoke. A hundred people stood in that tunnel and stared at the body on the floor and the man who'd put it there.

Doug stopped the video.

The conference room was its own kind of silent.

Not the shocked silence of people who couldn't process what they'd seen. We'd all seen death, all of us in that room, in our different ways and for our different reasons. This was the silence of recognition. Of seeing, clearly and without the mercy of distance, exactly what kind of man we were building a case against.

I realized my hands were gripping the edge of the table. I let go. The blood came back into my fingers in a tingling rush.

"That's first-degree murder on camera," Martinez said. His voice had gone flat and hard, stripped of the charm the way a weapon is stripped of its safety. "In front of a hundred witnesses who were too terrified to do anything about it."

"He wanted them terrified," Jack said. "That's the whole point. He killed Joaquin the way he did because fear is how he runs the operation. Every fighter in that room watched it happen and understood that if you step out of line, you end up dead."

Jack's phone buzzed in his hand. He looked at the screen.

"It's the crime lab," he said.

The room went still. Jack answered on speaker.

"This is Sheriff Lawson," Jack said.

"Dr. Wendt at the state forensics lab. I have ballistics results on the .22 caliber revolver submitted under your case."

"Please tell me you have good news."

"The rifling patterns and striation marks on the .22 recovered from both victims, Andre Washington and Terrance James, are consistent with test rounds fired from the submitted revolver. Both rounds were fired from this weapon. It's a match."

Jack closed his eyes. Just for a second, a blink that lasted a beat too long, the only outward sign that the words had landed somewhere deeper than professional satisfaction. Then he opened them.

"That's what I needed. Thanks for getting it back to me so quickly."

"It's not like I've got anything better to do in the middle of the night."

Jack hung up and said, "Kallas gets two counts of first-degree murder. Stavros gets first-degree on Joaquin, conspiracy on Dre and T-Bone, racketeering, and enterprise homicide. I want warrants before the sun comes up." He looked at Martinez. "How long has Vic been sitting?"

"Long enough he should be good and nervous."

"Good." He looked at his watch and grimaced. "Now I get to wake up a judge and someone from the DA's office."

"Better let me call the DA's office," Martinez said. "Leisa Slater has a soft spot for me."

"I guess that leaves the judge for me," Jack said.

Doug was still sitting at the table, his hands flat

on either side of Margot's keyboard, staring at the dark monitor. The wired energy that had carried him through the night was gone. What was left was a sixteen-year-old boy who'd just watched a man get murdered on video and was carrying the weight of it the way you carry something sharp.

"You should get some sleep," I said. "Jack's got a cot behind his office."

He shook his head. "Not yet." He was quiet for a moment. "I keep thinking about Dre. Sitting in that crowd. Watching Stavros kill that kid. And then going back. Week after week. Recording, documenting, building the case." He looked up at me. "How do you do that? How do you watch something like that and go back?"

"Because the alternative is letting it stand," I said. "And some people can't live with that."

Doug nodded slowly. He didn't say anything else, and I didn't push. Some things didn't need more words.

I found Jack in his office twenty minutes later, hanging up the phone.

"Judge Aldridge signed the warrants and sent them over electronically," he said. "Two counts first-degree murder on Kallas. First-degree murder, conspiracy, racketeering, and criminal enterprise charges on Stavros. She wasn't happy about missing out on her beauty sleep, so she told me we'd better make an airtight case or she's coming for me."

"I always liked Judge Aldridge."

"Martinez got Slater at the DA's office. She's reviewing the affidavit now and she'll have the formal charging documents ready by morning."

"So you think it was Leisa Slater's house Martinez was seen leaving in the middle of the night?"

"Your guess is as good as mine," Jack said. "But it wouldn't surprise me at all. She's got a thing for cops. She and Colburn went a few rounds several years ago."

"Oh really?" I asked, arching a brow. "Maybe that's why things always seem a little off between Colburn and Martinez."

There was a knock on the open door, and a uniformed deputy I didn't recognize leaned in.

"Sheriff, the suspect in interview two is asking to talk. His lawyer showed up about half an hour ago."

Vic talked for forty minutes. He told us everything we needed to make sure Stavros never saw the light of day again.

"Dre deserved better," he said, slumped in his chair like a man who accepted his fate. "He deserved the shot I never gave him. If putting Stavros away is the last thing I do for that kid, then I'm okay with it."

I guess that was as close to remorse as we would get.

When it was over Jack had everything he needed—Stavros's direct order on Dre, Kallas as the trigger-man, the three days in the back chamber, T-Bone's execution after Beckwith tipped the cooperation, and Cole's shooting, ordered as a tactical diversion so Kallas could get to T-Bone.

Jack found me in the corridor.

"We're done for tonight," he said. "Nothing happens until Stavros moves in the morning."

The building was settling into that strange pre-dawn quiet, the hour when exhaustion felt almost peaceful and the world outside hadn't decided what it was going to be yet.

Stavros was asleep somewhere, still believing the night had gone his way.

Morning was coming.

And so were we.

CHAPTER EIGHTEEN

Jack was already in the shower when my alarm went off at six thirty. I lay there for a moment, listening to the water run and the house settle around me.

I'd showered as soon as we'd walked into the house a few hours before, deciding it was best to get the grime of the day and the police station off of me before I got into bed. So I was downstairs and dressed, pouring coffee into mugs, when he came into the kitchen. He was dressed in dark jeans, boots, a white button-down with the KGSO logo stitched over the breast, and the shoulder holster he wore the way other men wore a suit jacket. His badge was already on his belt. He'd shaved, and he somehow managed to look like a man who was well rested and ready to make one of the biggest arrests of his career.

"Surveillance check-in was five minutes ago," he said, scrolling his phone. "Stavros is still home. He's up and moving. Hops said he's currently in his home gym doing a workout."

The plan was clean. Units had been staged since seven at the King George Yacht Club. He normally arrived just before nine according to the manager of the yacht club, and reserved the private terrace overlooking the grounds. While Stavros was enjoying his last civilized breakfast, a secondary team would be executing the warrant on his home and other vehicles.

We drank our coffee standing at the counter and didn't talk about what was coming because there was nothing left to talk about. The work was done. The evidence was locked. All that remained was the walk through the door and the words that would end Nikolai Stavros's life as a free man.

His phone buzzed. He looked at the screen.

"He's moving. Heading toward the yacht club right on schedule." A pause while he read. "Time to roll out."

"Creature of habit," I said.

"Everyone is, even if they don't want to be." He set his mug in the sink. "Let's go."

The drive took twenty minutes. Jack called Martinez. Unmarked units were already in position around the yacht club. Plainclothes at the entrance.

Marked cruisers on the access road, out of sight from the building.

The morning was cool and gray, the sky the color of old pewter, the fields dark with dew. It was a Virginia morning that hadn't decided what it was going to be yet. The river appeared between the trees as we got closer to the waterfront, flat and silver, and the road wound through a corridor of oaks that were so old their branches met overhead and turned the asphalt into a tunnel of green and shadow.

The King George Yacht Club sat at the end of a private road on a bluff above the Potomac. It was white clapboard with dark shutters, and it had a deep covered porch with rocking chairs overlooking the river. The grounds were immaculate, every hedge trimmed, every flower bed edged, the gravel drive raked smooth. The parking lot was already filling up —golf carts lined up near the pro shop, couples in tennis whites heading for the courts, families drifting toward the main entrance for the Sunday brunch that had been a King George institution for decades.

Stavros's Mercedes sat in the designated valet lot beside the building.

Jack pulled up to the front entrance. Martinez's unmarked sedan was already there. The marked cruisers sat back on the access road. Containment was the goal, not assault. If Stavros decided to run, he'd find every direction closed. But Jack didn't expect him to run. Men like Stavros didn't run. They sat in leather chairs and called their lawyers and believed that money could make anything go away.

We walked through the front entrance together. The lobby was bright and busy. The Sunday brunch crowd filled the main room, the clink of mimosa glasses, the low hum of conversation and laughter. A hostess looked up from her stand and Jack showed her his badge without breaking stride.

"Private terrace," he said. "Which way?"

She pointed.

Jack walked through the main room and I was beside him. Heads turned as we passed, not because anyone knew what was happening, but because Jack moved through a room the way weather moved through a valley, and people noticed. Martinez stayed near the entrance, positioned between the terrace and the front door. Not because he expected trouble, but because Jack didn't leave gaps.

The private terrace was separated from the main dining area by a set of glass doors and a century's worth of exclusivity. It was wide and stone-floored, open to the river on three sides, the railing running along the edge of the bluff. Below it the Potomac stretched wide and flat, the far shore soft with haze. The morning air was cool and damp and smelled like mud and salt and the green tangle of the riverbank. Rocking chairs lined the railing. A single table with a white cloth was set near the water.

Stavros was at the table. He had his back to the building and his face to the river, and he was reading the newspaper with unhurried focus. An espresso sat at his right hand, still steaming. A plate held the remains of toast and fruit. He was wearing a white linen shirt with the collar open, and the morning light caught the silver in his hair. From where I stood he looked exactly like what he'd spent decades constructing himself to be, a man of wealth and taste and absolute immunity from consequence.

Jack's boots sounded on the stone. Stavros heard them and turned his head, not quickly, but with a measured pause.

He saw Jack. He saw the badge. He saw me standing three steps behind Jack's shoulder. And something moved behind his eyes, fast and calculating, the machinery of a powerful mind processing an unexpected variable. But it wasn't fear. It wasn't even surprise. It was irritation. The look of a man who'd found a stain on his shirt at a dinner party. A minor problem. Manageable.

"Sheriff Lawson," Stavros said. He picked up his espresso and took a sip. Deliberately. Making us wait while he drank. "I have to say, you're persistent. But this is a private club and you're interrupting my morning."

"Nikolai Stavros, you're under arrest," Jack said. "Stand up and put your hands behind your back."

Stavros set the cup down and smiled. It was a real smile, wide and warm, reaching his eyes. "On what charges?"

"Conspiracy to commit murder. First-degree murder. Racketeering and criminal enterprise under the RICO Act."

"Murder." He said the word the way you'd say a mildly interesting piece of gossip. He folded his newspaper and set it on the table with care. "I assume you're referring to those unfortunate events in the dock district. Sheriff, I'm a businessman. I own property. What tenants do with that property is not my concern or my liability. My attorneys will have this dismissed by this afternoon."

"Your attorneys can try. Stand up."

"You're making an enormous mistake." Stavros looked at Jack with patient condescension. "I have resources you haven't begun to imagine. Legal resources, political resources, financial resources. The people who matter in this county. The people who fund campaigns and sit on boards and decide who keeps their jobs." He leaned back in his chair. "Are you sure this is a hill you want to die on?"

"Mr. Stavros," Jack said, his smile genuine. "My people would eat yours for lunch. I promise you don't want to start a power war with me or mine.

You'll lose. And you know that, just like I know you've already looked into my entire background."

"You're making a powerful enemy."

"I'll add you to my list," Jack said. "I've got video of you putting a knife into Joaquin Melendez's neck. Remember him? One of the boxers who made you money." He took another step closer. "Stand up. I'm not going to ask again."

Stavros' smile stayed and the composure held. But underneath it, in the place where the real man lived behind the construction, was a tremor in the foundation. The first crack in the certainty.

He stood. He took his time about it, smoothing his shirt and adjusting his cuffs. He was taller standing than sitting, and broader, and he held himself with the erect posture of a man who had never in his life allowed anyone to see him diminished.

Jack cuffed him. The steel clicked against his wrists. The sound carried across terrace and out over the water, and a bird startled from the railing and flew out over the river.

"You have the right to remain silent," Jack said. "Anything you say can and will be used against you in a court of law. You have the right to an attorney. If you cannot afford one, one will be appointed for you."

"I can afford plenty," Stavros said. The smile was

still there but it had gone thin and hard, like a blade turned sideways. "And I promise you, Sheriff, every one of them will be very interested in how this case was built. The methods. The sources. The corners that were cut."

"No corners," Jack said. "Clean warrants. Clean evidence." He leaned closer and whispered. "A clean judge and district attorney. I found your payroll. Looks like this county needs to clean house."

He took Stavros's arm and turned him toward the doors. Stavros walked without resistance.

As he passed me he slowed. Not enough to stop. Jack's hand on his arm kept him moving. But he found my eyes.

"Dr. Graves," he said. "I heard you had some trouble at the funeral home. It's a shame when we can't feel safe in our own city. You should talk to the police about that."

Jack walked him through the doors and into the club. I followed.

Martinez handled the transport. Jack watched them load Stavros into the back of the cruiser and close the door, and then he stood in the parking lot for a long moment with his hands on his hips, looking at nothing. The morning light was strengthening, burning through the haze, and I could see the exhaustion in his face.

"I want to swing by the hospital later," he said. "Cole should hear about the arrest from us, not the news."

I was silent.

"What's wrong?" he asked.

"I don't know." I wanted to shrug it off, but my gut instinct had always been strong. "Just something bothering me about Stavros."

"The fact that he's a psychopath?"

I looked at Jack. "That's twice now he's mentioned the funeral home. Why?"

"I would say because that's what psychopaths do, but I know that won't be enough to ease your mind. Do you want to go by and check it out? You still have T-Bone's and Dre's bodies down in the lab?"

"Yeah, they're ready to be released to family."

"I tell you what," he said, squeezing my shoulder and leading me toward the Tahoe. "Let's swing by the funeral home and check on your residents. Then I'll take you to breakfast. Someplace nice. With pancakes."

I almost laughed. It felt strange in my chest, rusty and unexpected, like a door opening in a room that had been closed all week. "Are you asking me on a date?"

"I'm asking the most beautiful woman in the

world to sit across the table from me and talk about anything but murder, dead bodies or police work."

"Hmm," I said. "That sounds like a challenge. You've got a deal."

We drove with the windows cracked. The morning was warming, the clouds dissolving, and the air coming through the truck smelled like cut grass and honeysuckle.

I leaned my head against the window and closed my eyes. Not sleeping. Just resting in the silence. The week was over. The case was closed. Stavros was in cuffs, Kallas was in a cell, Vic was talking, and dozens of others were being questioned and processed into the system. We'd dismantled Stavros and his organization. It was done.

Jack's hand found my knee. I covered it with mine.

We turned onto Catherine of Aragon and the funeral home came into view at the end of the block. Four generations of my family in that building—the three-story Colonial in dark red brick, the white columns flanking the front door, the two massive elm trees shading the yard with roots so old they'd cracked the sidewalk. It looked the way it always looked. Peaceful. Still. The windows dark. The parking lot empty.

Home. Not the house on the cliffs where Jack and I slept, but the other home—the one where I did the work that mattered, the one where the dead came to me and I translated what they had to say into a language the living could use. My great-grandmother's building. My grandmother's building. My mother's building. Mine.

Jack pulled the Tahoe into the lot and killed the engine.

"Everything looks okay from here," Jack said. "Don't let him get in your head."

"You're right," I said. "Let me run in and check downstairs, and then pancakes."

I unbuckled my seat belt and reached for the door handle.

The morning shattered.

The blast came from inside the building—a deep, concussive roar that hit the Tahoe like a wall of moving concrete and turned the morning into noise and heat and a blinding white flash that erased everything. The shockwave caught the vehicle broadside and lifted it off its wheels. Glass shattered inward and metal shrieked against concrete so loud it blotted out everything else, even thought, even fear, even my own voice screaming Jack's name.

The Tahoe came to rest on its passenger side. My side.

I was hanging in my seat belt, glass in my hair, blood on my hands from cuts I couldn't feel yet. The airbag had deployed and deflated, leaving a chemical smell that mixed with something worse—smoke, thick and acrid, pouring through the shattered windshield.

"Jaye," Jack said. "Jaye, talk to me."

"I'm here. I'm okay."

"Can you move?"

Arms. Legs. Fingers. Everything responded. There were cuts on my hands. But nothing structural. Nothing broken.

"I can move," I said. "I'm okay."

Jack kicked out the windshield with his boots, the safety glass crumbling outward in a cascade of green-white fragments. He reached back for me, and I unclipped my seat belt and fell into his arms and he pulled me through the opening.

The heat hit me first. Then the light. Then the sound—the deep, roaring breath of a fire consuming everything in its path.

The funeral home was burning.

Done Dirty

September 29, 2026

Chapter One

I had no plans to become a widow at the tender age of twenty-four.

I also had no plans to own a tea shop on a sleepy South Carolina island, but I've discovered life doesn't give two figs about my plans. Life on Grimm Island taught me that lesson. Here, the oak trees drip with Spanish moss and secrets hang just as heavy in the humid air.

The Perfect Steep—my tea shop and little kingdom of mismatched chairs and organized chaos —sat on the corner of Harbor and Lighthouse. From the outside, it was Grimm Island gentility personified —soft blue paint with crisp white trim, black shutters, and a sweeping wraparound porch where two rocking chairs waited patiently as if ready for Southern hospitality itself.

Inside was a different story entirely. Inside was pure me.

My name is Mabel McCoy, and I'd done a good job of pretending to be gentility personified since my husband died ten years ago. But I'd noticed lately there were times when I was starting to feel a bit frayed around the edges, and I wondered how long it would be before people started to notice.

My tea shop was what I affectionately called organized chaos with a tea obsession, a phrase that would have made Patrick smile if he'd lived to see it. Shiplap walls that should have been pristine white were instead painted a pale yellow on one wall, mint green on another, and a soft lavender on the third— the result of my inability to choose just one color and my stubborn refusal to start over once I'd begun. The heart pine floors creaked like they were telling secrets, especially in the three spots by the register that I'd learned to hop over during busy hours.

Ceiling fans with blades shaped like giant leaves spun lazily overhead, stirring the air that always smelled of whatever tea blend I was experimenting with that day. Today it was something with bergamot and cinnamon that made the whole place smell like Christmas morning, even in the middle of May.

I glanced at the hideous cherub clock on the wall

—a wedding gift from Patrick's grandmother that I couldn't bring myself to take down despite its beady-eyed stare. Five-thirty. The afternoon crowd had thinned out, and I had about thirty minutes before the Silver Sleuths would arrive for their monthly book club meeting.

I caught a glimpse of myself in the mirror and smoothed back a stray blonde curl. At least the island's humidity was good for something—my vintage waves actually seemed to like it. I reapplied my red lipstick, the one bit of glamour I never skipped, and hummed along with Frank Sinatra as he sang *I Get a Kick Out of You* through the speakers.

I'd just finished boxing up a special tea blend to deliver to Mrs. Pembroke when the bell above the door jingled. Deputy Mark Reynolds strolled in, his uniform crisp despite the late hour, that easy smile crinkling the corners of his eyes.

"Just in time," I said. "It's almost closing time."

"My timing's always been impeccable," he replied, removing his hat. His rust-colored hair had gone silver at the temples since I'd known him, but his pale blue eyes still held that same kindness they had since I'd been a kid. "Got any of that cinnamon tea left? Been a day."

"For you? Always." I turned to prepare his usual as he settled onto his regular stool at the counter. "Rough shift?"

Reynolds sighed, running a hand through his hair. "Milton left us a mess to clean up. This new sheriff's asking a lot of questions and digging through files none of us even knew existed.

"And that's a problem?" I asked, sliding his to-go tea across the counter.

"Can't say I blame him," he said. "But it's just stirring up the past. Sheriff Milton did a lot of damage and people are hurting. He even went through the case files from when those three girls went missing. That might have been before you were born. But those girls' families still live on the island. No need to dredge it all up and put them through that again. Some things are better left buried, if you ask me."

He took a sip of tea and closed his eyes in appreciation. "Perfect as always, Mabel. Don't know what I'd do without my evening fix."

I smiled. Reactions like his to my teas were my favorite part of the job. It might seem boring by most people's standards, but I didn't need much. I considered myself a simple, easy-going woman.

"So how's the new sheriff working out?" I asked, wiping down the counter.

"Beckett?" Reynolds shrugged. "By the book. Bit of an outsider, but seems decent enough. Time will tell if he sticks around." He glanced at his watch. "Guess my break is over. You closing up for your book club tonight?"

"How did you know about that?" I asked, though I wasn't really surprised. Nothing stayed secret on Grimm Island for long.

He tapped the side of his nose and said, "Hey, I'm a cop. I know things." He finished his tea and slid a five-dollar bill across the counter.

"On the house," I told him.

He put the five in the tip jar anyway and gave me a wink. "See you tomorrow."

As the door chimed behind him, I went to clear china cups from a corner table, wiping it down and giving my last customer a side-eye because he'd been sitting there for three hours and kept filling up his tea cup with whatever was in the thermos he'd brought from home. I was getting ready to shoo him along when he hurriedly shoved his things in his bag and hurried out the door.

"Rude," I said, cleaning up his mess. "Almost time, Chowder," I said to my French bulldog, who was sprawled across the window seat, his wrinkled face looking particularly judgmental today. "The Silver Sleuths will be here soon."

Chowder snorted and rolled onto his back, his stubby legs in the air.

"I'll take that as excitement. Just try not to con Walt out of all his treats this time. You know what the vet said about your cholesterol."

I wiped down the large round table by the front

window—the Silver Sleuths' preferred spot for their meetings. They liked to see and be seen, a requirement for five seniors who considered people-watching a competitive sport. I'd arranged six chairs around it, knowing that somehow they'd rope me into joining, despite my protests.

I gave my sea-green dress a final smoothing. It was vintage, with those puffed sleeves I loved, and paired perfectly with the pearl pendant Patrick had given me on our first anniversary.

Frank's crooning faded, and Ella and Louis came on, deciding whether or not they could be friends as they debated the correct pronunciation of the word tomato. Chowder gave a soft woof and rolled to his side so he could look at passersby out the window.

"I agree," I told him. "I could never fall in love with someone who says tamahto. A bit too pretentious for my taste."

Chowder woofed again in agreement. There were some moments when Chowder and I were in perfect accord.

I'd just finished arranging a fresh bouquet of flowers in the center of the table when the bell above the door chimed again.

"Do I smell lemon scones?" Deidre Whitmore called as she bustled in, fifteen minutes early as usual. Her silver hair was secured in a haphazard bun with what appeared to be a pencil, wayward curls flying in all directions. She carried an enormous tote bag, and I knew it was filled with books and enough butterscotch candies to survive an apocalypse.

"Fresh out of the oven," I confirmed, smiling despite myself. Ms. Whitmore had been Grimm Island's librarian for most of my life—a woman who had seemed positively ancient when I'd been a kid—only to finally retire a few years ago. Somehow, she looked exactly the same as she had twenty years earlier. I still couldn't quite shake the feeling that I should whisper in her presence. I also had trouble remembering to call her Deidre instead of Ms. Whitmore.

"Wonderful! I brought some of my lavender shortbread to share," she said, extracting a tin from her bag. "The recipe's from 1897. Found it in the historical society archives."

I smiled and took the tin from her. "You know you don't have to bring food, Ms. Whitmore. This is a tea shop. I'm happy to provide all the refreshments."

"Call me Deidre, dear," she reminded me for what had to be the hundredth time. Her bright red culottes were a blur as she made her way to the prepared table. She untied her red and white striped sweater from around her shoulders and put it on the back of her preferred chair to save her spot. "And nonsense. It's a book club, and book clubs have potlucks."

The bell jingled again, and Walt Garrison marched in with military precision, followed closely by Dottie Simmons and Hank Hardeman.

"Five forty-two," Walt announced, consulting his ancient waterproof watch. He wore pressed navy slacks with sharp creases, a matching windbreaker, and the thick soled shoes his orthopedist insisted he wear for fallen arches. "Right on schedule."

"We're early, Walt," Dottie corrected, adjusting her green cat-eye glasses. "The meeting doesn't start until six."

"Early is on time, on time is late," Walt replied with the air of someone who had been saying the same thing for at least seventy years.

"And late is unacceptable," Hank finished with a sigh. "We know, Walt. We've known since 1972."

Hank had spent a good part of his career as a federal judge and had finally retired a few years ago at his wife's urging. He was a no-nonsense sort of man, but he'd taken to wearing shorts since his retirement, showing off knobby knees and the black dress socks he wore pulled up to the middle of his shins.

"Where's Bea?" I asked, noting the missing member of their quintet.

"Picking up Mr. Whiskers from the groomer,"

Dottie explained. "That cat gets more salon appointments than I do." She patted her freshly cut bob that had been dyed the jet black of her youth.

"Tea will be ready in a minute," I said. "I've got Earl Grey for Walt, oolong for Deidre—"

"And chamomile for me," Dottie finished. "You're a dear to remember."

"It's not exactly difficult," I said. "You've ordered the same thing for the past three years."

"Consistency is the foundation of character," Hank declared.

I retreated to the counter to prepare their tea. This monthly ritual had become so familiar I could probably do it in my sleep. First Thursday of every month, the Silver Sleuths Murder Society would descend upon my shop for their book club meeting, which inevitably dissolved into island gossip and wild speculation about whatever mystery novel they'd selected.

The bell jingled again, and Bea Livingston swept in like a tropical storm. Today she wore a flowing caftan in a peacock print so bright it had its own weather system, paired with earrings the size of small chandeliers. Her red hair sizzled with electricity.

"Sorry I'm late," she announced, though she was actually ten minutes early. "Mr. Whiskers was uncooperative." She held up her hands to display several small scratches. "Battle wounds."

"I have some antiseptic cream," I offered.

"Don't bother. I've survived three husbands and more hurricanes than I can count," she said with a dismissive wave that sent her bangles jangling. "A few cat scratches are nothing."

She settled into her usual chair and immediately leaned forward. "Now, before we start, has anyone seen our mysterious sheriff today?"

I rolled my eyes. The whole island was fascinated by the new sheriff. Maybe because he'd been brought in because of a scandal. Maybe because he wasn't a local. Or maybe because none of the gossips could get any personal information out of him. But the Silver Sleuths' sheriff watch made the CIA look like a bunch of amateurs.

"Not since yesterday," Walt reported. "He was at the pharmacy picking up a prescription."

"Did you see what for?" Deidre asked, leaning in so eagerly she nearly knocked over her teacup.

"Couldn't tell," Walt said, clearly disappointed by this gap in his intelligence gathering. "Brown paper bag, folded at the top. Very discreet."

"Blood pressure medication, most likely," Hank declared with authority. "Law enforcement has the highest rate of hypertension of any profession."

"Could be pain medication," Dottie countered,

tapping her fingers thoughtfully on the table. "Did you notice how he rolls his neck? I bet it's arthritis. Unless he's addicted to pain pills. That's a whole other problem."

"Maybe it's something more...personal," Bea whispered, raising her eyebrows.

All I could do was shake my head. The poor sheriff would have an interminable disease by the time they got through with him. "Or it could just be allergy medicine," I offered. "I've seen him sneeze every time he walks past the magnolias on Harbor Street."

"Interesting that you've noticed his sneezing habits, Mabel," Bea said, her smile spreading like warm butter.

I felt my cheeks flush. "We live on a four thousand acre island. Everyone knows everything."

"Clearly not everything," Walt said, rubbing his chin thoughtfully. "Otherwise we'd know what was in that prescription."

"You all do realize that stalking the sheriff is probably illegal, right?"

"It's not stalking," Deidre protested. "It's community awareness. You should just ask Jerry, Hank. Don't you two play golf together?"

Hank grunted. "Jerry holds confidences better than a Catholic priest. He's a pharmacist with scruples."

"Imagine that," I murmured.

"He'll be here any minute." Dottie said with a meaningful glance at the clock. "It's almost closing time."

She wasn't wrong. For the past three weeks, ever since Sheriff Dashiell Beckett had been appointed to replace our disgraced former sheriff, he'd developed a habit of stopping by The Perfect Steep just before closing time for his evening tea. Black, strong, no sugar, splash of milk. It was the most predictable thing about him.

"He's very consistent," I said, trying to sound casual. "Professional habit, I guess."

"Or he likes the view," Bea suggested with an exaggerated wink in my direction.

I pursed my lips. "He likes the tea, Bea. That's all."

"Mmhmm," all five seniors hummed in unison, with identical expressions of disbelief.

"So what's the book this month?" I asked, desperate to change the subject.

"The Graves of Walter County," Deidre said, producing a worn paperback from her bag. "About a series of cold cases in a small Texas town in the 1960s."

"How many victims?" I asked, despite myself. These murder mysteries were admittedly a guilty pleasure.

"Seven," Dottie replied eagerly. "All buried in the woods behind the killer's house. But he didn't bury them deep enough and when heavy rains came one spring one of the bodies was washed into the creek and floated all the way downtown. Victim was a girl that had gone missing from the college in the next town."

"The killer strangled all his victims with his belt," Walt said. "Had a real unusual belt buckle that left an impression in the tissue."

"The author's research was impressive," Hank added, reaching for a scone. "Though I found myself quite irritated by his abbreviations of words. He kept using the word anal for analysis, as if that's some kind of shorthand those of us who deal in crime use on a daily basis. I can tell you I've never uttered the word anal in my courtroom."

I stifled a laugh, entertained by the absurdity of the conversation.

"Pass the clotted cream," Walt said, unfazed. "I enjoyed the book. It reminded me of a case in Annapolis back in '82."

The bell above the door jingled, and I didn't have to look up to know who it was. A hush fell over the Silver Sleuths as Sheriff Beckett entered, right on schedule.

He was still in uniform, dark pants and a short sleeved button-down that fit well across his broad shoulders and hugged his biceps. His dark hair was slightly tousled by the wind. A thin scar ran along his right jawline, barely noticeable unless you were looking for it because of the stubble he'd let grow.

"Evening, ladies. Gentlemen," he nodded.

"Sheriff," Walt replied.

"Good evening, Mrs. McCoy," Sheriff Beckett said, turning to me with a polite nod. "Hope I'm not interrupting."

I smiled at the formal address. After ten years as a widow, "Mrs. McCoy" felt like a well-worn sweater—comfortable, familiar, and something I had no desire to take off.

"Not at all, Sheriff," I replied. "Just in time for your usual?"

"Please," he said with a small smile that didn't quite reach his eyes.

Sheriff Beckett smiled with his mouth, but his eyes always remained watchful, alert. It was slightly unnerving and, if I was being honest with myself, slightly fascinating.

"Book club night?" he asked, glancing at the table where the Silver Sleuths had spread out their books and notes like battle plans.

"First Thursday of every month," Deidre confirmed, straightening her glasses with a librarian's precision. "We're discussing The Graves of Walter County." She held up the book.

"True crime?" he asked, raising an eyebrow. "I saw a TV special on that case. It was fascinating."

"We only read true crime," Dottie explained with a dismissive wave. "Fiction is too..." She paused, nose wrinkling like she'd smelled something unpleasant. "Unrealistic."

The corner of Sheriff Beckett's mouth quirked up. "How so?"

"Too many coincidences," Hank declared. "And the detectives—" he jabbed a finger toward Beckett, "—are too incompetent, so the amateur sleuth ends up solving the case. It's ridiculous."

"Unlike real detectives, who welcome civilian input," Beckett said dryly, his eyes crinkling at the corners despite his deadpan delivery.

Walt leaned forward, elbows on the table, entering what I'd come to think of as his intelligence briefing posture. "Depends on the detective," he countered. "And the civilian. Some of us have relevant expertise."

"Is that so?" Beckett asked, accepting the to-go cup I handed him, his fingers briefly brushing mine.

Deidre sat up straighter, fairly bursting with pride. "Walt was career military. He spent thirty years in Navy intelligence," she said, patting Walt's arm. "Worked for the Department of Defense before he retired. Appointed by the President."

"Really?" Beckett asked.

Walt nodded. "If I told you about it I'd have to kill you. Top secret security clearance."

"And of course Dottie was a pathologist with the Charleston medical examiner's office," Deidre continued.

"It's true," Dottie said, cleaning her glasses. "I've had my hands in a lot of bodies."

Deidre's eyes widened comically, but she continued as if that were a perfectly normal thing to say. "Hank was a federal judge."

"They called me The Hammer because I liked to put the final nail in a criminal's coffin as I sentenced them," Hank added.

Dottie rolled her eyes. "I've known you for forty-five years, and I've never heard anyone call you The Hammer." She patted his hand to soften the blow. "But you were tough on those criminals."

"I spent almost fifty years as a librarian," Deidre said. "But my true love is research. I can get lost for days in research. And then there's Bea..." Deidre paused, looking like she was unsure what to say. "Bea—"

"Had access to more secrets than the CIA," Bea said with a theatrical flourish of her bangle-laden wrist. "Society columnist. You'd be amazed what people will tell you at charity galas after two gin and tonics. I've got the dirt on every player in town if they've been here long enough. Of course, I've got the dirt on anyone who thinks they're anyone in the whole state. The south loves old money and family secrets."

Beckett looked thoughtful as he sipped his tea, his eyes moving from one Silver Sleuth to another as if reassessing them. "That's an interesting combination of skills."

"You never want to watch mystery movies with us," Dottie said. "We always figure out who did it."

"We call ourselves the Silver Sleuths," Walt said, puffing out his chest slightly.

"Catchy," Beckett commented, but he was looking at me as if he were waiting to hear what my special skills were. I hated to disappoint him, but I didn't think he'd be too interested in my ability to do crossword puzzles or how I can memorize song lyrics the first time I hear them. Neither of those things is helpful when watching mysteries on T.V.

"Storm's coming in," I said for lack of anything better, nodding toward the windows where dark clouds were gathering on the horizon. "Looks like it could be a bad one."

Beckett followed my gaze. "You're right about that," he said. "Weather service issued a severe thunderstorm warning not long ago. You might want to wrap up your meeting early tonight."

"Nonsense," Deidre said dismissively. "We've weathered worse. Remember Hurricane Matthew?"

"I remember you showing up on my doorstep because you ate all your hurricane snacks before the storm hit," Dottie said.

Beckett turned to me. "What time will you close up here?"

"We usually finish at seven," I said.

He nodded. "You'll be cutting it close. You'll want to get home before it gets too bad."

"I'm just three blocks away," I told him. "The white corner house with the piazza at the end of Harbor Street. I'll have time before things get too bad. Those clouds are still a good ways off."

"You can predict the weather?" the sheriff asked, arching a brow.

"I'm my father's daughter," I said, and left it at that.

"Right." His eyes met mine with that dark, direct gaze that never seemed to waver.

He paid for his tea, leaving his usual generous tip in the jar by the register, and then he nodded to the group. "Enjoy your book club. Try not to solve too many crimes in one evening."

"No promises," Bea called after him as he headed for the door.

"Have a good night, Sheriff," I said.

He paused at the door, glancing back. "Dash," he corrected quietly. "After hours, it's just Dash."

Before I could say anything else, he was gone, the bell chiming in his wake.

Five pairs of eyes immediately swiveled to me.

"After hours, it's just Dash," Bea mimicked in a deep voice. "Well, well, well."

"Don't start," I said with a small smile. "It's just tea and manners. That's all."

"I certainly didn't notice any arthritis in his neck," Hank said observantly. "He was able to turn his head to look at Mabel just fine."

"Did you notice the scar on his jaw?" Deidre asked, leaning forward conspiratorially.

"Bar fight in Charleston," Walt declared.

"Knife fight with a drug dealer," Bea countered.

"Military," Dottie guessed. "He has the posture."

"You're all ridiculous," I said, returning to the table with a fresh pot of tea. "He probably cut himself shaving."

"No way," Walt shook his head. "That's a knife scar. Clean, deliberate. Man's seen action."

"I heard he's from Virginia originally," Deidre offered. "Old family, fell on hard times."

"I heard he was FBI before this," Bea said, not to be outdone. "Undercover work. Very hush-hush."

"I heard he's just a normal person trying to do his job without being the subject of wild speculation," I suggested.

"Boring," Bea dismissed. "My version is better."

"We should invite him to join the book club," Dottie suggested suddenly. "He seems interested in true crime."

"Occupational hazard, I imagine," I said dryly.

"No, it's perfect," Deidre agreed, warming to the idea. "We need fresh perspectives."

"And it'd give him a chance to stare at Mabel more," Bea added with a wink.

"He's probably very busy with sheriff duties," I said, adjusting my pearl pendant.

"Not too busy for tea, apparently," Deidre pointed out, patting my hand.

"Mabel should consider courtship," Hank announced to the table, as if I weren't sitting right there. "A respectable widow of her standing would be quite eligible."

Bea nodded sagely. "In my day, ten years was more than sufficient mourning period. I married my second husband six months after my first had been buried. Of course, Leonard and I had something of a past if you know what I mean."

"If you mean you were having an affair with him while Earl was alive then we know what you mean," Deidre said, shaking her head. "The whole island knew."

Bea pursed her lips tightly, but she didn't dispute it.

"Patrick would have wanted you to move on,"

Dottie said softly, using the exact phrase she'd repeated at years two, five, and seven.

Walt cleared his throat. "Sheriff seems like a decent sort. Responsible. Reliable pension. Good posture."

I glanced between them, fighting both amusement and exasperation. They'd decided my future with the same certainty they used to plan the church bake sale or determine who was stealing Mrs. Peterson's newspaper.

So I did what I always did when I didn't know what to say. I started singing.

"Don't know why there's no sun up in the sky, stormy weather..."

"Ethel Waters or Lena Horne?" Walt asked immediately.

"Lena," I said. "Though Ethel did it first."

"Good taste," he approved. "My Margaret loved Lena Horne. Saw her perform in New York once, before we were married."

And just like that, we were back on safe ground, with Walt launching into one of his stories about his late wife that somehow always involved either naval intelligence or jazz music, often both. The tension dissolved, and I found myself relaxing back into the familiar rhythm of their conversation.

Outside, thunder rumbled in the distance. I sipped my tea and half-listened as Deidre started discussing the book, with frequent interruptions from the others. The storm was building, but in here, in this moment, everything felt comfortingly normal.

I'd spent ten years building this life—the tea shop, the routines, the careful distance I maintained from anything too emotional or complicated. Ten years as Mabel McCoy, young widow, tea shop owner, honorary senior citizen.

But as another rumble of thunder shook the building, I couldn't help wondering if maybe, just maybe, I was ready for a little storm in my life.

Not that I was thinking about Dash Beckett when that thought crossed my mind.

Not at all.

ACKNOWLEDGMENTS

Getting a book to publication takes an amazing team of people. I'm fortunate to have had these people in my corner for years.

To my editor—Imogen Howson for always making me better.

To my cover designer—Dar Albert for always blowing me away with your talent.

To my children—You're all so special. You have gifts and abilities beyond measure, and I'm excited to see what God has in store for each of you.

To Scott—thank you for answering a ridiculous amount of law enforcement questions and acting out weird scenarios with me. Any mistakes are mine alone.

Liliana Hart is a *New York Times*, *USA Today*, and Publisher's Weekly bestselling author of more than eighty titles. After starting her first novel her freshman year of college, she immediately became addicted to writing and knew she'd found what she was meant to do with her life. She has no idea why she majored in music.

Since publishing in 2011, Liliana has sold more than ten-million books. All three of her major series have made multiple appearances on the *New York Times* list.

Liliana can almost always be found at her computer writing, or spending time with her family. She calls Texas home.

If you enjoyed reading this, I would appreciate it if you would help others enjoy this book, too.

Recommend it. Please help other readers find this book by recommending it to friends, readers' groups and discussion boards.

Review it. Please tell other readers why you liked this book by reviewing.

Connect with me online:
www.lilianahart.com

facebook.com/lilianahartauthor
instagram.com/LilianaHart
bookbub.com/authors/liliana-hart

ALSO BY LILIANA HART

JJ Graves Mystery Series

Dirty Little Secrets

A Dirty Shame

Dirty Rotten Scoundrel

Down and Dirty

Dirty Deeds

Dirty Laundry

Dirty Money

A Dirty Job

Dirty Devil

Playing Dirty

Dirty Martini

Dirty Dozen

Dirty Minds

Dirty Weekend

Dirty Looks

Dirty Liars

Dirty Valentine

Fighting Dirty

Done Dirty

Mabel McCoy Mystery Series

Skin and Bones

A Bone to Pick

Chilled to the Bone

Bone of my Bones

Addison Holmes Mystery Series

Whiskey Rebellion

Whiskey Sour

Whiskey For Breakfast

Whiskey, You're The Devil

Whiskey on the Rocks

Whiskey Tango Foxtrot

Whiskey and Gunpowder

Whiskey Lullaby

The Scarlet Chronicles

Bouncing Betty

Hand Grenade Helen

Front Line Francis

The Harley and Davidson Mystery Series

The Farmer's Slaughter

A Tisket a Casket

I Saw Mommy Killing Santa Claus

Get Your Murder Running

Deceased and Desist

Malice in Wonderland

Tequila Mockingbird

Gone With the Sin

Grime and Punishment

Blazing Rattles

A Salt and Battery

Curl Up and Dye

First Comes Death Then Comes Marriage

Box Set 1

Box Set 2

Box Set 3

The Gravediggers

The Darkest Corner

Gone to Dust

Say No More

Laurel Valley

Tribulation Pass

Redemption Road

Midnight Clear

Forgiveness River

Atonement Trail